WHAT IF I TOLD YOU

ANAHEIM STARS
BOOK TWO

SUSAN RENEE

WHAT
IF I
TOLD
YOU

SUSAN RENEE

Editing by Brandi Zelenka, My Notes in the Margin

Reader Team: Kristan Anderson, Stephani Brown,

Jenn Hager, Jennifer Wilson

Cover Design by Quirky Bird Covers

 Created with Vellum

To Jeff.
Because you fucking deserve it.
I'm not sure I've ever hated anyone more.
You're the world's biggest taint stain
and one day Karma will knock on your door.
And I can't wait to be sitting in a lawn chair
in your front yard when she does.

CHAPTER ONE

AUGUST

"You going to shove that whole wiener in your mouth at one time?"

Griffin eyes the hotdog in his hand and then winks at me. "Nah. Just the tip this time." I watch in amusement as he licks the end of his hotdog bun and then bites off the end, chewing as his eyes roll back in his head. "Fuck, so meaty." He turns the end of his hot dog around so I can see where he took a bite. "And just look at that girth."

Harrison leans forward in his stadium seat and pulls his sunglasses down his nose. "Dude, do you need a minute alone with that thing? In a private room perhaps?"

"Hell no." Griffin smirks. "I like eating wieners out in the open. Right here in front of all of you. I know how much you like to watch." His brows shoot up. "In fact, I think you all need a good wiener experience. Where's that wiener man? WEINER MAN? I NEED YOUR BIG WEINERS!" he shouts as the crowd around us chuckles. I've never been more grateful to be wearing sunglasses but then this is Griffin's everyday behavior, so am I surprised?

Not in the slightest.

"Someone shut him up," Barrett mumbles from a few seats down before he tips back his beer and swallows what's left in his glass. "The last thing we need is the media writing headlines about the team's wiener obsession."

"You think I could deep throat this one, Bear?" Griffin asks, dangling the rest of his hotdog in front of his face with his mouth wide open. "Ten bucks says I could do two at one time."

"No bet,'" Barrett responds. I have to laugh as Oliver Magallan and I glance at each other. Even in the off-season Barrett "The Bear" Cunningham is in a grumpy mood.

"Dude, Bear, you alright down there big man?" I ask him. "You need someone to deep throat your wiener?"

"You offering, Blackstone?"

I rub my scruffy chin playfully and pretend I'm giving the idea some thought. "I tell you what, if the zombie apocalypse ever comes, I'll make sure you're well serviced right before we turn, alright? Instead of death coming for you, you will come hard for death."

"Fuck the zombie apocalypse. It's never going to happen." He shakes his head and wipes a few sweat beads from his forehead. Nothing like a ninety-five-degree July day to take in a baseball game with the guys. We're used to the cold temperatures around the ice so while this is a pleasant change, it's also hotter than Satan's taint out here.

"You know what you *should* worry about though?" Ledger Dayne adds to our conversation from behind us.

I turn my head slightly so he knows I'm paying attention. "What's that?"

"You should worry about the twat apocalypse, because that shit's already upon us, bro."

Playing along, I gasp, grab my phone, and swipe open my weather app. "A twat storm you say? Are we about to have an overwhelming number of twats at our disposal? You call that an apocalypse, but I call that a normal Saturday night."

"Riiiight." Griffin laughs beside me. "Like you've seen an influx of anything of the sort lately."

"What?" I shrug. "How do you know whether I have or haven't?"

"Uh, how about because you tell me about every piece of tail you capture. I'm like your virtual bed-post marker. The keeper of your fucks, if you will, and so I'll just come out and say, dear friend, it's been a hot minute for you."

My smile fades because damn, he's right. It has been a minute.

"Aww, it's okay August. We all go through dry spells once in a while."

"Hey look who's up to bat." Oliver motions to home plate. "That's Carter Matthews, he's the brother of one of Charlee's friends. And I think now brother-in-law to Zeke Miller."

Oliver's sister, Charlene AKA Charlee, lives in Chicago. She's married to Milo Landric who plays for the Chicago Red Tails, so now because of Oliver we've hung out a little with their whole team. Great bunch of guys. I wish we got to spend more time with players from other teams. Once or twice a year on the ice is never enough and we don't get to be us when we're on the ice anyway.

Carter swings at the first pitch.

"Strike one," Griffin says before he leans over to me and asks, "So why the dry spell?"

Carter swings again at the second pitch and misses for an 0-2 count.

"I don't know." I shrug. "I think I'm bored."

"Bored?" He laughs again. "How the hell are you bored? It's summertime. How are you not out tapping every woman you come in contact with? How are you not traveling to all the remote islands of the world?"

"Alone?" I scoff. "I'm not taking some stranger on vacation and I'm definitely not going alone."

"I don't know." Griffin shrugs. "It worked for Magallan."

Carter swings at the third pitch and makes contact with the ball. We watch as it flies to the outfield and Carter runs all the way to second base.

"What about me?" Oliver asks.

Oliver Magallan, our team captain, fell in love with a girl after accompanying her on her honeymoon over Halloween last year. Ledger's cousin, Scarlett, was ghosted at the altar. Poor thing. Apparently, she was a bit of a mess, but she took it in stride and put out an all-call on social media for a date to the year's biggest Halloween party that was supposed to be part of her honeymoon. Ledger thought it would be a clever idea for Oliver to go with her so he kind of set up their arrangement and the rest is history. Who knew he would fall for some girl on her honeymoon?

Me though...yeah, I haven't been that lucky. Not yet anyway.

"Oh, I'm just reminding August here that you were lucky enough to fall in love with Scarlett after taking her on her honeymoon."

"Yeah well, we'll call those extenuating circumstances," I say. "Ledger's related to Scarlett and he knew Oliver would be good for her."

Griffin huffs out a laugh. "Oh, so that's what you want?"

"What?" I ask, tossing back my beer.

"You want me to set you up with someone?"

I nearly snort at Griffin's suggestion, coughing when my beer goes up my nose. "No fucking thank you. I can find someone to eat my wiener perfectly fine on my own."

Griffin shrugs. "A warm body, yeah. But we're not talking about pussy."

"Then what are we talking about?"

"You said you were bored," he reminds me. "Maybe you need a woman. Like an honest to God relationship."

"And why would I do that? I'm not home for several months out of the year. Our schedule is rigorous and I have women throwing themselves at me everywhere we play. No girlfriend or wife wants to see that. It wouldn't be fair to her."

"Then how do you think Oliver and Scarlett make it work?"

"Easy," Oliver jumps in. "Scarlett is a social media guru. She travels just as much as we do. And quite frankly, she could follow the team wherever we go, doing whatever she wants to do, and her followers would follow us. So really, it's a win-win for them, for her, and the team."

"Alright wise ass." Griffin turns back, rolling his eyes. "You might be right about that, but what I'm trying to say is I bet you two aren't bored. You have each other. You have someone to wake up to every morning and go to bed with every night. You laugh, you talk, you enjoy each other's company. Life is better when you have someone to share it with and maybe that's what August needs."

"Says the single guy who hasn't had a serious girlfriend in at least three years and has been playing with his wiener in the middle of this baseball game."

"Ooh." He scowls. "Ouch. You wound me."

"Just telling it like it is. I'm not the only one in a dry spell."

"He's not wrong there," Ledger adds.

"Alright but I like to see my friends happy so leave it to me to play matchmaker. Ledger's in love with Marlee Remington so I've got to work on that one."

Ledger's eyes bulge and even in the summer sun I can see his face turn red. "What? I am not. Why would you say that?"

"Because it's true dude. We all see the way you look at her."

He slouches in his seat. "Yeah well, she never looks at me."

"She will Ledge." Griffin pats Ledger's knee. "I promise, one day, she will." He turns back to me. "Now, what about that girl?"

I roll my eyes and take another sip of my beer, watching the next batter for the Indianapolis Racers connect with the ball for a home run.

Dang. Anaheim is not having a great game.

"What girl?"

"You know," he adds, wiping his face with the hem of his t-shirt, "your friend. That one you facetime every week."

My brows peak and I nearly spit out my drink when I realize who he's talking about. "Ella?"

"Yeah. Her. How about her?"

Now I do laugh. "Dude, she lives on the entire other side of the country first of all. Secondly, she's nowhere near my type and thirdly, if she would've heard you just now suggesting that the two of us hook up she would be laughing even harder than me. And she'd probably give you the finger."

"Oooh. Right up the butt, I hope. Man, I enjoy a girl who likes to get dirty."

"Fuck off, Ollenberg," I say to Griffin. Ella and I don't have to be dating for me to know I don't like other people talking about her. Or her fingers apparently.

Griffin frowns. "I guess I just assumed you two were in love or you had this secret relationship you didn't want to tell anyone about."

Harrison raises his hand but continues to stare out at the field. "Not going to lie, August. I thought that too."

"Same," Oliver adds.

"Yep," Barrett says with a belch.

I shake my head emphatically. "No way, guys. Ella's just a friend. My very best friend. I've told you that. We've known each other for...pfft...basically since we could walk. We were neighbors so we hung out a lot as kids. Her parents were kind of hard on her growing up so she spent a lot of time at my house. I guess I was kind of her getaway. Her safe space." I take another gulp of my beer and swallow it down. "Anyway, if we were going to be an item, that would've happened a long fucking time ago. And if we were having a secret relationship, you certainly wouldn't ever see me fucking other women in a goddamn hotel after a game. Not that you see that, you know, literally. I'm just saying. I would be loyal as fuck to her. She's too good of a person to be cheated on. I'd fuck up the asshole that ever did that to her."

Griffin gives me a little side eye and then shakes his head. "So, you two never...?"

I snicker with a shake of my head as well. "Not a chance. Well—" I stop short. "We did kiss once."

"See? I knew it!" Griffin's eyes bulge as he points at me. The rest of the guys laugh quietly.

I lift my hands in front of me. "Whoa, slow down. It wasn't like that, I promise. We were like twelve. Maybe thirteen but not quite in high school yet."

Griffin twists his mouth. "Oh."

"Yeah. We agreed to kiss each other, you know, be each other's first, so we could both learn what it felt like, and it was terrible. And by that I mean we were both terrible at it. First it was this tiny peck on the lips and then we didn't know what to do with our tongues so let's just say it was a gross wet mess that tasted like Swedish fish and sour cream and onion Pringles."

"Oh, my God." Ledger snorts. "Okay, that's funny shit."

"Yeah we both laughed about it after the fact and promised

never to tell anyone and certainly never to try it again. So don't tell her I told you anything."

Griffin crosses his heart with his fingers. "Cross my heart."

I don't miss Ledger and Oliver crossing their fingers and giving each other a high five. I roll my eyes, frustrated with myself for breaking my own rule. Never tell the guys anything you don't want coming back to bite you. That little tidbit I just dropped is definitely going to bite me in the ass one day.

"Anyway, we watched each other date lots of," I shake my head, "wrong people over the years. We've always had, and still have to this day, one of those relationships where I can tell her anything, you know? And I know she doesn't judge me for it because she knows me and I know her. And I've always reciprocated that for her. She tells me all sorts of random shit whether I need to know it or not."

"What does she do?" Harrison asks.

Griffin tilts his head. "Isn't she like, a professional cheerleader or something?"

"No. She's a cheerleading coach back where we went to college."

"And how would you feel if she lived out here?" Barrett asks from the end of the row. Seriously, I didn't think he was paying attention to this conversation.

How would I feel?

Elated.

Happy as fuck.

Like my life is complete.

Like I have someone to really share life with.

"Why do you ask?"

"Because I heard Marlee Remington talking to one of the other ladies in the front office about how Stockler is moving and they're thinking this might be an opportunity to retire Astro and come up with a whole new mascot."

All of us turn our heads toward Barrett, our jaws dropped in shock.

"Kingston Stockler? As in our team mascot?"

He nods. "Yeah. His wife got a promotion at work which means they're moving to Seattle. He's going with her to help with the kids. He's always said his family comes first."

"You think Ella should apply to be the team's mascot?" I ask him, but he merely shrugs.

"I'm not saying yes and I'm not saying no because I don't know who the fuck Ella is except that she appears to be some imaginary friend you supposedly talk to every Tuesday night. But if you're as close as you say you are, you might want her to be out here and her background sounds like she might have the right experience. I guess you would have to talk to the front office."

My thoughts start to run with the idea of Ella applying to be the team's mascot.

Would she want that?

Could she do it?

Of course she could do it.

She would be great at it.

And she'd probably love every minute of it.

"So, they're replacing Kingston?"

"I imagine they will, yeah." Barrett nods. "There's nobody else that does his job."

Oliver places his hand on my shoulder. "Do you think your girl would want to give it a go?"

"She's not my girl, and anyway..." I turn back in my seat. "I seriously doubt it. That would mean a huge move for her. Not sure that's really something she wants. She seems happy where she is."

CHAPTER TWO

ELLA

"So, then Timmy Randulph, remember him from high school? I mean he's fully grown now obviously and has a wife and two kids, but anyway, he pulled his pants down right there in the middle of the drive-in and gave us all a good look at his full moon, and Auggie," I pause to finally take a breath. "The man has the whitest ass I think I have ever seen."

"How did we get on to the subject of Timmy Randulph and his white ass again?"

I scoff. "August Blackstone are you even paying attention to me?"

"What if I told you I wasn't?"

"Wouldn't be the first time," I respond with a quick roll of my eyes. "What if I told you this facetime call is over?"

He gives me a smile and a quick wink because he knows I hate it when he's not paying attention to me. I only get to talk to him once a week so I really value our time together.

"I'm just kidding Montgomery. Don't get your panties in a twist. Timmy Randulph has a white ass. Noted. Also, because of that statement, I'm now making myself an appointment to have my ass spray tanned."

I laugh at his retort. God, I love that he can always make me laugh. I love that we laugh a lot when we're together like this. It's like no matter what's going on in life, our Tuesday nights are always a happy night.

A night of hometown comfort.

A night with my best friend.

I miss the old days.

I miss him.

The day we graduated from college back in Indigo Bay, Massachusetts, we knew we would be taking different paths. August would go wherever his hockey career would take him, and I would stay in Indigo Bay to become one of the new cheer coaches while working as one of the resident directors. I've done a few other odd jobs to make extra income since being an RD doesn't pay all that much, but I've always been great at pepping up a crowd. I enjoyed cheerleading growing up and was always good at it. To be honest, I think August was surprised when we graduated and I didn't try out to be an NFL cheerleader. He always said they'd be lucky to have me, and I always appreciated how much he supported my efforts. Instead, though, I stayed behind and made him promise we would always stay in touch. Hence, our weekly facetime calls. August hasn't been home in almost two years but seeing his face every Tuesday evening, even if it's after a game and he's exhausted or I'm tired because I've waited up for him due to the time difference, have always been one of my favorite things. It's like I can finally be me again. And he can be August Blackstone, the guy from small town Mass-achusetts instead of August Blackstone, pro hockey player for the Anaheim Stars.

"I'm sure your ass isn't nearly as white as Timmy's, Auggie. Don't forget you live in California."

"And don't you forget that just because I live in California does not mean I walk around in the sun with my assless chaps on all the time."

"Oooh are you saying you actually *have* assless chaps?" I gasp, sitting up on my bed ready for a show. "Oh, my God, you have to show me!"

My enthusiasm for his non-tanned ass makes him laugh. "I'm not showing you my ass, Ella."

"Come on, I saw it when we were like..."

"Four," he finishes, leaning back on his bed, his head resting on his arm behind him. Damn when he does that it makes his arm look massive. "Maybe even younger. Trust me, babe. It looks much different now."

I'm sure it does.

"Right," I giggle. "It's all swole now because you're a big bad hockey star. My bad."

He chuckles softly. "Something like that."

"Well, I'm certain many other women have gotten to see August Blackstone's ass. I'm your best friend, which means I love you more than all those women combined and I am still in the dark."

"And the dark is where you are staying."

"How am I supposed to talk you up to all my friends and all your fans? I could be telling them all what a fine as fuck ass you have."

"You gonna show me your tits?"

I scrunch my nose and squeal with laughter. "What? No!"

"Why not? I could be telling all my friends what beautiful tits you have."

"Ugh. You're incorrigible." I roll my eyes and give him a goofy grin.

He chuckles again, softer this time, and I can tell he's a little tired. "And I'm right. So, I rest my case."

I lie back on my bed and release a loud sigh. "Fuck my life."

"Why? Just because I won't show you my white ass?" He passes me a sideways smile. "Now you think your life is that bad?"

"Alright. Alright. Subject change. Did I tell you Paige is falling for a goat man?"

He almost chokes on his water. "Come again?"

"Okay so he's not a goat man. But he owns a goat. More than one I think. She's in Tuft Swallow for the summer filling in for her aunt and uncle. They own that antique store there. Anyway, she met a guy and I think she's falling for him and you know what that means?"

"Nope but I'm sure you're about to tell me."

I rest my arm across my eyes like I can't bear to say it. "It means she's finding someone to spend her life with. And now I'm all alone!"

"You're not all alone. I'm right here."

I lift my arm. "Umm, no offense but you're all the way on the other side of the country. And you've got your hockey career and all the sex, love, and rock and roll that comes with that."

"You're making my life sound much more glamourous than it really is, you know."

"You don't have to lie to me, Auggie. You're a celebrity. And you deserve all the things a celebrity athlete could possibly have in life. I'm just jealous because I'm stuck here in stupid Indigo Bay with nothing and nobody."

There really isn't much in Indigo Bay. It's a small college town where everybody knows everybody else. Honestly, Auggie was right to get out, but it killed me that he was leaving me with no promise of when I would ever get to see him again.

"Quiet around campus this summer I assume?"

"Of course. It's always quiet in the summertime. I'm starting to hate it. You guys are out there living life and loving every minute of it I'm starting to regret staying here."

"Okay, then change things up. Make a move. Do something new."

"Like what?"

He's quiet for a minute and I can tell he's thinking something. "Well...actually, what would you think about becoming a hockey team mascot?"

I cock my head. "A what? What are you talking about?"

"Astro, our mascot. The guy who wears the costume is leaving the team," he explains. "His wife got a promotion and they're moving to Seattle. So, the Stars are going to have to do a search to find the next Astro, only Bear mentioned something about them creating a whole new mascot and retiring Astro so I guess I don't really know all the specifics yet."

Me?

A hockey mascot?

The wheels begin to turn in my head. "You're serious about this?"

"Why would I bring it up if I weren't serious babe? I wouldn't do that to you."

My smile widens and the sparkle returns to my eyes for just a moment. "You think I could really do it though? You think I could seriously wear the costume and do all the things and like, be the face of the team?"

"Of course. You're great at what you do now. As long as you can skate on ice, and I know you can because I'm the one who taught you, you can do this job."

Oh, my gosh! How cool would it be to be a freaking team mascot! Wait..." My smile morphs into an uncomfortable cringe. "Uh...what does a job like that pay? California has a much higher cost of living than Indigo Bay. I might end up living on the streets. Hmm, maybe I could substitute teach by day and mascot by night. I don't know. It sounds cool but I'm sure there are more qualified people out there. Honestly, it's probably too good to be true."

"Don't sell yourself short, Ella. Hang on," he tells me as he swipes through something on his phone. "Okay so I'm sure I can find out what Kingston was making but Google says starting salaries run anywhere from sixty to seventy thousand per year."

"WHOA! Sixty to seventy thousand! That's way more than I make now! Ugh...but we're talking about California. Is that enough?" I cringe. "I mean I feel terrible for even asking that because to me that's more money than I could ever dream of and I realize I'm talking to a millionaire hockey star but still. It's a ton of money compared to what I'm making now but California is California. I'm pretty sure just breathing costs a couple thousand dollars a day. Can I get a nice place on that salary Auggie? You would know better than me. Where would I live? Would it be like a relatively sturdy carboard box in an old, abandoned parking lot somewhere or would there actually be an apartment with working doors and windows?"

He chuckles lightly on the other end of the line and looks straight at the camera on his phone "What do you mean where would you live, Ella? Why wouldn't you live with me?"

Wait.

What?

My brow furrows. "Uuuh, why would I do that?"

"Uuuh..." he mocks. "Why wouldn't you? My place is huge. It's more than enough space for two people. We're friends who haven't gotten to really see each other in...how long's it been?"

"Two years at least."

Two years, five months, and fourteen days, but who's counting?

"Right. Two years. Plus, for about eight to nine months out of the year, I'm not here, so you'd have the place to yourself."

I give him a gentle smile and clear my throat. "Auggie. My dear sweet Auggie. You're forgetting one thing."

"What?"

"If I move out there, it's because I'll have the job as the new Anaheim Stars team mascot. So that means for eight to nine months out of the year, I also won't be there much."

"Damn," he mumbles, shaking his head. "Guess there goes the getting a cat idea."

I spring up in my bed, my eyes widening in surprise. "WHAT DID YOU JUST SAY?"

He shrugs, but I see the tiny smirk on his lips. He knows what he's doing. "I was just thinking man, it would be cool to have a pet around here. Some rascally cat that makes me laugh but keeps me company. Thought maybe if you moved out here we could get one together."

I've never jumped out of bed faster. "SOLD! OH, MY GOD! I'M MOVING TO ANAHEIM! NO TAKE BACKS, AUGUST!" I point at him with a seriously serious face even though he's laughing at me right now. "You said cat! And you never say cat! You hated cats when we were younger! You threatened to put my cat in the microwave when we were ten!"

"I didn't mea—"

"Do you remember that day?"

"Yes but—"

"Do you remember how much I cried?"

"How could I for—"

"Wait!" I narrow my eyes and lower my voice to a low whisper. "Do you have a microwave in that palatial home of yours? Because if you do, it better not be there when I get there or so help me—"

"ELLA!" August's guttural laugh is one of the most comforting sounds I could ever hear. He doesn't laugh like that often but when he does it makes me miss the younger version of ourselves. When we would run free all day through the fields or play in the creek or ride our bikes into town to grab ice cream sandwiches. It never mattered what we were up to in those younger years. As long as we were together.

"What?"

"I promise I won't put our new cat in the microwave, okay?"

"Will you let me name him?"

"Not a chance." He shakes his head, his smile fading.

"What? Why?"

"Because if I let you name our cat, he'll end up with a name like Sunflower Teapot."

It's my turn to laugh now. "Don't be absurd. I would never."

"You totally would. We would have a little Sunflower Doily Teapot walking around our house and our cat is going to be a manly cat. The manliest cat we can possibly find."

"Alright, alright. Just promise you won't name him something weird like Cletus or Dickface or...Greg."

"How about we pick it out and name it together?"

"Okay that sounds wonderful." Feeling a little calmer now, I climb back into bed and take a few silent breaths. "Am I really doing this, Auggie?"

"Moving to California to start a new chapter of your life next to your lifelong best friend who loves you and can be here to support you through it? Yes."

"Wait...we didn't talk rent. I can pay you. How much do you want? I think I have a good bit in my savings to start."

He blinks ever so slowly, staring at me like I just said I was walking to California. "You're not paying me, Ella."

"But—"

"No."

"Aug—"

"No."

"What if—"

"Nope."

"I have to gi—"

"No, you don't."

"Why?"

"Because I fucking said so, El."

"Auggie."

"Ella, listen to me. I make millions of dollars a year. Not hundreds. Not thousands. MILLIONS. Do you understand that?"

"No. No I don't," I answer honestly with a shake of my head. "I can't begin to understand that kind of money. I don't know how you even do it."

"So, on top of those millions of dollars, the last thing I need, the very last thing I need is to charge you even a dime to live in my space. Believe me when I say there's enough room for you, and ten cats if we—"

Too late.

He said it.

My eyes bulge and my jaw drops and I gasp. "OH, MY GOD are you saying—"

"No." He shakes his head, staring me down and giving me the parental point of his finger. "No, I am not saying anything. I said one cat."

"You just said ten."

"I meant one. And then a zero after that. One and then none. So, one."

A huge smile spreads across my face at the prospect of my life taking a completely new turn. "August?"

"Yeah, babe?"

"I'm really doing this."

He nods, giving me that sweet smile I remember. "You really are."

Realization of what has to come next hits me and I fall back against my pillow. "Oh fuck."

"What? What's wrong?"

"I have to tell my parents."

PAIGE

> GIRL! Where have you been? Did you not get my last text? I've been wanting to talk to you for DAYS!

DAYS? She's been waiting to talk for days? Did she get wind of my impending move and now she's mad at me for not telling her sooner?

Shit.

I should've told her weeks ago when the idea was brought up, but I know she's been busy with the antique shop and falling for the hot goat-dad guy and I didn't want to bother her until all my plans were made. I certainly didn't want her to talk me out of it. August is right. This is a good move for me. After emailing the Stars front office a video of my cheer work, and having an initial phone interview, they offered me a chance to interview in person so they can really get to know me better before deciding. Gah! This could be a super fun job opportunity that would earn me tons of new connections. The last thing I want is for my best friend to think it's a bad idea.

ME

> Why? Did you hear something? What did you hear? Who told you?

PAIGE

Uh...was I supposed to hear something? Now I'm intrigued.

ME

Oh. Umm, hehe welllll I might have some news.

PAIGE

You're not pregnant! Tell me you're not pregnant.

ME

Wait, what? Why would I be pregnant? I'm single AF right now.

PAIGE

That doesn't mean you can't go out and get yourself knocked up.

ME

Truth. Okay but rest assured, I'm not pregnant. But I do have news and I'm sorry I haven't been answering my texts over the last couple of days. It's been a little stressful and a lot busy and HOLY SHIT HE KISSED YOU?

PAIGE

Oh, NOW we're talking about the kiss? What's your news?

ME

Not until you tell me about this kiss!

PAIGE

What do you want to know? It was a kiss. His lips touched my lips. And then we moved them together in a slippy-slidey kind of way.

ME

LOL. Okay but was it like...sweet and slow? Or did he grab you and take what he wanted?

PAIGE

Definitely sweet and slow. It was almost like he was nervous and then once he actually went through with it he was like "yeah, that's right. I'm good at this. I remember now." I mean, I know I joke about it but it really was a moment with him I don't think I could ever forget.

ME

AAAAAHHHHHH!!! This is so exciting! So, have you seen him since? How does he seem? Did you bone him yet?

PAIGE

There has been no boning. And yes I've seen him since. Obviously. He's kissed me a few more times now. Well, pretty much every time he's around me. It's kind of cute, but he'll stop in when I'm working and drop something off like a drink or a cookie but really it's just his excuse to kiss me.

ME

Oh, my goodness that's so sweet.

PAIGE

It is. I know he's always come across as grumpy to everyone else but he's actually a super sweet guy. I really think I like him a lot. But more on that later. What's your news?

ME

Right. Soooo ummmm I'm moving to California.

PAIGE

"WHAT THE FUCK? CALIFORNIA?"

ME

OH, ARE WE TALKING IN CAPS NOW? OR ARE YOU ACTUALLY SHOUTING IN REAL LIFE?

PAIGE

ELLA!

ME

Okay, okay. Yes. California.

PAIGE

You're seriously leaving me? What are you going to do? Where are you going to stay? Have you had this plan this whole time and never told me? I thought I was your person?

ME

You are Paige. You are my person. Which is why you also know I haven't been happy sticking around Indigo Bay any more than you have been. I need new. I need the unknown. I need a challenge. And Auggie told me there's a job I could apply for with the team and he said I could move out there and stay with him. It's a fantastic opportunity for me.

PAIGE

Have to go for a bit. Customers need me. Talk later. Love you E!

ME

Yes! Go be an antique star! Love you, P!

"Well, that wasn't nearly enough time to talk to you about all this new stuff." I get it though. My best friend is having the summer of her life in Tuft Swallow and I couldn't be happier for her. I really hope things work out between her and this goat-dad guy. I've really got to find time to find out more about him. I sigh as I toss my phone onto my bed and stare at the three boxes I'm shipping to California. If all goes well, I can just travel with two suitcases. I think I have enough winterish clothes packed, but seeing as I'll be living in the warm sunshine state, hopefully I won't need too much.

PAIGE

OMG so sorry I never got back to you. I'm a terrible friend right now. Tell me you're still in Massachusetts and I didn't miss the big move!

ME

Nope! Still here. Boxing up all my shit. Just confirmed my flight reservations.

PAIGE

Tell me more about this move to California. What's the job? And you ARE coming to see me before that happens, right?? (You had better say yes!) Also how did your parents take the news?

ME

Of course, I'll come and see you! A couple of hours drive is nothing compared to an entire country between us. And the job is to be the new TEAM MASCOT! Also, my parents weren't the happiest but they know I'm an adult and will do whatever I want anyway so they'd rather know where I'm going than have me move away and not tell them.

PAIGE

Well, that's…mature of them. Team mascot!? OMG are you SERIOUS? 😂

ME

Yes! Apparently the one they've had is leaving California with his wife and Auggie says I have all the qualifications and it actually pays pretty decently. I mean much more than I make now anyway.

PAIGE

Holy shit, Ella! What an opportunity!

ME

Right? That's what I said. Even if it's a steppingstone…it's something new and exciting and I need new and exciting.

PAIGE

Okay so, when do you leave?

ME

Mid-September, so a couple weeks. Once they finally posted about their job search I applied and had a phone interview. Then I waited several days while they interviewed the rest of their top contenders and then I got an invitation to fly out and interview in person but their person in charge is going on vacation so they asked if I could do the interview in a couple weeks.

PAIGE

And so, you're not waiting to see how the interview goes before moving your whole self out there?

ME

Would you? I mean, I've been in Indigo Bay my whole damn life. And something just felt good on the phone with them. It felt right. I'm getting all the good vibes.

PAIGE

No, I guess you're right. It makes me sad that you could be leaving me but this could be a wonderful opportunity for you. I'm positive even if this job doesn't work out (which I'm sure it will if Auggie has anything to say about it), you'll have no problem finding something! And as long as you're living with Auggie, you won't have to be immensely stressed about living expenses while you're looking.

ME

I really hope Aug doesn't insert himself too much into trying to get me this job. I really want to earn it on my own. The last thing I want is for someone to say I got the job because of who I know.

PAIGE

Meh. I wouldn't worry about that. It's not like you're sleeping with someone to get the job. You just know one of the players. Shit like that happens all the time. Sometimes a connection is what we need to get our foot in the door. After that, you have to show off how awesome you are! Trust me, you're going to be great!

ME

So, tell me more about the hot kissing goat daddy!

CHAPTER THREE

AUGUST

"Come on asshats! Shoot the fuckers like you mean it!"

"Yikes, Barrett," Griffin says with a quick smirk. "Are we really deciding to start the preseason with last season's stick still up your ass?" Griffin circles the net and comes up on Barrett's left, shooting the puck toward the net, but Bear blocks it with ease.

"Stick feels pretty good up there." He grunts and gestures to Griffin's hockey stick. "You'll see what I'm talking about if you don't learn to shoot harder and faster the next time you try to sneak around the net. You're too predictable."

Griffin flips him off as he skates toward me, but I'm hyper focused on pulling one over on our grumpy goalie.

"Slide it in pretty boy," Harrison says, standing not far from me. "I'll distract him for you."

I smile at myself as Harrison skates toward Barrett, weaving around our teammates and shuffling a puck down the ice with his stick. As he circles around the net, I prepare for my shot, passing another practice puck back and forth between Oliver and myself as I change positions on the ice. Edging closer to the net, Barrett is focused on Harrison's position, so I take my shot, forcefully hitting the puck toward him at the same time as Harrison. I watch in awe as Barrett lowers into a split, successfully blocking Harrison's shot with his left thigh and my shot with his stick.

"Dammit," I groan with irritation.

I really thought I had that.

Barrett lifts his goalie mask so he can wink at the both of us. "Nice try fuckers. Better luck next time."

If there's one thing I can say about Barrett, "The Bear", Cunningham, he's a true beast when he's out on the ice. Best goalie in the league by a mile.

"Anyone see that article about the hotshot kid, Bodhi Roche?" Ledger asks as several of us step into the shower after practice.

"Read it last night," I answer. "He's got some great stats, that's for sure."

Griffin scoffs. "I hear he's a little diva dick though."

Oliver scowls. "Where did you hear that?"

"Social media," Griffin explains. "Sports news won't report that kind of shit but leave it to social media to hear what a few people who have played with him think."

"Oh yeah!" Ledger nods. "Like that one guy. The dude who got hurt several years ago during his rookie year and can't play anymore. What was his name?"

"Jeff Furbling," I mumble.

"Yes!" Ledger points at me. "Jeff Furbling! I swear I saw a social media post where that guy was complaining about Bodhi's stats. He rambles on and on about how much better he was than this kid."

"Guess we'll never know though, will we?" Griffin shrugs as he lathers shampoo between his hands. "Dumbass went and got himself injured before he could really make something of himself."

Jeff is right though.

He was better.

In his day.

Before he got hurt.

Before I knocked him into the wall during a game that shattered his knee and fractured three vertebrae in his neck.

We were friends once, Jeff and me. Well, friendly rivals, anyway. Both graduated from the same high school and then attended rival colleges. We knew each other very well and it helped both of us when we faced off on the ice. I knew his strengths and weaknesses like the back of my hand. I knew his directional pivots were never fast but the guy had eagle eye vision when it came to shooting the puck from anywhere on the ice. Fuck, if I didn't use that knowledge to my benefit anytime I could. He boasted his scoring stats all the time, but the fucker never pushed himself to be faster on his feet. I always equated him to the kicker on a football team. He was good for one thing only and that was shooting the puck, but he would never win a race skating down the ice. I knew I would always be able to kick his ass when the time came. We played against each other numerous times early on in our hockey days, but I'll never forget that game in the first year of our pro hockey career.

The game that ended his before the end of the second period.

All because of me.

But none of these guys know I was the one who checked Jeff into the wall. It happened before I was traded to Anaheim and at the time neither of us was a big enough name for the story to take off. Lucky for me, I guess, but that doesn't mean I don't feel bad for ending another player's career. It was an accident nobody saw coming. I mean yeah, I wanted to check the son of a bitch and show him who was boss, but I didn't plan for a pile up to occur just before bashed him back into the wall. That hit caused parts of his body to literally snap.

That wasn't my plan at all, but it happened all the same.

He's blamed me for it for years, I know.

He bashes me on social media every now and then, but I've learned to tune him out. He's angry. I get it, but accidents happen. I felt bad then, but I've made my peace and moved on.

"Well, if Jeff Furbling is right about Bodhi Roche, it'll be interesting to see where he ends up after the draft next year."

Ledger laughs. "Let's hope he goes to Chicago. Let the Red Tails deal with the prick," right Oliver?"

"If he knows what's good for him, he'll check his tiny penis sized ego at the door if he ends up in Chicago," Oliver says with a chuckle. "Landric might end up putting a fist through the kid's face like he did to McClacken."

I narrow my eyes. "Wasn't Landric just protecting your sister when he attacked McClacken?"

"In that instance, yes, and I have no doubt the fucker deserved every punch Milo threw at him. Also, Milo didn't know she was my sister at the time, so to him, he was just protecting his girl. Landric is a great guy. He was definitely worthy of marrying my sister after that night, though if you ask me, he was worthy of her the very first night he took her in, but that's a whole other story. He keeps Charlee happy so I'm not complaining one bit. But he has no patience for egos when it comes to being on the ice. He's a team player through and through."

"Hey, speaking of girls," Griffin mentions before turning off his water and grabbing a towel. "What's the status on your non-girlfriend girl...friend? She coming for that interview?"

"Actually yeah." I nod, finishing with my shower and also reaching for my towel. "Her stuff was delivered to my place two days ago and I'm picking her up from the airport this afternoon."

"Wait...her stuff?" Ledger asks from a few shower stalls down. "What does that mean?"

"Her stuff. You know, her belongings."

"Oh, so she found a place to live and everything? That's awesome. Which area did she decide on?"

"Uh, she didn't, actually. She's moving in with me."

Silence falls over everyone in the room. The only sound is that of the few showers still running but one by one, the water is turned off and a towel is grabbed. Griffin is staring at me as if I just told a joke and he doesn't understand the punch line. Harrison comes out from his shower stall, wrapping his towel around his waist.

"Did you just say she's moving in with you?"

"Yeah."

"OKAY, HOLD THE FUCKING PHONE!" Ledger shouts from the shower, still drying off. "Blackstone is skipping the fuck-around-and-find-out and going right for the move-in-with me?" He jumps out of his shower stall staring at me like I'm an alien as he steps toward Griffin, whose head is cocked to the side as he eyes me mysteriously. "Who is this guy and what has he done with August Blackstone?"

"That's what I want to know," Griffin mumbles back to him.

"Alright, alright, this isn't that big of a deal guys." I toss on a pair of shorts and grab my t-shirt from my locker.

A towel wrapped around his waist and still dripping from the shower, Ledger crosses his arms over his chest. "Uh...I beg to differ. Moving in with a woman is kind of a huge deal."

"So, you guys really are a thing, then?" Griffin asks with a twinge of unhappiness in his voice. He almost seems disappointed, as if I've been keeping a secret from him. Like I would keep a secret like that from my best friend.

"Hell no." I shake my head with a scowl. "I told you, we're not a thing. We've never been a thing. We're not going to be a thing."

On the other side of the room Barrett lets out a laugh but says nothing. He lets his towel drop to the floor, his bare ass on display for the rest of us. Not that this is anything new.

"What's so funny, Cunningham?"

"You are, Blackstone," he says, pulling on his boxer briefs. "Not a thing, never been a thing, never going to be a thing? I call bullshit. If that girl moves in with you, you'll have your dick inside her before the end of preseason."

Fury almost chokes me as I march across the room, my fists clenched at my sides. I step up against Barrett's huge frame. By all means I should be intimidated as fuck at the sheer size of him. He stands at least a head taller than me and probably has a solid fifty pounds on me, but I don't give two shits how big of a man he is. I'll be damned if I stand here and allow someone to talk about Ella that way.

"Say that again to my face *cunt*-ingham." I pin him with a cold stare but he remains unfazed. The corner of his mouth turns up and he calmly takes a breath before he opens his mouth again.

"I said, you'll have your—"

"Ooookay." Griffin steps in between us, pushing me away while patting Barrett's chest lightly. "I think we heard what you said the first time, big Bear, but thanks for offering to remind us again."

Not really wanting to sport a black eye on the day my best friend is finally coming to town, I step back over to my locker and continue getting dressed, only to hear Barrett mumble, "Am I wrong?"

I turn toward the rest of the team, eyeing each one as they

look between Barrett and me. My jaw drops and I shake my head. "Well, don't all speak at once."

"Yeah," Ledger speaks slowly like he's unsure of what he's saying. "No, you're very...uh...wrong, Bear. Very wrong indeed."

Harrison leans over and whispers loudly, "Dude that was so not convincing."

Ledger shrugs. "I know, but what was I supposed to say?"

"Wait," I speak up. "So, you all agree with Bear? You think I'm going to fuck my best friend? Simply because she has a pussy and will be living in my house?"

It's quiet in the room for a long awkward minute before anyone answers. Finally, Oliver asks, "Have you ever lived with a woman?"

"No."

"Ever even had one in your house?"

"You know I haven't. My house is my safe space. It's not for random hookups."

"And how long have you known her?"

"What does that even matter? She's my childhood best friend, assholes. We grew the fuck up together. I know what kind of tampons she used in high school. I know what she sounds like when she's hungover puking in the middle of the night or early in the morning. I know she likes her coffee with way too much sugar and way too much cream. I know who her favorite celebrity crush was when she was ten. I know she used to smash up her peas and spread it over toast when she was in first grade because she thought it was good and because it made her giggle to tell people she peed on her toast. I was the one she ran to when her parents would come down hard on her for stupid reasons like she didn't clean her room or she got a B on a test. I was with her to see her first rated R movie. You know what it was? *We're the Millers*! I know she stuffs her face with cinnamon rolls when she's nervous, and I know she gets nervous all the time over stupid shit because her parents made her that way. And I've watched her pop more pimples in our high school days than I ever want or need to see in my lifetime, because we are friends. The best of friends. We know everything about each other and we have since we could walk. Why do you all find it so hard to understand that a man and a woman are very capable of sharing a living space without fucking?"

Griffin nods and then steps over to me, capping my shoulder with his hand. "I'm with you, August. If you say you're not fucking, you're not fucking."

"Thank you." I inhale a deep calming breath and release it in a heavy sigh.

"But does that mean we could fuck her?"

My head spins faster than Linda Blair in the *Exorcist*, but the moment my eyes meet Griffin's he points at me and winks. "Got ya."

I flip him off and grab my baseball cap, slipping it backwards on my head. "Asshat. Get out of here."

"So, when is she coming?" Ledger asks. "And what's her name again?"

"Her name is Ella and I'm picking her up in..." I check the time on my phone. "One hour."

"Better get moving then." He gestures to the door with his chin. "Airport traffic is a bitch."

I say goodbye to the guys, grab my keys, and head out the door. No sooner does the locker room door close behind me than I hear one of them say, "They're totally going to fuck."

The rest of the guys agree and they have a good laugh at my expense. For a moment I consider walking back in there and raising hell, but instead I take a deep breath and keep walking down the hall with an annoyed shake of my head and roll of my eyes. Once I'm out of the building and in my car, all anger dissipates from my body, replaced only by genuine excitement. I get to see my best friend for the first time in over two years and I couldn't be happier.

I make it into the airport just in time to see her plane has landed so I head to the escalator where I know she'll have to come down to baggage claim. Less than ten minutes later, I'm watching her on the escalator chatting with some guy. Something inside my chest flips, causing me to stand up a little straighter, puff my own chest out a little more.

Who the hell is that guy?

She smiles at him and although it's pissing me off that he's smiling back at her, just taking a minute to look at her from afar when she doesn't know I'm here is good because holy shit.

She's gorgeous.

I mean I've always known she was pretty, but wow. The years have...wow, we're not kids anymore. I suppose after only seeing her face for the past two years when we chat, I shouldn't be surprised seeing the rest of her. I think I allowed myself to forget just how beautiful she is.

Damn...

Her chestnut-colored hair that she always used to wear in a ponytail is now in soft ringlets and dusting just past her shoulders. She wrinkles her dainty nose before scratching the top with a finger. Ella was never the tall and stick-thin type of girl. She always had curves. I spent many nights sitting on her bed while she paraded out from the bathroom in one outfit and then another only to ask me if I thought her hips looked too wide or her boobs too big.

The answer was always no because to me she was Ella.

She was perfect.

But now those very same curves have me unable to look away from her. And if I'm struggling to look away, I know exactly why that asshole won't leave her alone. She's dressed in a pair of black leggings that hug her body perfectly and a white crop top that shows off her fit body. The zippered sweatshirt jacket she's wearing over top looks familiar. I cock my head, studying it, and realize it's not just any sweatshirt, so I quickly pull my phone from my pocket and type out a text as quickly as I can.

ME

Is that my college hockey sweatshirt?

I know the moment she gets my text because her head snaps up and she looks around, but still doesn't see me. Stepping away from the column I was leaning on, I turn my hat around backwards so she can see my face, making myself more visible. When she finally spots me, the way her eyes light up with excitement and her smile broadens across her face calms all my anxiety about the guy next to her, who she immediately ignores. Finally seeing her in person after all this time brings back every single fucking feeling...every single memory I have ever had with Ella Montgomery.

She's here.

I can't believe it.

She's fucking here.

And now I'm home.

CHAPTER FOUR

ELLA

"Auggieeeeee!" I squeal as I run toward him after stepping off the escalator. I swing my backpack off my shoulder and drop it on the ground before leaping into my best friend's arms. I wrap my legs around his waist and my arms around his neck in a hug so tight I worry I might squeeze the air right out of him.

But judging from the grip his strong arms have on me right now, I'm guessing that's not going to happen. God, he feels good.

Like comfort.

And happy.

And everything is right in the world.

"Hey babe," he murmurs into my ear as I bury my face in the crook of his neck. Hugging Auggie has always been one of my very favorite things. The number of bad days I had growing up that ended with me rushing to his house for a comforting hug were more than I can count. He's always been my source of happiness. My emotional support. My safe place.

A light chuckle rises from his chest. "Ella?"

"Hmm?"

"Did you eat a cinnamon roll on your flight?"

Shit.

How does he always know?

I finally release him and he lowers me until my feet touch the floor. With a cautious wince, I nod. "One before my first flight, one during my layover, and cinnamon roll bites on this last flight."

His brows peak and he chuckles again with a grin. "Shit, Ella. Do I make you that nervous?"

I'm crazy, I know.

I like to eat cinnamon rolls when I'm nervous.

It's a habit now.

I can't help it.

"Not exactly. I mean flying makes me nervous too but..." She shrugs. "I haven't seen you in over two years, Auggie. What if you took one look at me and decided your offer was a terrible mistake? What if we no longer have anything in common whatsoever? What if you don't want me here but you were just trying to be nice in offering me your place to live? Also, damn." I place my palms on his chest. "How the hell did you somehow get even bigger and harder than the last time I saw you? Are they force-feeding you protein powders everywhere? Sneaking it into your swole juice or something?"

He laughs, circling my wrists with his hands, which surprisingly also feel bigger and stronger. "They're feeding me just fine, babe. It's my job to stay fit. Plus we've been in preseason workouts." Still holding my hands, he steps back so he can get a better look at me. "And you look great too. This is a great look for you," he says, nodding to my leggings and crop top. "I half expected you to come down the steps in your pink sweatpants and Jonas Brothers t-shirt. And also," he tugs on the zippered hoodie I'm wearing that just happens to be his old hockey sweatshirt from freshman year of college, "where the hell did you find this?"

"It's been in my closet for years, remember? You leant it to me that one night after that concert on the quad when that drunk asshole spilled his beer all over me. I tried to return it to you but you told me to keep it...so I did. Now it's just become one of my comfort pieces. When I'm missing you, I just throw it on and pretend it's you."

He smiles with a shake of his head and pulls me back into his chest, wrapping his arms around me again. "Well, you won't have to pretend it's me anymore because I'll be right by your side. You're here now. Right where you should be. And for the record, there is zero chance in hell I would ever turn you away or not want you here, alright? If I didn't want you here, I wouldn't have offered in the first place and you'd still be living in Indigo Bay."

"Okay." I sigh, allowing myself to breathe him in.

August Blackstone.

My person.

"I believe you."

"Good," he says. "Because I'm really fucking glad you're here. Now let's go get your luggage."

"Seriously, what do they put in the water out here?" I take another glorious bite of the pepperoni pizza August bought for dinner. "This has to be the best pizza I've ever eaten."

"Mmm." August shakes his head as he swallows his bite. "That's because you haven't been to Chicago. Wait till we play the Red Tails this year. I'll take you out for the real deal. Chicago has the best deep-dish pizza in the world as far as I'm concerned."

"Yeah?"

"Hands down."

"So, tell me about the guys on the team. What are they like? Will I like them?" I lean back against the couch from my place on the floor, twisting my mouth. "Will they like me?"

He scoffs lightly. "Of course they'll like you. What kind of question is that?"

"A sincere one." I shrug. "I just want to know what they're like. I mean, I don't want to interfere with your day-to-day life but if I get this job, I'll obviously be around a lot. I wouldn't want your friends to think I'm some sort of flake or something."

"Trust me. They won't think that. They're not like that."

I curl my hand in that *come* gesture. "Okay...I'm listening. Tell me more."

August takes another bite of his slice before he speaks again. "Oliver Magallan is a great guy. He's the team captain and he's the only one of us who has a girlfriend. Well, fiancée actually. He's got a solid head on his shoulders and pretty much always does the right thing. He's like the Captain America of the Anaheim Stars. Fun fact: his sister is married to one of the players on the Red Tails so we've struck up a nice relationship slash rivalry with their team. They're good guys."

"Okay. Oliver's a ten but he's married. Got it. Next?"

August's brow rises as he watches me warily. Why I'm all of a sudden getting a chilled look from him, I have no idea.

"What? Did I say something wrong?"

He shakes his head and then clears his throat. "No. Uh, then there's Griffin. He's my best friend."

"What?" I rear back, a little hurt. "I thought I was your best friend?"

"You are babe." He smiles, wiping his mouth with his

napkin. "Okay think of Griffin more like my brother. My very humorous, sometimes crass, and inappropriate but would kill anyone for hurting you kind of brother."

I incline my head and smile. "Sounds like the perfect kind of guy. Teddy bear with a sense of humor but cross him and pay the price?"

"Yep. Exactly like that."

"Swoooon," I breathe, leaning my head back on the couch.

August laughs. "I wouldn't go that far. Also, he has this fascination with pajama pants. I can't remember if I've mentioned it before."

I cock my head. "Pajama pants? How so?"

"He collects them. He's always wearing a different pair anywhere and everywhere. He's got them in all colors and with all sorts of random designs. *Scooby Doo* pants, *Transformers* pants, *Batman* pants, *Star Wars* pants, ones with cats, ones with sloths, ones with eggs and toast. Seriously, you name it, he's probably got them."

"That sounds like fun! At least he sounds like a guy who appreciates his comfort."

"I keep telling him one day he's going to find a girl just like him and it's going to be hilarious."

"Okay, who's next?"

"Harrison," he says with a nod. "Really great guy. Hard worker. Loves kids. He helps coach the youth league whenever he can and helps run a few hockey camps over the summer during the off-season. He's one of those guys who will literally give you the shirt off his back if you ask for it. Or he'll rip it from you on the ice."

I giggle. "Really? A shirt ripper, eh?"

"These guys are all beasts on the ice. I'm telling you. They all have great personalities off the ice, but when we're on the ice and it's game time, we leave it all out there. Nothing gets through us when we're really playing well."

I purse my lips, making a mental note of all August is telling me. "Got it."

"Ledger is like another big brother. A little goofy. He has an enthusiastic sense of humor, but he's got a huge crush on one of the girls who works in the front office. He's been too scared to ask her out so sometimes he denies he has a crush at all, but we know. We see the way he is with her. It's cute. One of these days he'll come around."

I gasp, sitting up a little more interested. "Oh my gosh that sounds like cute juicy gossip! Who is she?"

"Can't tell you." August laughs. "At least not until after you get the job."

"Aww man! Why not? What if I don't get the job?"

He looks at me dismissively. "One, you'll get the job and two, if you don't, I'll absolutely tell you. I promise."

"Then why can't you just tell me now?"

"Bro code," he says plainly.

"Ugh! So unfair!"

Ignoring my cries, he continues. "Listen the only one of us who seems to have a proverbial stick up his ass is Barrett. He's our goalie and he's a grump probably a solid eighty percent of the time. So, when you meet him, don't be shocked if he comes across that way. It's just his personality."

My brows crease and I tilt my head. "Why do you think he's grumpy a lot?"

"Beats me. He works harder than anyone of us and he's fucking good at what he does. Best goalie in the league hands down though you'll never hear him say it. But he's also had a few knee issues lately. I know that bothers him more than he admits."

"Married?"

SUSAN RENEE

He shakes his head and leans forward to grab another slice of pizza from the box. "Nope. Like I said, Oliver is the only one who is in a committed relationship though they're not married yet. Honestly, I'm not sure Bear would ever get married. He doesn't seem the type."

I wag my brows. "So, a bunch of single hockey players, huh? Any of them good dating material?"

He nearly chokes on his bite at my question. "For you?"

"Yeah."

"No. Absolutely not."

I give my best friend a goofy smile. "What? Why not? You just said they were all single."

"And they're all sluts," he explains. "I'm sure Griff has had more than one sexually transmitted disease. I love the guy but he'll sleep with just about any pussy that walks by. Ledger has a tiny dick. Trust me, I've seen it. Plus, like I said, his interests lie elsewhere."

"But—"

"Harrison is never around. He keeps a remarkably busy schedule so you'd hate that too and Barrett's an asshole so...you know. I wouldn't if I were you."

"Uh huh. Okay. Well, speaking of dating...should we come up with some sort of...I don't know, ground rules or something?"

"Ground rules? What do you mean?"

"Yeah ground rules. You know, like leave a sock on the door when you have a woman here." I tap his hand with my own. "Cause as much as I love you, Auggie, I do not want to walk in on that! And I don't really want to have to hear it either." I twist my mouth. "Though I guess I could get a sound machine or something."

"Ella."

"What?" I look up from my pizza to find him staring me down.

"We don't need ground rules."

"Why not? What if—"

"I don't bring women here, Ella."

I cock my head, studying him. "What, like ever?"

"Never." He shakes his head slowly and I'm flabbergasted with his answer.

"You're serious?"

"Very serious."

I stare at him for a moment, taking in his rigid demeanor, and then I let out an uncomfortable laugh. "What the fuck, Aug? You live in this..." I flail my arms. "Palatial apartment in the swankiest of buildings. You literally have everything here you could ever want that would certainly make any woman happy and you're telling me you've never invited a woman back to your place?"

"Hell no," he says. "This place is *my* place. My private safe space. If fans knew where I lived, I would have lines of crazies at my door all the fucking time so no. No way. I don't bring anyone back here. Nobody knows where I live except the other guys on the team because a few of them live in this same complex."

I narrow my eyes, taking in his words. "So, you've never... you've never slept with a woman in your own bed?"

How can this be?

He shakes his head quietly having swallowed another bite of pizza. "Ella, I don't usually *sleep* with women if you get my drift."

"You don't..." I gasp, hearing his words in my head. "August Blackstone you don't sleep with women?"

"No."

"But you fuck them?"

I see the slight lift in the corner of his mouth. Like he's proud I came to the correct conclusion. "All the time."

Something in my stomach drops.

I'm shocked by this news.

Why am I shocked by this?

My shoulders droop as my body slouches. "You're a pump and dump guy?"

He shrugs, popping the last of his pizza slice into his mouth. "I like to think of it as an adrenaline deposit. And you know this about me, Ella. When was the last time I had a relationship of any kind?"

He's right. I know this about him. But still. I thought maybe I was wrong. I thought maybe somewhere in that professionally cold soul of his there might be some sort of a heart.

"Ugh!" I roll my eyes and wipe my mouth with my napkin. "You're the worst."

"How am I the worst? I've never given any woman the wrong idea. They're all willing participants. Fucking is just..."

"What...?" I ask him, standing from the floor and crossing my arms over my chest and suppressing the feeling that I want to cry. Ugh, why is crying my go-to emotional response? I hate this about myself. "What is fucking, exactly, to you?"

And why is this news upsetting me more than I thought it would?

It's not like I didn't know he sleeps around.

"Fucking, for me, is just a way to help me unwind after a game. There's nothing emotional about it." He shrugs. "It's fun. It's physical and it gives me the release I need after a hard day... pun unintended." He smirks. "What's so bad about that?"

I cock my head. "So, then, what about me?"

"Uh...what about you?"

"Well first of all, what if I don't see fucking as just a physical..." I shake my head trying to find the words. "Deposit of adrenaline as you so nicely put it."

His brows lift. "I'm guessing from the look on your face that fucking is more of an emotional thing for you."

"Yes. Of course it is, but that's not what I meant when I brought up me. I meant, what happens when I want to bring a man home to my bed?"

He shakes his head adamantly. "No, no, no, no, no. That's a hard pass. Nobody touches you. Certainly not in my house."

Okay, now he's just pissing me off. I jut my hip out, my jaw dropping as I scoff. "So, it's okay for you to run around fucking whomever you want, but I can't have a boyfriend if I want one?"

"You can fuck whoever you want. Just don't do it here and honestly, I'd probably be better off not knowing about it."

"But unlike you, I'm the relationship type, Auggie. So, if and when I find the right guy for me, I'm going to want him to meet you and spend time with me and us, here, in my home. We're going to want to be physical because that's important to me in a relationship. You said I could live here."

"And I meant it, but—"

"So really you meant I can sleep here, but if I want to do any kind of living, which may or may not include a relationship with someone, or God forbid, sex of any kind, I better do it somewhere else."

"Listen Ella, I—"

I can feel my heartrate rising with every passing second. "What happens when one of your teammates falls madly in love with me, huh? What then?"

My challenge amuses him. "Right. Like that's going to happen."

I shift back a step, my mouth hanging open. "Oh, so now I'm not good enough for your teammates?"

His smile fades, his brows pinch, and he shakes his head. "That's not what I'm saying at all. Why are you getting all—"

"You know, I'm not really liking where this conversation is

going." I raise my hand to stop him from saying anything else. The last thing I want to do is fight with my best friend on my first day here.

"Ella." He steps toward me but I take another step back again.

"No. I get it. I hear you. Loud and clear."

Resigning himself, he pushes his hand through his mussed hair, fumbling his words. "Look if you...sleep with whoever you want. It's none of my business but—"

"That's right. It's none of your business, but alright. I'll play by your rules, August. So, just so you know, when I don't come home one night it's because I'm obviously out having the best fuck of my life."

"Ella."

"I'm tired from traveling. And I have a big day tomorrow."

We didn't even get to talk about my interview. It's fine though. I'll be fine. Everything's fine.

"I'm going to bed."

Frustrated and disappointed.

"Ella."

"Good night, August."

I rarely call him August.

He's always been Auggie to me.

It actually hurts to walk away from him as I head to my room and shut the door. Leaning against it, I inhale a deep breath and release it slowly.

Maybe we're both tired.

Maybe we have to get through a few growing pains after moving in.

Maybe this won't be as easy as either of us thought.

I just hope it's all worth it.

CHAPTER FIVE

AUGUST

I didn't sleep a fucking wink.

I've been in the gym downstairs since five and even that wasn't enough so here I am pounding the pavement before the sun even comes up.

I don't like the way I left things with Ella last night. I don't like that she was upset and I don't like that I had to watch her walk away from me when really, I should have been her biggest supporter. I don't even know where our conversation went wrong. One minute we were talking about the team and the next minute I'm a male whore who won't allow my best friend out of her room to socialize.

I don't know what came over me, but the minute she talked about having a relationship, or the mere thought of some sleezeball with his hands on her, I shut down. I want her to be happy here, whatever that means for her, but I never really sat and thought about how I might feel if she were to start dating someone. She's my best friend. My ride or die. I would do anything for her, and I love her more than I could ever explain, but how do I tell someone I'm not romantically involved with that watching her fall in love and grow alongside some other man isn't something I think I can do? It was easy in high school because I knew in the back of my brain that whatever boyfriend she may have had at the time wouldn't last. She wouldn't marry the guy and she would somehow or another always be my Ella.

But now?

She's a grown ass woman with dreams and aspirations. And she deserves everything in life that she wants. But having it all happen in my house while I stand by and watch?

No.

Nope.

I can't do it.

It would crush me.

Ella's right. She's a relationship kind of girl. She always has been. She's the super romantic type with wishes of love notes and flowers and little acts of kindness that make her swoon. She's always been a sucker for heartfelt romcom movies or the dramatic love saga television shows. Her mindset was always if it can happen on the screen, it can happen in real life. She's still that girl even after all these years. The pain and heartache that life throws at her still hasn't dampened her spirit.

I think she still hopes Richard Gere will drive up to her house in a limo with flowers in his hand like he did in *Pretty Woman.* I think she wants Andrew Lincoln to stand outside her door with a sign that says *"To Me You Are Perfect."* like he did in *Love Actually.* She definitely wants Ryan Gosling to kiss her in the rain and then build her dreamhouse for her like he does in *The Notebook.*

Consequently, she always refused to watch shows like *Alien* or *Dexter.*

Sweat soaks my body as I take my last few jogging steps into my building. I bend over at the waist momentarily to catch my breath, and then make my way to the elevators. Once the door closes behind me, I feel my chest tighten and I start to panic.

Shit.

Is this fixable?

Is she going to be mad at me when I walk in the door?

I should've apologized last night.

I should've made sure she was okay.

I should've fucking checked on her at least once instead of lying in my bed wide awake.

Was this all a horrible mistake?

Did I fuck up by asking her to move in with me?

Maybe I should look into buying her her own place.

Like she would ever let you do that, Blackstone.

Fuck.

She would be heartbroken if I even mentioned her going somewhere else now.

A surefire way to lose my best friend.

And that's the last thing I want.

The elevator dings for my floor and before the doors open, I'm already cringing at the smell permeating the air. That distinctive smell that tells me exactly what's going on inside my apartment. The scent that tells me to drop every thought or feeling of doubt I was having about my best friend because she needs me.

"Dammit." I bring a palm to my forehead. "Her interview."

She needs me and I wasn't here.

I left her this morning and now the entire floor of the building, along with most likely many others in proximity, smells like a goddamn cinnamon roll.

Pushing open my apartment door, I expect to see Ella in the kitchen or at the dining room table stuffing her face with ooey gooey goodness, but that is not the case. What I do see, however, is my living room looking like a department store at the end of a Black Friday sale.

"What the fuuuuck?"

Ella's clothes are everywhere. Literally on every surface of the room. Several pairs of shorts, pants, and even a few skirts are strung over the couch and chair along with six different colored tank tops, a black blazer, a solid red shirt, a blue shirt, a pink and green striped shirt, a purple flowery blouse, and four different pairs of shoes. Two bras, two thongs, and three pairs of panties are hanging from the television causing my mind to wander to places it should dare not go.

Do not think about Ella in a thong.

For the love of God do not think about it.

What size was that bra? B cup? C? Double D?

Fuck. Stop it August.

Her makeup is scattered across my coffee table from end to end along with a hairbrush, four hair clips, hairspray, and a bottle of perfume.

Trying my best to shut out the mess that is now my apartment, I focus on following the scent of cinnamon rolls filling my nostrils.

"Ella?" I shout, hoping wherever she is she'll hear me and feel better that I'm home.

"Hmmm?" she murmurs from somewhere in the apartment.

I take one glance into the kitchen and stop in my tracks.

"Oh, my God, you've got to be kidding me," I mumble to myself at the sight before me. On the counter next to the stove are at least a dozen boxes of Cinnabon cinnamon rolls in varied sizes. A few of them lay open with strings of icing the only remaining evidence of Ella's anxiety.

"Auggie, I need your help!" I turn just in time for Ella to come around the corner into the kitchen, a cinnamon roll box in hand as she stuffs another piece into her mouth.

Also, she's not wearing clothes.

Okay, she's in a black bra and matching panties so she's wearing clothes but she is sooo not wearing clothes.

"Whoa. What are you doing?" I ask, immediately squeezing my eyes closed and covering them with my hand.

"What do you mean what am I doing?" she cries. "I'm trying to get ready for my interview Aug and I need your help! I don't know what to wear! I've been through every fucking outfit I own and nothing feels right and I don't know what they're going to expect. Do I wear a suit? Like dress pants and my blazer? Do I go casual and wear leggings and one of your hockey t-shirts?" She pops another bite of cinnamon roll into her mouth. "I'm at Defcon-five over here and where the hell were you this morning? You left me and didn't tell me where you were going."

"Shit. I'm sorry. Force of habit," I tell her with a shake of my head. "Morning workout downstairs and then I went for a run."

She doesn't say anything for a minute before I hear, "What's going on? Why aren't you looking at me?"

"Because you're not wearing any clothes."

"Pfft," she scoffs. "Okay Mr. Pump and Dump, like you've never seen a woman in her underwear before. It's me Auggie. Not your grandmother."

"Thank God for that. Grandma's been dead for fifteen years."

"Would you please uncover your eyes and look at me so you can help me? I'm not sure I can be more nervous than I am right now and you're not helping."

Slowly I open my eyes, reminding myself that she's my best friend. Not some puck bunny I bend over from time to time.

She's Ella.

She's my absolute best friend.

I knew her when she had no boobs.

But hell, does she have boobs now.

I glance at them as haphazardly as I can without looking like a perv.

Fuck me. They're nice boobs too.

Pretty.

Perfect size. Perfect shape.

Perky too.

Ugh.

Get a fucking grip.

My eyes land on the part of her I had forgotten about over the years. Just above her heart sits a small owl tattoo. It was the very first tattoo she ever got and I remember she wanted me to hold her hand as she got it. She was so fucking brave that day. She didn't need me, but I was happy to be there for her.

A tightness pulls in my chest so I gesture to the obscene number of cinnamon rolls on the counter. "Babe, did you really order all this?"

"Yeah. You didn't have any I could make so I just Door-Dashed the whole menu." She tears another piece off and shoves it in her mouth. "You know I crave cinnamon rolls when—"

"When you're nervous." I nod. "I remember. This looks more like you're going to be nervous for the rest of the year."

"I know, I know." Her eyes are watery as she twists her hair around her finger. "But what if I told you I have no self-control when I'm nervous and so I couldn't help myself and once I saw the menu I wasn't sure how much I would want to eat because I was hungry but then like, not hungry at all, you know? Because the last thing I want to do when I'm nervous is eat but then I get this craving and I just have to have it and I couldn't stop myself this time so before I knew it I had clicked though the entire menu and hit submit."

Another thing my best friend does when she's nervous?

She rambles.

"I was sure to give one to the doorman when he brought my

order up this morning though so that was nice. And of course you should eat some. Obviously, I won't be able to eat all of this, but I can save them. Maybe freeze them for another time." She wraps her hand around my wrist. "Oh, and I promise I'll clean up this mess, okay? I just needed space to lay everything out so I could decide what to wear, only I couldn't decide on business professional or business casual since, well, you know, a mascot doesn't usually wear dress pants and heels, but I don't have the job yet so I wasn't sure and now that's where you come in because—"

"Ella." I stop her with the placement of my hands on her shoulders.

She finally swallows the bite of cinnamon roll in her mouth. "Yeah?"

"Take a deep breath with me."

I take a slow deep breath, my eyes locked on hers as she breathes in with me. We both breathe out as I count to ten in my head.

"Team colors. Navy blue dress pants are fine. Yellow top. A small pair of earrings and wear your hair in a ponytail. The curly kind you do when you're cheering."

"Heels?"

I nod and give her an approving smile. "Heels. And you don't need a ton of makeup. You're stunning just the way you are."

Her cheeks pinken as she tilts her head in a nod and then reaches up to kiss the side of my face. "Thank you, Auggie."

Trying to break her anxiety I glance down at her chest and wink. "The lace bra is nice but a little much for a job interview... you know, if you were wondering."

She rolls her eyes. "I don't care about my bra. This one makes me feel good. And pretty. And confident. But I'm ninety-nine percent sure nobody at the Anaheim Stars is going to see my black lacey bra today so that's inconsequential but thank you just the same."

"My pleasure. I'm going to hit the shower."

I give Ella a little time to herself to finish getting dressed, which gives me the opportunity to walk away from my nearly naked best friend before my mind starts playing tricks on me. Once I'm stripped down and in the shower it dawns on me that I haven't called on any of the puck bunnies usually on standby in weeks.

Since I offered my place to Ella.

Fuck.

I invited my best friend to live with me and now she's the cock block I never saw coming.

Coming...

Christ, I may never be coming again if this keeps up.

I stare down at my hand as if it just stood up and offered its services to my deprived cock. "No way, man. Not doing it," I whisper to my hand. "Especially not with Ella in my apartment."

Yep.

I just talked to my hand.

Fuck, this is how it starts, isn't it?

I'm going crazy.

Quickly moving through the rest of my shower, I grab a pair of shorts and a t-shirt and pull them on before checking on one more time Ella before she leaves for her interview.

"Want me to drive you?"

"What?" She shakes her head. "No, no. It's fine." She tries to square her shoulders as she tilts her head to put an earring in her ear. "I should do this myself, you know? Independent and all. Besides, I don't want it to look like I got this job because of you." She blinks, hearing what she just said. "I mean not that I would get it because of you. I just mean, well—"

"I know what you mean, babe. It's fine." I pull my keys out of my pocket. "Want to take my car?"

"Oh, uh," she says with a furrowed brow. "I can probably just get an Uber."

"Nonsense. Why pay for that when you can literally drive yourself? There's a parking pass in the car. You won't have to pay a thing. Here." I hand my keys to her. "You'll be safer in my car than with some stranger anyway."

"You're sure?" The look of apprehension in her eyes has me wrapping my arms around her.

"Of course I'm sure."

Holding her against my chest, I feel her inhale a deep breath and slowly release it. "You smell nice," she says.

"Not as good as you." I give her a kiss on her forehead and tilt her face up to mine. "Listen, you're going to do great today. I have no doubt that job will be yours within the hour and when that happens, we'll celebrate."

"What if it—"

"Nope," I say confidently, shaking my head. "There are no what-ifs right now. Only positive vibes for what will be."

She nods decisively. "Right. Okay. I've got this."

"You've got this." I repeat her words back to her with a smile and then playfully spank her ass. "Now get out of here and do your thing, Ella Montgomery. I believe in you."

CHAPTER SIX

ELLA

I head downstairs to the parking garage and tap the lock button on the remote August handed me. A black car honks several feet away, its taillights blinking twice. I cock my head a bit confused because the black car that belongs to the remote in my hand is not the one he was driving when he picked me up from the airport. That car is sitting a few spots down. This one is much fancier looking. A quick glance at the back of it as I approach makes me smile.

"Son of a bitch, he finally did it." My smile widens with a sense of pride for my best friend as I marvel at the shiny black Ferrari California T convertible parked in spot number eleven. She's the most beautiful car I've ever seen. "He's always wanted this car," I whisper to myself, smoothing my hand over the back. "I can't believe he didn't tell me."

A rush of anxiety shoots through my chest at the mere thought of trying to drive this car out of the garage and to my interview.

Why the hell did he offer me this car?
What makes him think I could drive this thing?
Or that I would want to?

Especially without him with me.

Morbid curiosity gets the best of me though because who wouldn't want to sit in one of these babies if given the opportunity? Smiling, I click the button to unlock the car and open the driver's side door and then slip into the driver's seat.

Daaaaaamn.

This is sleek!

I run my hands over the leather steering wheel and across the dashboard.

And makes me feel sexy as fuck!

Speaking of sex...I wonder what that feels like in a car like this.

Wait.

Ew. What if he's...

Has he...

No...he wouldn't...

But then again...

"Nope. Can't do it," I mumble to myself as I step out of his stunningly sexy car trying hard not to envision my best friend inside with another woman.

It shouldn't matter, and it doesn't really, but even the thought that he may have driven some woman he barely knew to a random fuck pad or hotel, or hell, even on a date, suddenly gives me the ick. And even worse, what if he made out with someone in here? What if some nasty ass puck bunny used him and the adrenaline rush that comes after a game? What if she took advantage of his fame and fortune for nothing more than a romp in the sheets?

What if I punch her face in for using my best friend or for... for...

Fuck.

"Too far, Ella. Calm your tits." I stand beside Auggie's beautiful new car and take a deep steadying breath.

"It's okay. Too many bells and whistles anyway and besides,

I don't even know where I'm going." Shutting the door behind me, I click the remote to lock the car and then pull out my phone to order a quick Uber.

It was nice of him to offer but no way in hell am I going to be the one who wrecks his car on the way to a job interview that won't even pay me enough to afford a replacement vehicle in the first place.

"Thanks, but no thanks, Auggie."

AUGGIE

Okay, three things: 1. It's been hours since I've heard from you. 2. Are you out moping somewhere because you didn't get the job because so help me I will wring someone's neck if that's the case and 3. You didn't take my car? It's still parked downstairs. WTF? Are you ok? Did you walk to the interview because if you walked you're probably only just getting there which means you're really late which means you missed your interview and didn't get the job and now I'm worried about you. Please tell me where you are and I'll come get you.

ME

Dude! You got the car! You got the car of your dreams and didn't TELL ME! What the fuck is up with that?

AUGGIE

Uh…yeah about that. I'm sorry. I got it that day you had an injured cheerleader who ended up in surgery. It didn't feel like the right time to bring it up and I didn't want to brag. I guess I forgot I hadn't told you after that.

AUGGIE

But what the fuck is the car still doing in the garage? You were supposed to take it this morning!

ME

Psh Not a chance. I was not going to be that person who messed up your brand-new car. Plus, it had too many bells and whistles anyway. It made me nervous.

AUGGIE

Babe, I would've driven you. You should've told me. Where the heck are you now? What about the job? Are you okay?

ME

What if I told you I got the job and I'm out celebrating? 😌

AUGGIE

What if I told you I'm now crying in my agent's office because you're celebrating without me? Did you really get it?? Is that a yes?? You're killing me here!

ME

Yes Auggie. That's a yes! I GOT THE JOB!!!!! 😊 And I'm not really celebrating but I did stop at the mall to buy myself a new outfit (or three, don't judge me!) and I want to take you out to dinner tonight if you're free to celebrate with me!

AUGGIE

How about I take YOU out for dinner? You're the one who deserves to be celebrated.

ME

Ugh. Auggie! You can't always pay for everything!

AUGGIE

Why not? It's just money babe.

ME

Because I didn't move here just to mooch off of you and I shouldn't be your burden.

AUGGIE

Okay, let's get one thing straight right now. You have never been, nor will you ever be a burden. So, get that shit out of your pretty little head right now.

ME

Geesh. Bossy much? 😥

AUGGIE

I mean it, Ella.

ME

Okay, okay. I'm not a burden. But I also meant it when I said I didn't move here to be your financial responsibility. Please just let me take you out to dinner. I found this really cute diner that looks fun!

AUGGIE

Ziggy's Diner?

ME

Yeah! Have you been there? Is it any good?

AUGGIE

They have the best meatball subs in the entire city.

ME

Well, who am I to say no to a fantastic meatball sub? I can be home in fifteen!

AUGGIE

Stay there. I'm leaving my agent's office now. I'll come to get you.

My hero 🖤

"So, then she said to me, 'Ella, I'm not going to beat around the bush anymore. Your experience on paper and your energy just sitting here chatting with you make you perfect for this job so before we let you walk out that door today, we would like to offer you the position'."

Auggie shakes his head, swallowing a bite of his meatball sub. He offers me a high five but when I reach my hand to his, he clasps his fingers with mine joining our hands. "Fuckin' right they did! I had no doubt you would knock 'em dead in there today. Congratulations, babe. Seriously, I knew this would be the perfect opportunity for you."

I'm all smiles watching how happy my best friend is for me. "And they said they're making me a new suit because the one they had me try on was a little big on me. I worried for a minute that maybe I wasn't tall enough for the job given the suit but they said they've been wanting to give Lumin an upgrade and now is their chance. And I actually got to have a little input on the new design!"

"Lumin. What's Lumin?"

"Oh! Lumin is the name of the new mascot! They said they wanted to change it since Astro is retiring. Just wait till you see her, Auggie!" I clap my hands excitedly. "She's going to be so cute when she's finished and I'm super pumped to get to debut her."

He sits back against the booth where we're seated in the diner watching me in awe. "I can't believe you're going to be our new shooting star. I mean I totally believe it, but like, God, you're here." He beams and a sudden wave of warmth rushes through my chest. "You're really fucking here and you're staying. You'll be at every one of my games. We'll be doing all this together."

Strangely, I'm flattered by his excitement.

"Just like we dreamed when we were kids, huh?" I scrunch my nose as I smile, remembering the days and nights of our childhood spent lying under the tree in my backyard dreaming of what life would be like as adults. August always knew he wanted to play hockey but I never aspired to be a professional sports team mascot. I thought I would be a teacher or nurse or, thanks to August, maybe some sort of sports announcer. After all, I had been to every one of his games growing up. I knew all his stats. I probably knew his strengths and weaknesses better than he did. I was his biggest cheerleader, even more so than his parents. I loved watching him excel at something he loved doing. I never expected I would grow up and actually get the opportunity to cheer him on and get paid to do it.

He looks at me like he's photographing me with his eyes and with an affection I've never seen before. It's enough to cause butterflies to flutter through my stomach, which is weird because I don't get butterflies around Auggie. Not since early high school anyway.

"What are you thinking about over there?" I ask him when the silence between us becomes a little too close to awkward.

He swallows with a tiny shake of his head and with a smile tells me, "The guys are going to love you."

"I can't wait to meet them. I can't believe you haven't taken me to Griffin's apartment yet. Didn't you say a lot of you live in the same complex?"

He nods. "Yeah but fuck them. If I'm going to be forced to

share you throughout the season, I want to keep you to myself for as long as I can."

"Share me?" I giggle. "Sounds like kinky fun. Where do I sign up for that?"

Auggie's smile fades and his face turns red. "Not at all what I meant, babe."

"Relax, I'm just kidding with you." I pass him a wink even though I haven't forgotten the conversation we had about my ability to have a life inside or outside his apartment. "I think it's sweet you don't want to share me. I've missed you so damn much, so I'll take all the Auggie time I can get."

"Good, can we go home now? Because I kind of want to be able to chill with you before life gets hectic again."

I wipe my mouth with my napkin and take one last sip from my drink. "Absolutely. I paid with the QR code so we're good to go," I tell him, slipping a twenty from my wallet as a tip for the table.

"Don't worry about it. I've got the tip," Auggie says, pulling cash from his wallet and laying it on the table between us. My jaw falls open when I see he's laid down a one-hundred-dollar bill.

"Auggie are you insane? That's one hundred dollars!"
That could feed me for a month!

He eyes me under his ballcap and gives me a slight shake of his head. "No, I'm not insane. I'm a professional athlete eating in a very public diner. People know who I am."

I shrug. "Okay. So? Our bill was only—"

"Doesn't matter what the bill is," he adds. "I can't be known around town as the pro hockey player who only tips twenty percent."

"Twenty percent?" I scoff. "I'll have you know that twenty-dollar bill was a forty percent tip."

"And now it's a four-hundred percent tip." He eyes me as he

stands from the booth waiting for me. "And it's no big deal. It's just money and it'll make the waitress's day. Besides, who else am I going to spend it on? Come on. Let's go home."

Taking my hand in his, I follow him out as he waves to a few customers who recognize him.

It's just money.

Easy for him to say.

I suppose he's right though.

I wouldn't want his reputation to go down the drain over a tip in a diner.

He really is a good guy.

"You know what you need, August?"

He chuckles as he opens his car door for me. "No, but I'm certain you're going to tell me."

"Yeah I am. Because what you need is a steady girlfriend to spend your money on."

Closing his door and clicking his seatbelt he laughs softly again. "How about I just spend all my money on you?"

"Me? No, no, no. I'll make my own money thank you very much. I just mean you've had a bunch of hookups here and there with all the women you've...well, you know."

Let's not think about the number of women Auggie has slept with.

That's a rabbit hole of depression waiting to happen.

"But maybe what you need is a real woman in your life. Like a solid relationship. Maybe I need to help find you a girl you can fall head over heels for. Then you'll have something and someone to spend your money on."

As he pulls out into traffic he nods and then casts a quick glance my way.

Damn if he doesn't look hot in those sunglasses.

"And you think you're the perfect person to help me with that?"

"Yeah of course." I shrug. "Duh. I know you better than any woman. Well...I mean, I haven't seen those assless chaps you talked about a while back so if you want to pull those out for me..."

"I do not."

Damn!

I tried.

"Ugh. Okay. No chaps. And so, maybe I don't know you like...you know, biblically and all that, but I know your brain and I know your heart. Who could be better at finding you a girlfriend than me, your best friend?"

CHAPTER SEVEN

AUGUST

Ella talked about finding me a serious girlfriend the whole way home and wouldn't take no for an answer. I have a feeling I'm in for an extremely uncomfortable night if Ella has anything to do with it. I know this girl and when she puts her mind into something, she doesn't relent. At least I got her to understand how important it is to not create an online profile for me. Fuck, that would quickly become a feeding frenzy for the tabloids.

"This is so exciting." Ella claps as we ride the elevator to our floor. "I'll get my notebook and we can spend the whole evening creating you a lover girl list."

I lift my brow. "A what?"

"A lover girl list. You know, a list of all the qualities you find attractive in a woman and some of your biggest turn-offs."

Ugh.

"Did I agree to this?"

She bumps me with her hip and chuckles. "Yep. It's complimentary because we're roommates."

"Is it too late to kick you out?"

The elevator door dings and then slides open. Ella doesn't even look at me as she steps forward into the hallway. "Afraid so. Oh, hello…"

She stops mid stride before we reach the door to the apartment. I nearly run into her and then look ahead to see why she stopped. There in front of my door are my five brothers from other mothers. Griffin, Ledger, Harrison, Oliver, and even Bear.

"What the hell are you guys doing here?"

"Well, asshole," Griffin starts with a smirk. "We heard there's a new mascot in town and you've been holding her up here in your high tower."

High tower.

Like they don't all live near the top of their respective buildings.

Ledger grins. "Yeah. So like the gentlemen that we are, we decided to come meet the Tuesday girl who's had your heart since before you could grow a boner."

I shake my head. "Oh, for fuck's s—"

"Aww. I guess that's me!" Ella smiles and waves at the guys. "Hi. I'm Ella. It's a pleasure to meet you all."

Griffin steps out of the group and offers Ella his hand. "Hey. I'm Griffin. It's great to finally put a face to a name."

"Ah, the guy with the pants," she says with a smile gesturing to Griffin's choice in pajama pants. Today's pair has tacos all over them with the words 'Let's TACOBOUT it' scribbled around each one. "Auggie talks about you all the time. Love your choice in comfortable apparel by the way."

Five sets of eyes shoot to me when Ella says my name, causing me to wince. She's the only one who calls me Auggie. She's done it since we were kids.

"Well thank you very much," Griffin drawls, grinning like the damn Christmas Grinch and I can tell whatever he's doing, it's going to piss me off. I watch as he wraps an arm around

Ella's shoulder and gestures towards the door. "Auggie here can't get enough of my penchant for fun comfy pants, isn't that right...*Auggie?*"

Ugh.

They're never going to let me live this name down.

"Isn't it time for you all to leave?"

"What?" Ella squeals. "No way. You guys have to come in!" She turns, still in Griffin's arms. He glances my way when she's not looking and winks knowing damn well I'm hating that he's openly flirting with my girl right in front of me.

Okay, she's not really my girl, but close enough.

"Oooh, actually Auggie and I were just planning to sit down and talk about his lover girl list. Maybe you guys could help!"

Harrison's eyes bulge as a smile grows across his face. "Oooh, a lover girl list huh? What's that about...*Auggie?*" He offers his hand to Ella. "I'm Harrison by the way."

"Right. Yeah. Sorry. Pleasure to meet you, Harrison. "I hear you're the Captain America of the team."

Harrison's gaze turns to me as his he cocks his head and sighs. "Aww, Auggie really does like me. Thanks, pal."

Yep. I'm never living this down.

For as long as I live.

"And this lover girl list is being created so I can find my best friend a serious girlfriend," Ella explains, patting my chest. "He needs someone to spend his money on. He's too rich and lonely."

I shake my head, unlocking the door and pushing it open. "I'm not lonely. I never said I was lonely."

Ledger shakes his head, clapping my shoulder. "Oooh, I disagree Auggie. A serious girlfriend is just what you need." He offers his hand to Ella next. "Hi. I'm Ledger."

"Hi Ledger. I'm Ella."

"Ella, I'm Oliver...or Oli, whichever you prefer." Oliver adds gesturing to Cunningham on his left. "And this is Barrett, but we all call him Bear." They both shake her hand. "And I think you're right. We should absolutely help you find the right girl for our friend Auggie. Good thing we showed up when we did, huh?" The fucker has the audacity to wink at me when I glance back at him.

"Great! It's settled." Ella claps her hands like a giddy teenager. "Come on in, guys. Make yourselves at home."

We stop just inside the apartment letting the guys move past us and then Ella rounds on me and in an excited whisper says, "Okay, first of all, oh, my God! You cleaned the apartment and I told you that you didn't have to do that. I promised I would do it when I got home. And secondly," she lays her hands on my chest and the contact alone makes me feel oddly fuzzy inside. "This is okay, right? We're just having some fun and I really want to get to know the guys." She leans in closer. "I really want them to like me."

The slightest bit of trepidation in her eyes melts me.

Fuck, I would give anything to make that look in her eyes disappear. I'd lasso the fucking moon if she asked me to.

"Yeah, babe. We're good. And stop worrying. They're going to love you."

She pats my chest twice more and then kisses my cheek. "Thank you. Come on," she says, taking my hand. "This will be fun."

For her.

It'll be fun for her.

For me?

It'll be pure torture.

"Mmm! Smells good in here, Auggie," Griffin states as he walks toward the kitchen. "Did you make cinnamon rolls?"

"DUDE, she's helping you find a girlfriend?" Ledger asks on one side of me when Ella leaves the room to grab her notebook and pen.

"Don't ask."

"You better tell us quick," Griffin adds from the other side of me. "Are we describing some random woman you've fucked before or are we describing her?"

My head snaps to Griffin. "What?"

"You heard me."

"Why would you describe her?"

Griffin's lips form a wide grin. "You're cute, Blackstone."

I shrug. "What?"

He leans a little closer to my ear. "First of all, look at her. It's no wonder you've kept her to yourself all these years. She's hot as fuck and any one of us would easily drool over her but—"

"Shut it, Griff." My face heats at the mere mention of any one of them putting the moves on Ella.

"But," he continues, lifting a finger and making me pause, "she chose you. She loves you. She's living with you."

"I told you it's not like that with us though. It doesn't mean anything," I quietly spit back at him.

He looks me in the eye and then smiles as Ledger pats my leg. "Mmkay. You keep telling yourself that big guy."

I hear what Griffin's saying but until today—right this second—I've been able to deny all feelings of attraction toward my best friend because she's just that. My best friend. I can't allow myself to think about her in any other way because it just wouldn't work. Sure, she's unfairly attractive with a personality that would rival anyone's. She's kind, compassionate, and has a spirit I've always appreciated.

But she's Ella.

She's my best friend.

My person.

There's nothing I wouldn't do for her.

And that includes ruining the relationship we have had for our entire lives just because I find her attractive.

"Hey Ella, congratulations on the new job," Griffin tells her when she pops back out of her room. "We can't wait to support you in the Mascot Tournament this year."

She stops dead in her tracks, her eyes widening. "Mascot Tournament?"

"Yeah." He nods. "Nobody told you about the Mascot Tournament? It's a huge fundraiser event."

Ella shakes her head and glances at me with trepidation. "What's the Mascot Tournament? Should I be scared?"

I give her a confident shake of my head and explain, "Nah, it's just a fun event with a bunch of mascots from our conference. They do a skills competition on the ice for the fans and they play a short hockey game and then there are picture opportunities and all the fun stuff the fans like."

"Yeah." Harrison nods, adding, "It's a fun day. And it's for a great cause. The proceeds go to St. Jude so, you know, it's for the kids."

I can see Ella's heart melting already. "Aww," she says, bringing her hand to her chest. "That sounds wonderful. I can't wait to do my part."

"I bet you could do a number on those other mascots," Ledger tells her.

Ella flexes her arm, showing off her muscles. "Bring it on. I'll invite them all to my gun show."

The guys whistle and laugh and Oliver says, "That's right

you will. And we'll be there to support you one hundred percent. We're hosting this year, so you'll want to be on your game for sure."

"I hope you'll all train me first!" Ella laughs. "I'm good on the ice, but Auggie's the hockey player. Not me."

"You'll be great, El," I tell her. "Don't worry. We're not going to let you fail. We'll make sure you're ready."

"Phew!" She wipes her brow with the back of her hand. "Good. Alright then." She holds up the notebook and pen in her hand. "So, let's get this ball rolling, shall we?" Ella walks through the group of us seated around the living room and finds an open spot on the floor. "We're all here to help Auggie find the love of his life."

I'm doing this for her.
I'm doing this for her.
I'm doing this for her.

"Wait," Bear says, holding up his hand. "Before you start, I'm going to need you to tell us an Auggie story. Something about him none of us would know."

I shake my head. "That is totally unnecces—"

"Oh, that's easy," she says, smiling. "Did he tell you about the day he thought there was a badger in the bushes behind his house and told me to run for it while he stood there and peed all over his yard because he heard from some older kid that the smell of urine would deter angry animals?"

The guys all burst out laughing as I lower my forehead to my palm. "Okay in my defense I was like eight or nine years old and heard it from someone on the bus."

"The visual," Harrison says as his body shakes with laughter. "It's the visual for me."

"Or that time when he took several of his fish out of their tanks and walked them around the house in his hand," Ella continues. "Because he wanted to give them a tour of the rooms they couldn't see from their tank. Poor fish, by the time the tour ended they were dead."

More laughter from the guys.

Ella's brows shoot up. "Oooh wait! Wait! This one is a doozy! When we were like, six or seven Auggie was hanging out at my house and we found a used condom in my parents' bathroom and didn't know what it was so Auggie put it on his foot like a sock."

Cue even more laughter.

"Neither of us had any idea what it really was at the time. I don't think we figured it out until we were teenagers!"

"Oh my God!" Ledger wheezes. "This is too good!"

"Bet you had the softest feet in the whole damn world that day," Oliver cackles.

"Damn right I did," I tell him. "And I was pissed there wasn't one for my other foot."

That comment earns another round of straight up belly laughs from everyone in the room. After a few minutes of continued laughter pass, Ella looks at the guys and clicks the tip of her pen.

"Alright, gentlemen, let's dive into this list, shall we? Describe for me the type of girl Auggie seems to find the most attractive."

"Oh, that's easy," Oliver says, crossing his arms. "He likes blondes."

I huff a quiet laugh but Griffin shakes his head and speaks up. "No, I don't think so."

"Of course he does." Oliver smiles. "Remember the last two girls he fu—"

"Nah, I'm pretty sure he really prefers brunettes," Ledger argues on my behalf.

Ella peers up at me, pen at the ready. "Well, which is it, Auggie? Blondes or brunettes?"

Oliver is right. Up until now I've always gone for the blondes. The last four or five women I've fucked after a game were all blondes. Box blondes or not, they were still blonde, but now...

I study Ella's soft brown hair for a minute. What was hanging down in a cute but messy bedhead this morning is now tied up in a messy bun on the top of her head. Still just as beautiful either way she wears it. "Definitely brunettes." I swallow the lump in my throat as I watch her take notes.

I feel the guys look my way but I ignore them and remain focused on Ella.

"Okay," she says, finishing whatever it is she was writing. "How about size? Tall? Short? Skinny? Curvy?"

I twist my mouth as if I'm thinking about it, but Griffin beats me to an answer. "Ella can you stand up for a minute? I need something to compare to."

"Sure." She stands and holds her hands out like she's on display and Griffin nods. "Yeah. Probably someone built kind of like you. Not too tall but not too short. Curves in all the right places. Not too much of a skinny rail."

Ella wouldn't be a skinny rail at all.

She'd be a perfect rail.

Fuck, I can't believe I just thought about railing my roommate.

Blackstone, what is wrong with you?

"Perfect." She scribbles a few more things on her notepad.

"He likes tits over ass," Bear mumbles.

"Oh, he does?" Ella asks even though I know she already knows this about me. We may not have always talked about every detail of our sexual experiences during our Tuesday night chats, but she knows enough about my preferences to know I appreciate a nice pair of tits.

Like the way hers looked in that black lace bra she was wearing this morning.

"Mhmm." Bear nods. "If you've got tits, I can guarantee you he's looked at 'em."

"And so has every last one of you in here," I add in my defense.

"To be fair," Ella says, "he didn't want to look at mine this morning."

Harrison nearly spits out the beer I gave him earlier. "I'm sorry, WHAT?"

Griffin turns his head toward me. "What the fuck is wrong with you?"

"What?" I ask, eyes bulging.

"Dude," he gestures to Ella seated on the floor, "a beautiful girl shows you her tits and you refuse to look at them?" He holds his wrist up to my forehead. "Are you ill? Or just plain stupid?"

I flail my arm in her direction. "She...she waltzed into the kitchen this morning with no clothes on. I was trying to be a fucking gentleman!"

"I was nervous as hell and needed your help Auggie!" Ella explains.

Ledger scoffs beside me. "Yeah, Auggie, the fucking hot girl with no clothes on needed your help." He slaps me upside the head. "What were you thinking?"

"I was just trying to be nice and really, I was more concerned about the number of cinnamon rolls in my kitchen. Besides, it's not like her tits were going to turn me on anyway. They're Ella's tits. She's not some smoking hot puck bunny. She's just Ella."

Smiles fade on the faces around me and the energy in the room shifts. A few of the guys sit back in their chairs, trying to look anywhere but at me or Ella who has stopped writing in her notebook; her head bowed as she silently nods to herself. It feels like all the air has been sucked out of the room. I toss a glance to Griffin who winces and whispers, "Dude…"

I don't understand.

What just happened?

I turn my glance at my best friend assuming she'll back me up but her smile is gone too.

"Ella…"

She doesn't make eye contact at all.

Fuck.

What did I say?

They're Ella's tits. She's not some smoking hot puck bunny. She's just Ella.

Fuck!

"Ella that's not what—"

"You know, on second thought, I'm getting pretty tired," she says in a pained mumble. She finally lifts her head and I swear to God my heart tumbles into my stomach. It's like I've been sucker punched in the gut. Her red-rimmed eyes glance quickly around the room. She tries to smile and I know without a doubt she's trying as hard as she can to not cry.

Fucking fuck!

Her voice trembles slightly, giving her away. "It's been a long day and if you guys don't mind, I think I'll just uh…" I watch a tear slip down her cheek.

Fuck fucking fuck!

I start to get up from the couch to get to her but she springs up from the floor, stepping away before I can get there. "It was nice meeting you guys. If you'll excuse me."

"Ella, wait!"

Griffin nudges my leg and when I look down at him he's shaking his head. I watch in shock as my best friend retreats to her room and shuts the door and then I take a step to go after her but he stops me. "Let her go."

"But—"

"She needs a minute, August."

"But I didn't mean it the way it came out."

Bear frowns. "Yeah, but that's how it came out."

Thank you, Bear, for stating the obvious.

Plopping back down on the couch, I lean on my knees and hold my head in my hands. "What the fuck have I done?"

Ledger pats me on the back. "Well son, you basically told her that her tits aren't pretty and she's not nearly as attractive as the nameless women you fuck on the daily because she's just...Ella."

"But I meant—"

"Doesn't matter what you mean, August," Oliver explains softly. "It's what you said and the way you said it."

"Yeah, man." Griffin nods. "We know what you meant. But she one hundred percent didn't hear it that way."

"Fuuuuuck. What am I supposed to do now?"

"Let me ask you something. Because honestly I'm curious."

"Okay."

"This morning when she came out into the kitchen, the bra and panties...did they match?"

My head snaps to Griffin again. "Seriously Griff? I just insulted my best friend and you want to know if her underwear matched?"

His face remains stoic as he nods again. "Yes. Did it?"

I think back to what she had on. "Yeah. Black lacey bra and matching panties."

Griffin tosses a glance at Harrison and Oliver who both nod in agreement.

"What?" I ask, exasperated. "What they fuck does the color of her underwear have to do with anything?"

"It's not the color, August," Harrison explains. "It's that they matched. She wanted you to see them."

I roll my eyes at their ridiculousness. "What are you guys even talking about?"

"August, trust me when I say this," Oliver whispers, "girls don't usually care about matching their undergarments unless they want someone to notice."

"She said they made her feel pretty."

"Right." He nods. "And she wanted you to see them."

I shake my head. "That's insane. I've told you guys a hundred times Ella and I aren't like that. There's nothing there between us. There never has been and—"

Griffin raises his finger to stop me. "Don't say there never will be because from the look on her face just now, one of you doesn't have the same feelings as the other."

I fall back against the couch cushion completely flabbergasted at what the guys are trying to tell me.

"How can this be? She's never...

"We've never...

"We've always just..."

My shoulders fall as I release an overwhelming sigh. "Guys, tell me what to do. Should I go in there?"

Ledger shrugs. "Give her some time and then maybe check on her. We'll get out of here in case she needs to cry it out so she's not embarrassed."

"But at some point," Bear stands from his chair, "you'll have to get your shit together and figure out your feelings."

My brows remain furrowed as I say goodbye to the guys and lock the door behind them. I turn, staring at the living room, replaying the last twenty minutes in my mind about a thousand times, and experiencing the clusterfuck of emotions I did not see coming over and over again. I have no clue how I should manage this situation. I stand in front of Ella's door for what feels like hours trying to come up with the right words to say because I want to apologize but everything I consider saying sounds lame and stupid. Eventually I muster up the courage to knock softly on her door.

"Ella? You awake?"

She doesn't answer me. Instead of knocking again and risk waking her, I lay my palm against her door and then rest my forehead there as well, closing my eyes and inhaling a steady breath.

"I'm sorry, Ella," I whisper against the white wood. "I'm so fucking sorry."

CHAPTER EIGHT

ELLA

"I t's not like her tits were going to turn me on anyway. She's not some smoking hot puck bunny. She's just Ella."

"Just Ella," I whisper to myself when I step inside my ensuite bathroom and stare into the mirror. The lifeless face staring back at me pisses me off and depresses me at the same time. My eyes are red and my mascara is now running down my already splotchy cheeks. For as hot as I thought I was looking earlier, now all I see is a hot mess of emotional shit. I pull a tissue from the box on the counter and blow my nose quietly, refusing to allow August to hear me crying.

I shouldn't care what he thinks.

I'm a confident, smart, kind human being and I am proud of the person I am.

But when my best friend announces to a room full of breathtakingly gorgeous professional hockey players that I am, indeed, ordinary, unattractive, and just...Ella...yeah, that stung a little more than I was ready for.

So, there it is.

After all these years of friendship, I finally know what

August Blackstone really thinks of me. "I'm crazy enough to love but not at all pretty enough to fuck."

And now there is most likely a room of professional athletes sitting out in my living room discussing just how unattractive I am and how I'm a nice girl but it would never be good enough for any of them.

Fucking August.

He was supposed to be my biggest supporter, not the one who would tear me down. And especially not in front of new colleagues.

I love August. I do.

He's been my very best friend. My person. The one I run to when I'm happy, when I'm sad, when I'm pissed off, and when I'm depressed. But when he becomes the cause of all those feelings, when he's the one person to say something so cold and hurtful, I don't know what to do. I've never felt more alone than I do right now.

Slipping down to the floor of the bathroom, I curl my knees to my chest and wrap my arms around my legs and allow myself to cry out my feelings.

It's dark outside when I hear August knock on my door.

"Ella? You awake?"

Yeah, I am.

But I don't want to talk to you.

That's a lie.

What I want is for this evening to have never happened.

What I want is to swing open my door and laugh with you over some stupid movie.

What I want is for you to tell me I'm fucking sexy and actually mean it.

I remain still and stare at my door from my bed where I'm seated with my favorite Amy Daws book praying he doesn't turn the knob and barge right in. When he doesn't, I inhale a deep breath and release it slowly, inwardly thanking him for realizing I need a hot minute away from him to process all my feelings.

What I want is for you to tell me my tits are the prettiest mounds of flesh you've ever seen.

I twist my lips and narrow my eyes at my last thought because when have I ever wanted August Blackstone to say anything whatsoever about my tits?

That's a big never.

I mean I've asked him plenty of times over the years if my boobs look okay in a particular outfit and he's always chuckled and shaken his head and said yes.

But tonight was different.

It wasn't just about my chest or lack thereof. For him to blatantly tell other people that I'm not a turn-on...

Ugh.

Why?

Why August?

Why did you have to be such a thoughtless asshole?

His words tonight just made it feel so real. Like from a real man's perspective, because let's be honest, August is who I picture any time I talk about masculinity or men in general. He's the hot guy with the strong jaw, the sexy man bun, and the well-kept short beard. He's got arms of steel and rock-hard abs. There's nothing about him that isn't perfect. Me on the other hand, I'm simply an average Jane with features that wouldn't turn on a horny dog let alone some random hot guy.

Once I hear August close the door to his bedroom I toss back my covers and tiptoe to my bathroom one last time before I go to sleep. Standing in front of the mirror in my sleep shorts and frumpy t-shirt, I tilt my head and study my reflection. I know my body isn't perfect. I have my flaws and areas I don't love just like every other woman on this earth but dammit, I like my body. I'm proud of the woman I've grown up to be. I'm not a little kid anymore. Feeling a wave of confidence and courage I march back to my room and pull open the top drawer of my dresser. I rifle through the assortment of sexy lingerie I bought before moving here in case I met my soul mate and needed to look my best and pull out my favorite piece. A plum-colored lace crop cami with matching lace trimmed shorts that show off the shape of my ass perfectly. Tearing off my clothes, I slip into the sexy sleep set and study myself in my bathroom mirror once again, only this time I'm smiling and giving myself a confident nod of approval.

"You are a sexy ass queen." I push my breasts up with my hands and then tell myself to, "Just look at those beautiful tits. Auggie can fuck all the way off with his bevvy of big, busted women." I flip the bathroom light off and head back to my bead, slipping under the sheets and feeling like a million bucks in my sexy outfit. "Some hot man out there will appreciate whatever I have to offer because I'm a fucking catch."

Setting my book on the bedside table, I hit the button to turn off my lamp and fall fast asleep, the memories of hours ago slipping from my mind, replaced by whatever dreams may come.

I'M startled awake by the sounds of glass breaking and items crashing to the floor. My bed rocks underneath me causing my entire body to freeze, my muscles tightening in fear. My hand grips at the sheets beside me and my heartbeat races as I glance around my darkened room for any explanation.

Am I dreaming?

Is this a dream?

What the hell is happening?

"AUGGIE!" I scream with a tremor to my voice. The rumbling sounds grow in intensity, my bedside table shakes causing my lamp to tip over and roll to the floor.

This is not normal!

"AUGUST!

"ELLA!" I hear him scream back at me from somewhere outside my room. "ELLA, I'M COMING! STAY THERE!"

"AUGUST!" No way in hell am I staying where I am. I need the fuck out of here right now. Trying to get to August as fast as humanly possible, I jump from my bed and reach my door just as he pushes it open.

"Ella!" He takes one look at my frightened face illuminated by the moonlight and whatever streetlights glow from outside and instinctually pulls me against him, his arms covering my head as he buries me against his bare chest. "It's an earthquake Ella. You're okay. We're going to be okay."

"Auggie," I whimper, gripping his bare skin as hard as I can, wishing I could do more to get closer to him, forgetting that just hours ago he pissed me off and hurt my feelings. August has always been and will always be my safe space. "Fuck, Auggie. That scared the shit out of me."

"I know. I'm sorry." He has to speak loudly in order to be heard over the knocking of furniture against walls and items falling to the floor. "This is one of the stronger ones we've had in a while. We had a few mini ones just before you got here so I had a feeling a bigger one was coming. I'm so sorry. I should've told you."

"What do we do? We can't just stand here, right? Shouldn't we go hide or something?"

"No babe. Right here in this doorway is actually the safest place for us until it stops. We're away from anything that could fall off a wall. Just stay right here with me." He squeezes me against him as if I could possibly get any closer and smooths a hand down my hair. Furniture rattles around us and a few more knickknacks from around the apartment can be heard falling off their respective shelves and tumbling to the floor. My body flinches with each crashing sound and I squeeze my eyes closed.

August leans his head down so his cheek rests against the top of my head. "Just breathe, Ella. I've got you, alright?"

"Mhmm."

"Take a deep breath. This won't last more than another couple seconds. I won't let anything hurt you. I promise."

I nod my head against his chest and try to take a deep breath. It's a shaky one for sure, but the mere scent of him helps bring me back to my senses. Finally, the movement around the apartment stops and all is quiet except for a few car sirens we can hear from somewhere outside.

"There. See?" August murmurs softly as he strokes his hand up and down my back. "All done. You just lived through your very first California earthquake."

"Yeah, I'll be okay if that never happens again."

He chuckles against me. "Uh, I hate to break it to you, Ella, but California and earthquakes kind of go hand in hand. In fact, there will probably be aftershocks throughout the rest of the night. But if it makes you feel any better, you do get used to it the more times it happens."

"Aftershocks?"

"Yeah. Tiny little quakes. I like to think of it like the Earth is trying to go to sleep but it's just not quite comfortable yet so it has to shift until it finds a comfortable spot."

"Ugh. I don't think I'll ever get used to this," I say with my eyes still clenched shut. "I don't ever want to be startled awake to the feeling of a poltergeist under my bed ever again."

August curls his hand around my hair and softly brushes through it with his fingers. "Do you want to sleep in my room for the rest of the night?"

I don't even have to think about it. "Yes please. No way am I falling asleep alone after that."

"Okay, come on." He takes my hand and turns to lead me to his room but I stop him. "Wait. What about the mess? Don't you want to clean up the broken glass?"

He shakes his head. "It's not going anywhere. It'll still be there to clean up in the morning. And if some of the aftershocks are sizable, I don't want to have to clean it up twice."

Fair point.

"Alright."

August leads me to his room where a king-sized bed covered in cream-colored sheets and a light tan colored duvet acts as the focal point. The lamp connected to the wall next to his bed gives the space a warm glow that contrasts with the cool temperature. August clearly likes to sleep in Alaska given how cold it is in here.

"Dang, Auggie. Why do you sleep in an ice box?"

"It's not that bad," he says with a chuckle. "Don't worry. I promise you'll be warm enough. I'm a living furnace."

He turns around with a smile on his face but the moment his eyes land on me his expression changes. My eyes bulge in response and I turn quickly to glance behind me wondering what he's looking at.

"What?"

"Ella what..." He shakes his head and grasps the back of his neck. Clearing his throat he asks, "What are you wearing?"

I look down at my outfit quickly having forgotten completely that I changed into my favorite sexy sleep set before going to bed.

"Pajamas."

"Those are...not...pajamas," he tells me, his voice strangled. "You can't sleep in that."

"Why not? You're sleeping like that." I gesture to a half-naked August standing in the middle of his bedroom wearing only a pair of black boxer briefs. And yes, for the record, his body is fire but I can't focus on that right now no matter how much I want to. "Look at you. You're literally in your underwear."

"As are you."

"So, we're even then. And anyway, I'm still dressed more than you."

He gestures to my body. "Yeah, but you can't—"

"Why?"

"Because..."

"Because why, Auggie?" A hand on my hip, I tilt my head and scowl. "Is it because I look fucking hot?"

He doesn't answer.

But he also can't seem to look away.

"I mean, I don't see the problem here," I tell him, smoothing my hand down my side making sure to put on a show for him. I even push my breasts up with my hands causing him to step back. "I mean I know my nipples are poking through the material because you keep it cold as fuck in here but you made it clear just hours ago that these tits don't turn you on because what did you call me? Oh, that's right...just Ella."

"Ella, you know I didn't—"

"So, I am absolutely sleeping in this because I look fucking amazing and it makes me *feel* good and you..." I say, poking my finger against his rock-solid chest. "You are not going to say one fucking word."

Knowing he's not going to win this battle because I'm in my power clothes, he relents with a sigh. "Fine."

"Fine. Yeah." I nod with him. "Okay then." Without asking

what side of the bed he sleeps on I step over to the far side and pull back the comforter freezing in place when I spot something next to his pillow that I recognize.

Is that what I think it is?

He still has it?

In his bed?

I haven't thought about that thing in years!

Gasping, I reach for the old Beanie Baby crab I gave to August when we were in middle school and hold it in my hand. "Crabby?"

My heart melts at the sight of the gift I bought for August all those years ago. "August? Is this really—"

"Yeah," he answers with a gentle nod.

Speechless, I stare at the small stuffed toy in my hands. A little ragged looking now, I'm shocked it's still in one piece let alone in his bed. My brows furrow as I ponder the appearance of the old gift. "And do you—"

"Every single night." His eyes finally meet mine and suddenly I'm finding it hard to form words.

"But..." I shake my head. "I don't...I mean...this is..."

"It's no big deal."

"Auggie you've had Crabby since we were thirteen. I think that's kind of a big deal."

He shrugs but his demeanor has changed. He's softer now. "It helps me sleep," he says. "And it helped me feel closer to you over the years when we weren't...you know, like we are now."

Like we are now?

Should I be reading more into this?

August and I have never really spoken about furthering our friendship or crossing that line. In fact, that one time we kissed in high school, when we were young and curious to know what kissing felt like, we specifically promised each other we would never cross that line. But then I look down at my hand, at the stuffed toy I gave him nearly fifteen years ago that he still has, and I wonder if his feelings have changed in some way.

"Like we are now?" I question.

The corner of his mouth turns up slightly and he nods, stepping toward me. "Yeah," he says, wrapping his arms around me and pulling me against him for another hug. "Who needs Crabby now when you're here? In the flesh."

"I guess that's true," I murmur against his warm skin. I close my eyes for a quick beat while he holds me in his arms, the sound of his heart beating in his chest reverberates against my ear. He's right. His hold is strong and warm but tender and loving.

"I really am glad you're here with me, El. You mean more to me than I could ever begin to explain. You've always been that comfort from home, you know? You're my best friend and I don't know what I would do without you."

My ribs grow tight and there's a sudden heaviness to my body, but I will away the feelings of uneasiness and wrap my arms slowly around August's torso. My palms rest against his heated back, his muscles moving under my touch.

"I'm so sorry about what I said earlier, Ella," he says, his chin resting on the top of my head. "It was a douchey thing to say and I didn't mean it the way it came out."

It *was* a douchey thing to say.

I offer him a weak smile even though he can't see my face. "I know."

"Your tits are beautiful, okay? You're beautiful," he emphasizes. "I've always told you that and I've always thought it."

I nod knowing deep down that what he said earlier was, in fact, the way he really feels. It's moments like those where you learn someone's true colors and I learned August's. I know now he'll only ever see me as his childhood best friend and that's okay, but why I'm suddenly feeling saddened by that revelation

I cannot explain. I squeeze him a little tighter and tell myself to let go of my hurt and my anger and simply spend the moment breathing in his heady scent.

"Thank you, Auggie."

"Yeah," he whispers. Once our moment together passes, and I climb into his bed and cover myself with his ultrasoft duvet. August turns off the lamp and then climbs in on the other side coming up behind me and wrapping an arm around me.

A random thought shoots through my mind as he curls himself around me, cocooning me inside his body. "You know I'm not Crabby, right?"

He chuckles softly behind me. "Yeah. I know, but when was the last time I got to fall asleep next to my best friend? You'll have to forgive the intrusion because I'm taking full advantage while I can."

He folds his body around mine, his warmth encapsulating me. His strength protecting me. His...

Hooooly shit.

Is that...?

It is, right?

It has to be.

Oh, my God. Is he?

I shuffle slightly against him, like I'm trying to make myself comfortable and I don't miss the sudden inhale of his breath from behind me.

"El?"

"Yeah?"

"Keep that up and this sleepover will get very awkward very fast."

It's my turn to giggle. "Well, why is it poking me in the first place?"

His hand palms my stomach as he pulls me against him and though he can't see my face, my eyes bulge and my cheeks heat.

This is sooo not the way two friends fall asleep.

"Because for the first time ever, there's a girl in my bed," he explains. "And not just any girl but a fucking hot as hell one with tits any man would be lucky to get the chance to handle, so please excuse my dick if this knowledge excites him just a little bit. Give him a few minutes and he'll calm down, I promise."

Hearing August's surprising words sends a jolt of lust through my body that I have no choice but to ignore because doing anything other than ignoring it would mean crossing a line neither one of us is prepared to cross. Instead, I slowly inhale a deep breath and release it with an open mouth, biting down on my lower lip and trying hard not to smile.

"Good night, Auggie."

He nuzzles me from behind, his voice low and sleepy. "Night, El."

CHAPTER NINE

AUGUST

After a double dose of caffeine and a solid workout on the ice this morning, I'm finally feeling a little more like myself. I may have missed a few easy shots but I feel like I can finally get my head straight for tonight's opening game and be a productive member of the team. Damn good thing too, because after all the incredibly inappropriate thoughts I was having last night as I fell asleep with Ella in my arms, I woke up worried I wouldn't be able to get my mind off her.

Who am I kidding?

I haven't stopped thinking about her at all.

As if waking up in a panic hearing her scream during the earthquake wasn't bad enough, I offered to share my bed with her only to realize she was dressed like a goddamn walking wet dream.

Christ.

The way that dark purple lacey top molded to her tits, pushing them up just enough to allow my imagination to run wild. And the satiny bottoms that left me wondering how much I would see if she were to have bent over and touched her toes.

Fuck me.

I was wrong when I said what I said to the guys last night.

Dead fucking wrong.

She's not just Ella.

And her tits are not at all unattractive.

Just the opposite.

My best friend is sexy as hell.

And I'm finding myself desperately attracted to her.

Any other woman lying next to me and looking that amazing would've been on her back with her legs open wide for me in a matter of seconds, but this wasn't just any other sexy woman. It was Ella.

My roommate.

My best friend.

She's like forbidden fruit and although I slept amazingly well knowing she was in my arms right next to me, not allowing my hands to roam might be on the list of one of the hardest things I've ever done.

Grateful to have woken up before her this morning I jumped into an extremely cold shower to help calm me down from the three vivid dreams I had, each of which included Ella Montgomery in some kind of sexual position somewhere in my room.

Bent over my bed with her beautifully silky ass in the air.

Lying on my duvet with her arms above her head, her back arched, calling out my name.

On her knees with my stiff cock between her lips.

Yeah, it was like that.

And I don't think I've ever woken up with a morning wood as hard as I did this morning. It took all of ten seconds under the warm water before I was exploding onto the shower floor silently screaming her name, then I punished myself with the coldest water I could physically withstand.

I'm a hypocritical asshole.

I dissed my best friend in front of my teammates and then

spent the night holding her and wondering what it might feel like to be eight inches deep inside her.

Alright, alright. Seven inches.

Six and a fucking half. Alright? I'm no sex God and we can't all be Barrett Cunningham.

"How about that earthquake last night, huh?" Griffin gives me a wide-eyed nod as he slips on a clean pair of pajama pants —these ones blue with hockey sticks all over them—and t-shirt after a quick shower.

"Yeah. Definitely couldn't sleep through it," I answer. "That's for sure."

"How'd Ella do? Was that her first quake?"

"And what happened after we left, by the way?" Ledger adds, stepping back into his tennis shoes.

I'm quick to say, "Nothing...happened."

Ledger eyes Griffin who glances at me and then back to him. "Do you believe nothing happened Ollenberg?"

Griffin shakes his head with a laugh. "Not in the slightest." He points at me, his eyes narrowed. "I know you, man. And you're different when it comes to that chick. So, you may as well spit it out and tell us what's going on with you two because she's in the building today."

"So?"

His brows raise and he passes an ornery grin. "Sooo, if what you say is true and nothing happened...or is happening...you won't mind if I ask her out because she is hot as fuck and if you don't want to look at her, I will." He pushes the door to his locker closed and takes a step toward the door. My body reacts of its own accord, my arm stretching out and my palm resting against his chest.

"Over my dead body."

Griffin jumps back with a wild smile, pointing at me now with both hands. "A ha! I KNEW IT!"

"What did we know?" Harrison asks when he comes around the corner after his shower.

"Blackstone's got the hots for his roommate."

Harrison doesn't even have to look at me before he snorts a laugh. "Shocker."

"Well after last night, it was definitely not a shock," Griffin explains happily. "I just needed to get him to say it."

"I still haven't said it," I manage to say with a straight face, but Griffin isn't buying it. He stares at me, his eyes narrowing again, and he cocks his head as if he's trying to read my expression that I'm trying extremely hard to keep neutral. Knowing exactly what he's doing, he crosses his arms in front of his chest and nods to me, never once looking away.

"Alright wiseass. You're right. You haven't said it, but I bet my next goddamn paycheck that you're about to."

"Pffft. What makes you think that?"

"Because you haven't denied it, for one, like you were denying weeks ago. And you missed three shots at this morning's skate which is also not like you. And that can only mean one thing."

"Maybe he's constipated," Ledger suggests but Griff is quick to shake his head while still holding my stare.

"Nope. That ain't it. Blackstone's got something on his mind."

"Probably those unattractive tits," Oliver murmurs having walked into this mess of a conversation.

"Fuck off, Magallan." Realizing my response just gave me away, I close my eyes and release a resigned sigh as Griff chuckles in front of me.

"Told you. Now spill."

Maybe he's right.

Maybe it's okay for me to talk to the guys about this. Who else would I have if not them?

Bowing my head, I lower myself to the bench in front of the lockers and let my thoughts escape my mouth.

"Alright listen, nothing...happened last night. At least not in the way you all think it might have."

Griffin nods. "Go on."

"She was asleep when I knocked on her door. Either that or she just wanted nothing to do with me because she didn't answer me when I knocked. So, I went to bed and figured we would talk about it this morning, but then the earthquake happened and she's never experienced anything like that before."

Harrison cringes. "Yikes. Was she freaked?"

"Freaked is an understatement." I nod. "She was screaming for me. Her cries woke me up and I ran to her and assured her everything was safe and then told her there might be after-shocks—which she wasn't at all excited about obviously—so I told her she could sleep in my room if it would make her feel better. No big deal."

An understanding smile hits Harrison's lips. "Right. No big deal."

"Except then it was a huge deal because I didn't notice what she was wearing until we got to my room and I turned around to say something to her when she whined about how cold it was in my room."

"Wearing?" Griffin asks, his brow furrowed.

"Yeah." I wipe my hand down my face still in disbelief. "She had on this sexy little plum colored number."

The guys start to whistle and pass on their ooohs and ahhhs. "The top was this part satin, part lacey bra thing and the bottoms were these matching silky extra-short shorts and fuck..." I sigh. "She looked..." I shake my head. "Amazing."

"Yeah she did!" Ledger teases. "Was she mad at you about what you said?"

"She wasn't mad per se, but she gave me hell when I mentioned what she was wearing and refused to change."

"Wait, wait, wait." Harrison waves his hand. "She was wearing something sexy and you told her to change? What the fuck, man? Are you really that stupid?"

"Yeah because I was about to share a bed with her!"

"So?"

"So, the last thing I wanted to happen was to be hard as fuck all night long. We're supposed to be friends, remember?" I shake my head, blowing out a breath in exasperation. "Anyway, she said it made her feel good and then said something about me saying she wasn't attractive and therefore I shouldn't be at all bothered by what she was wearing." I hold my forehead in my palm.

"Oooh, she got you there, *Auggie*." Griffin laughs, teasing me with Ella's nickname for me.

"Yeah she did because she climbed into my bed and I knew I had to have my hands on her in some way so, I held her and... fuck me...the dreams I had last night coupled with the world's most uncomfortable morning wood when I woke up..."

"Let me guess," Oliver adds. "You can't stop thinking about her now?"

I nod grudgingly. "Bingo."

"Can't stop picturing her in that outfit?"

"She's everywhere I look."

"But you don't know what to do because she's your best friend and she doesn't see you the way you see her?"

"Exactly." I sigh. "She's like forbidden fruit. I can't do that to her. I can't cross that line."

Ledger shrugs. "Why not?"

"Why not?" I repeat back to him. "Have you not been listening? She's my best friend. We've known each other for longer than I can even remember. And because of my big mouth she thinks I don't find her attractive. She thinks I don't see her in any other way. And what if I said something and it all went to shit?"

"Then convince her," Oliver tells me.

"What?"

"Convince her."

"Convince her of what? That I think she's sexy as fuck and can't stomach the thought of her being with anyone else but me?"

"Yes." He laughs. "Exactly that."

"How am I supposed to do that?"

He grins and pulls his cell phone from his locker, unlocking the screen and tapping on it a few times.

"You're calling someone?" I ask in disbelief. "Now?"

"Yep. I know just the person to help us with this one."

While I appreciate Magallan using the word *us*, making me feel like I'm not alone in this new pursuit to convince Ella that we should be together, I can't for the life of me think of who he could possibly call to help with this situation. He lays his phone down on the bench, having turned on the speaker so we can all hear.

"Oliver?" a female voice says on the other end of the line.

"Hey Sis," he says into the phone with a smile. "I'm calling for my friend August. He's here with me. Well, actually pretty much all the guys are here with me. Except for Cunningham. He's still training."

"Oh. Hey guys," she says. "How is everybody?"

Those of us in the room all say our hellos before Oliver continues. "Anyway, we're calling because August has the hots for his childhood best friend who just happens to also be his new roommate."

"Aww, how sweet! I love that!" Charlee coos.

"Right but she doesn't know he has the hots for her."

"Ooooh. So, it's like that."

Oliver chuckles. "Yeah. It's like that."

"So, he's got to convince her!"

Oliver winks at me and then wags his brows. "Exactly! And since you're into all that romance book stuff with your editing job, I thought maybe you might have a few ideas on how August can convince Ella that they're meant to be. I'm sure you've read stuff like that before in your editing, yeah?"

Charlee Landric, whose husband plays for the Chicago Red Tails, giggles on the other end. "Like you would not believe. August," she says confidently. "You came to the right place but listen. Don't think about this in terms of convincing her you like her. If you're up for a little fun to see where her head really is, then this needs to be more of a situation where you convince her that *she* likes *you*."

"Ahh, so drive her a little crazy and then go in for the kill?" Oliver says.

"Yes," she says with a chuckle. "Something like that. You can definitely have a little fun with it. Flirt with her a little but not so much that it's painstakingly obvious. Make it so she has no choice not to notice you so you're always on her mind."

"Alright." I nod. "Sounds easy enough. Where should I start."

She's quiet for a beat before she finally asks, "Do you have a pair of gray sweatpants?"

"Hey." I poke my head around the corner of Ella's dressing room and find her on the couch with her laptop in front of her. "What are you doing?"

"Oh hey. I'm watching mascot videos," she tells me. "Why? Did you need something? Am I supposed to be doing something else?"

"Nope." I smile and shake my head. "Just thought I'd check on you. Big first day and all."

"Tell me about it." She gives me a sideways smile and I can tell she's getting nervous.

Understandable.

I'd be surprised if she weren't.

"I figured maybe watching a few videos to see what some of the league's favorite mascots have done would help me get in the zone for tonight and give me a few pointers on things the crowds enjoy, you know?"

"Smart idea," I tell her, stepping farther into her room. "But remember, you were hired because the team loves who you are. You don't have to try to be someone else."

"I know." She taps the cushion next to her. "But they're still fun videos to watch. Want to join me?"

I nod and plop down next to her. "Sure. I've got a few minutes before I need to go tape my stick."

"This one is hilarious. Check this out." She clicks the arrow on the screen and the video shows the mascot for the Seattle Sea Brawlers unable to stay upright on his skates. Ella giggles the whole way through it. "It's like they forgot to tell whoever they hired that they were going to need to skate! I mean I feel bad for the guy but this is too funny!"

"Damn right it is." I huff out a laugh. "Let's hope you play against that guy in the Mascot Tournament. You'll skate rings around him."

"Oh my gosh, and this one," she says, pointing at the screen as the next clip runs. "This guy just walks around and throws pies in peoples' faces and they love him for it."

Her disbelief makes me chuckle. "Oh yeah, that's Grizzy.

He's with the Minnesota team. We love playing there. That guy's a freaking hoot!"

"I just can't believe fans are okay with getting a pie to the face! That's crazy to me!"

"Meh." I shrug. "They usually then get heavily rewarded with team merch so it's a win-win. The mascot gets the laugh and the fan gets some merch. It's all in playful fun."

"Aww but watch this one! I had no idea Remi Red Tail did this last year!" The next video pops up and shows the Zamboni driver on the ice doing her thing when the wives of the Red Tails players line up with Remi along the wall each holding a different poster board in their hands. The first poster is turned over and it reads

GIANNA, LOVE IS A SMILE FROM A FRIENDLY FACE

Several more poster boards are flipped, each with another phrase about what love is and then finally Remi flips his which says

REMI REALLY LIKES GIANNA (BECAUSE LOVE IS A STRONG WORD WHEN WE HAVEN'T EVEN KISSED YET.) WILL GIANNA GO OUT WITH REMI?

The Zamboni driver hops down from the vehicle and gives Remi a huge hug and the crowd goes wild.

"Oh yeah, I forgot this happened. Milo Landric told Oliver all about it. Apparently their Zamboni driver is a woman, which is rare in this industry, and there were some drunk fans at their home games that were giving her a tough time. Sometimes it was more like sexual harassment. Anyway, the guy who is their mascot has had a crush on the Zamboni driver for some time and at that game," I say, pointing to the screen, "he finally got the Red Tails wives involved to let her know he liked her. Pretty sure it was Valentine's Day or close to it if memory serves me right."

Ella melts next to me, bringing a hand to her chest. "That might be one of the sweetest most romantic gestures I've ever seen!"

She likes romantic gestures.

Noted.

"Yeah. I guess it was a pretty wild game."

"And did they end up getting together?"

"I guess you'll have to ask him when we play them next month. And if I had to guess, you'll probably meet the Red Tails hockey wives too. They're a cool bunch of ladies."

"You've met them?"

"Yeah. A couple times now. Oliver and his fiancée Scarlett got together at an Anaheim-Chicago game. Well, really they got together on Scarlett's honeymoon but—"

"Wait...Scarlett's honeymoon?" she asks wide-eyed.

"Yeah. It's a cute story. You should ask Scarlett. She loves talking about it."

Ella beams back at me. "I will absolutely ask her." She shuts her laptop and takes a deep breath. "I guess I should get ready. I have some promo videos to make with Marlee this afternoon before the game."

"Want to know a secret about Marlee?"

Her brow furrows. "Umm, is it going to change my perspective on her? Because maybe I don't want to know."

"Nah, this is cute gossip."

"Oh, well then by all means, lay it on me."

"She's the one Ledger has had a crush on. Remember I mentioned it before you moved here?

"Oh, my God! Yes, I remember! Why doesn't he just ask her out? She's super nice."

I shake my head. "She was dating some rich dude in the corporate world for a while. Honestly we think maybe they broke up but she might still be with him. I'm not positive, but we like to tease Ledge about it."

"Aww, poor Ledger."

I stand from the couch. "Alright, I'll let you get yourself ready." I offer her my hand and help pull her up from the couch.

"Can I give you a good luck hug?"

She smiles. "I'd be pissed if you didn't, Auggie." She wraps her arms around my neck and I pull her against me, covering her with my arms. "You give the best hugs."

"Do I?"

Maybe hugs are my superpower.

She likes hugs?

I can give hugs.

I can give lots of hugs.

"Mhmm," she says. "I'm anxiously nervous for tonight. Is that a thing to be? Anxiously nervous? Like I'm super excited to be out there but nervous as hell at the same time?"

"Yeah, that's a thing you can be," I tell her, squeezing her a little tighter and wishing I didn't have to let go. "But you're going to be great and you're going to have so much fun. And I'll be around the arena all day so if something happens or you need me, just call."

"Thank you, Auggie."

"You're welcome. Good luck out there." I place a swift kiss on her forehead and then give her a fist bump before walking out of her room.

LITTLE THINGS that make her think of me.

This one might not be on Charlee Landric's list but it's an obvious one for Ella's first day as the team mascot for tonight's season opener. As I walk down the hall toward Ella's dressing room, I hear music playing in the arena so I make my way up the tunnel to see what's going on. Assuming they're running sound checks before tonight, I'm surprised to find Ella on the ice. Dressed in full costume she dances for the camera as Lizzo sings about getting loose and blaming it on the juice.

Look at her go.

Doin' her thing.

The new Lumin costume is so perfectly her. The character almost resembles that of a cat with bright yellow fur and a yellow tail tipped with a glittery star. The cat-like face has star shaped ears and little stars in the pupils of its eyes. Three blue tufts of fur sit between the ears like a bow in her hair and of course she's wearing a STARS jersey with the name LUMIN printed across the back.

She's adorable as fuck out there.

"That's fantastic Ella," Marlee tells her with an amused chuckle. "You make those moves look way too easy in that costume."

Ella doesn't say anything in response, but she does twirl on the ice and then gives Marlee a high five.

Marlee smiles from ear to ear. "I think we got the shots we need. We'll put this out on social media within the hour. With any luck, the crowd tonight will eat this up."

My chest swells with pride as I stand here quietly observing her from the shadows. She looks great and seems like she's really in her element. Not that any of this should surprise me. Ella was made for a job like this. She knows how to work a crowd and I have no doubt that's exactly what she'll do tonight.

Looking down at the two cinnamon rolls in my hand, Ella's

nervous habit of choice, I decide leaving them in her dressing room might be a better idea than waiting for her here in case she's not done. I wouldn't want to embarrass her in front of her new colleagues and plus this way, I can leave them with a quick note for luck.

Perhaps the gesture will be that first something to stick with her.

Something to show her I'm thinking of her even when I'm not with her.

I take a deep breath and head for her dressing room.

Here goes nothing.

CHAPTER TEN

ELLA

"That's fantastic Ella," Marlee says with a smile. "You make those moves look way too easy in that costume."

I don't reply because mascots don't talk. Staying in character, I twirl myself around on the ice and then give Marlee a high five.

"And seriously, this new costume is adorable if I do say so myself," she says. "It's the yellow fur and the star tail. It all just looks so stinking cute." She shakes her head in wonderment as I skate around on the ice chasing my own tail.

"Come on goofball, I'll walk with you to your dressing room."

Marlee and I walk ourselves carefully off the ice and down into the tunnels. I finally take off the head of my costume, unable to contain the smile on my face.

"Oh my gosh, that was so much fun!"

Marlee laughs. "Girl, you seem like you were made for this. How you can move that way in a costume like that is beyond me. Oooh..." She grabs onto my fur-covered arm. "And just wait until we do the formal welcome of Lumin to the team and give you your very own hockey stick. I got a look at it last night and it is so cool!"

Her enthusiasm brings a smile to my face. "Can't wait!"

"Alright, if you don't need anything else for right now, I've got to run back upstairs to handle a few other schedule issues with some of the players."

"Yeah sure, no problem," I tell her, waving. "I'll catch you later."

Marlee walks on down the hall and when I turn into my dressing room, a recognizable scent fills my nose as I step inside. Immediately a huge smile spreads across my face because I know only one person could have possibly left this gift for me and that person is August Blackstone.

"No, he didn't..."

I find the source of the yummy, sweet scent on the counter to my left. Making quick work of my costume, I pull my gloves off dropping them to the floor and then peer into the bag spotting not one, but two boxes of cinnamon rolls.

"Oh, yes, he did."

Attached to the bag is a note that I unequivocally recognize as August's handwriting.

El,

For you on your special day.

I'm so fucking proud of you and can't wait to watch you shine.

Knock 'em dead tonight and then we'll celebrate together!

Welcome to the team! - August

He knew I would be nervous on my first day.

He knew exactly what I would want.

He did this for me.

My heart swells as I tuck the note into my bag for safe keeping and then rip open the first cinnamon roll box. I tear off a piece of the warm gooey goodness and drop it into my mouth, savoring every pass over my tongue as my phone rings in my locker. Grabbing it from the shelf, I smile at the name on the screen and tap it excitedly to answer the call.

"Paige!"

"Ella!"

"Oh, my God! It's so good to hear from you!"

"You didn't think I would leave my girl hanging on her first official day as Lumin the shooting star, did you?"

I chuckle as I take a seat on the small couch in my dressing room. "Of course not. Hold on, I'm gonna switch to facetime so I can eat my cinnamon roll while we talk."

"Uh oh," she says. "Cinnamon roll, huh? You feeling okay?"

"Yeah, of course," I say, attaching my phone to the cell phone holder near me. "But you know me. Cinnamon rolls are my nervous habit. Now I feel like I have to have one, you know?"

"Right." She nods with an understanding smile. "For good luck."

"Yeah."

"Well, I don't think you have anything to worry about. I'm sure you're going to be great tonight!"

"Thanks, Paige." I tear off another piece of my roll and toss it in my mouth. "So, how's the hot goat dad? What's the goat's name again?"

She sighs. "His name is Winston. And his hot dad is dreamy in every sense of the word. I swear since he asked me to move in with him and stay in Tuft Swallow he is a whole new person. Even my friends in town are talking about how outgoing he is now. It's crazy. Good crazy of course, but crazy."

"Why do you think that is? That he's so different, I mean."

"Honestly, I think he's finally forgiven himself for the accident he was in with his sister all those years ago. He had been holding on to that pain all this time and I really think that did a number on him. It's like since she wasn't here he wasn't allowing himself to be happy."

"I'm sure he has you to thank for that change, huh?"

She smiles. "Maybe. I mean I don't want to take credit for his strength or his resilience because he's worked through his pain all on his own, but I'd like to think my being here has had some kind of small impact on him."

"It's not small, Paige. You changed his life."

"And he's changed mine. But speaking of life changing... how are things in California? How's Auggie?"

My cheeks redden at her question and she notices the coy expression on my face and gasps. "Noooo you did not!"

"What?"

"Ella! Did you sleep with August?"

"No. Of course not." I shake my head adamantly and give her a nervous giggle. "It's not like that. Although we did sleep together last night but we—"

"Whoa, whoa, whoa," she says, stopping me and waving her hands at the camera. "Let's back up here. What do you mean you slept together last night but it's not like that?"

Leaning forward on the couch, I bulge my eyes and as over dramatically as I can, tell her, "Paige, I lived through my very first earthquake last night!"

Paige gasps. "Oh my gosh! No way! Tell me everything. I've never experienced an earthquake before! What's it like?"

"Scary as fuck, that's what it's like!"

She laughs. "Were things falling off the walls? Does Auggie

live in a tall building? Did it sway? Did you have to take cover? Did the ground open up and suck everything down inside this deep black hole? Ella how are you even still alive?"

I laugh at her barrage of questions. "Okay first of all, you watch too much television. There was no sucking of the world down into an open earth hole. At least not in Auggie's apartment. But yeah, things were falling off walls and onto the floor and I woke up to my bed shaking and I screamed for August because I didn't realize what was going on."

"So, you weren't sleeping together then obviously," she states.

"No, but as soon as he mentioned aftershocks I was like, oh hell no, and so he offered to let me sleep with him so I wasn't alone if those happened throughout the night."

"Aww that was sweet of him. He's such a good guy."

"Yeah, but there's more."

She smiles and rests her chin on her palm. She must be at work in her antique shop.

"Do tell girl! And don't leave out any details!"

I recount for Paige what happened earlier in the evening when I finally met the guys on the team and what August had to say about my unattractive breasts.

"What the fuck was he thinking?" She seethes. "I can't believe he said that!"

"Right? That's what I thought, which is why it stung a lot. I mean I know we're not like...a couple or anything but geesh. A little compliment would've been nice, you know? Especially in front of his friends."

"I'm going to have to have a talk with that guy," Paige mumbles. "He doesn't get to treat you like that."

"Well, he may have made up for it last night."

Paige quirks her brow. "Oh?"

A sly smirk spreads across my lips. "Yeah. So, I may have

been wearing this sexy little purple number when the earthquake hit. After I walked out on August and the rest of the team, I decided I was going to bed looking and feeling like a million bucks so I put on this sexy sleep set. Purple lace and satin. Paige, I can't lie, I looked fabulous."

She beams. "I have no doubt!"

"So, when he took me to his room we were laughing about the temperature in there because the man sleeps in an arctic tundra. Seriously my nipples were screaming. And when he turned around to say something else he finally noticed what I was wearing."

Paige squeals. "Aaaand?"

"And let's just say he was extremely uncomfortable and I didn't give two shits. He tried to tell me I couldn't wear the outfit to bed but wouldn't give me an answer as to why so I threw it in his face that he said I was unattractive and so therefore it's no big deal what I wear. And then I climbed myself right into bed." I shrug, tearing off another bite of cinnamon roll. "I mean it didn't stop him from climbing in behind me and pulling me against him."

Paige's gaze latches onto mine and her smile grows. "Uh huh, aaaand?"

"Aaaand he may have been a little turned on because he was poking my ass!" I can't help but giggle especially when my friend does the same. "And because I'm a pot stirrer when I'm in the right mood, I wanted to drive him a little crazy. We'll call it punishment for being an asshole earlier in the evening. So, I may have shuffled back against him a little. And he may have told me if I didn't cut it out he would end up having an extremely awkward night."

She laughs even harder.

"And when I asked why, he told me it was because for the first time ever there was a girl in his bed—side note, he's never brought a woman back to his place! Can you even believe that?"

She bobs her head. "Makes sense I guess. Privacy and all."

"Yeah. That's exactly what he said. Anyway, he said I was the first woman to be in his bed and then said I was hot as fuck, his words not mine, and that I had tits any man would be lucky to have the opportunity to handle."

Paige nearly chokes on her drink. "No, he did not say that!"

I nod. "Yes he absolutely did."

She gasps. "Ella Montgomery, does he like you? I think he likes you! Like, likes you likes you!"

I crinkle my nose. "I don't think I would go that far."

"No?"

"Nah. He meant what he said in front of the guys. It was one of those statements you make when you're not thinking and usually those are the ones you mean, you know?"

"Then why would he say otherwise with you in his bed last night?"

I shrug. "To save face would be my guess, but..."

She waits a moment before asking, "But what?"

I lean forward toward my phone and lower my voice so nobody walking by my room can hear me. "Paige, I think I liked it. I liked being in bed with him. There was this moment when his palm rested against my bare stomach and I liked his hands on me. And even if he didn't mean it, hearing him say those things to me last night, right in my ear as he held me, it felt... nice. I found myself getting a little hot and bothered."

Paige beams back at me through the phone. "Of course you did! Also, this doesn't surprise me. I think it's to be expected. First of all, you two have been best friends since you were tiny humans. You have this bond that few people have. You've always been that way. Secondly, you were feeling great, looking like a gazillion bucks, and you were in the arms of your best friend in the entire world who also happens to be a hot as hell professional hockey player. So, the question is, when are you going to just drop the good-girl act, and go for it with him?"

Sometimes I wish...

"Why would I do that? It could mess up everything if it were to not go well and as you said, our bond is too strong for me to want to fuck it up over crazy physical attraction."

She shrugs her shoulder. "The way I see it, the only reason it might not go well is if the two of you can't get your heads out of your own asses."

Her words sit with me, soaking in and spreading through my mind.

"Do you have feelings for August, Ella? Like more than just friends?"

I take a deep breath mulling over my answer.

"I...maybe? I think part of me always has. I'd be lying if I said he wasn't hot as sin and that I haven't thought about...you know, stuff."

She grins. "Yeah. Stuff. And I think you've liked him longer than you want to admit to yourself and that's totally okay. So, maybe it's time to take the next step and see where he is. Maybe he feels the same. If he was poking you in the back last night, then there's obviously a part of him that was attracted to you."

"Yeah," I giggle. "The horny part. The part who hasn't gotten laid since I got to town because I think I've become a cock block for him."

"Good. Then it's time to drive him crazy and show him his eyes need to be on you and you alone."

"What? How am I supposed to do that?"

"Come on, Ella. You can do this. Surely you can come up with a few ways to flirt with him or challenge his thoughts so that he's constantly coming back to you. Turn on the hot girl charm. Ooor the bad girl charm. Read the room. You're good at that. Make him want you. Make him desire you. Show him what he's missing by not making a move and then when he finally does make a move, you'll be right there with him."

I nod my head at her suggestions. "Do you really think that's the way to go?"

"Yeah. I really do. Auggie is headstrong. You know that. If he has feelings for you, and I kind of think he does, he might be just as scared to talk to you about them. So, play with that a little bit. Have a little fun. You have one week to make a couple moves and the next time we talk I want a play by play."

"What do you think I should do first?"

She laughs on the other end of the line. "The only obvious choice."

"Which is?"

"Go on a date," she says. "A date with another man. Make the guy squirm." A bell rings in the background and Paige looks away from her phone. "Hi welcome to The Nest." She glances back at me and whispers, "Okay I've got to go. Customer just walked in." She blows me a few kisses. "But lots of luck tonight! I'll be sending you all the positive energetic vibes I can."

"Thanks Paige. Love you girl."

"Love you too! And good luck with August! Take the bull by the hornies." She gives me one last wink and then she's gone.

"Take the bull by the hornies..."

I end the call with a smile on my face and an eye roll for Paige's creative word mashup but then sit in silence for a moment going through everything she had to say about August.

Maybe she's right.

Maybe I should do this. Because if I'm really not interested then would his words have hurt so badly yesterday? If I'm not interested, would I be okay knowing he's out getting his needs met by random women in every city he plays in?

Yeah, that's a hard no.

I don't think I could stomach knowing that.

But could I see the woman he sleeps with being me?

Kissing me?

Touching me?

The warm flutter in my stomach tells me all I need to know.

It also tells me I need to sit here and eat every last bite of these cinnamon rolls if I'm going to have the courage to do any of this.

CHAPTER ELEVEN

AUGUST

"Hey knock 'em dead out there, Ella," Griffin says to her, offering her a fist bump. Dressed head to toe in her new mascot uniform, Ella returns the fist bump and then claps her hands without saying a word. One by one each of the guys wishes her good luck and then it's my turn. I offer her a fist bump too, but I know her better than that. She swats my fist away and comes in for a hug. The embrace might be a bit awkward when I'm in full gear and she's in a big fur suit but we make it work.

"I'm so fucking proud of you, El. You're going to be great."

"Thank you, Auggie," she whispers loudly enough for me to hear from inside her costume. "For everything."

"Anything for you, babe. Good luck out there." Those are my last words to her before my skates hit the ice.

Our pre-game warm up is amped by an excited crowd and music blaring through the arena. By all means I should be focused on one thing only and that's doing my job to sink as many pucks in the net as possible. Instead, adrenaline is coursing through my veins knowing my best friend is about to make her debut as Anaheim's newest mascot and I'm fucking nervous for her.

What if the crowd doesn't take to the change?

What if they don't like her?

What if they think yellow fuzzy creatures are stupid?

What if they boo her out of the arena?

What if she falls on the ice and gets hurt?

What if she spends the rest of the night in tears regretting this move?

What if she quits and moves back home?

Shit.

What if she blames me and I never get to see her again?

Fuck.

I bend over at my waist, pretending to stretch my back, when Ledger and Harrison skate up to me stopping at either side.

Ledger pats my back. "Relax man. She's going to be great."

I lift my head to find his amused face staring down at me. "How did you..."

Harrison laughs on the other side of me. "Because you keep skating in circles and looking around like you're looking for her dude." He gestures behind him. "She's in the tunnel, remember? We all passed her on the way out here."

Standing tall, I pretend to fix a part of my uniform when I finally confess, "I'm nervous as fuck for her guys, but she's great at this. She was made for this and I know she's going to be just fine so what the hell is my problem?"

"Meh, you're crushing on her. No big deal," Ledger says. "But don't let Coach catch you being a dumbass out here or he'll put your ass on the bench."

"Man crush?"

He rolls his eyes. "Yeah. Man crush."

"He's right," Harrison says, gesturing to the pucks being

slung around the ice in our warmup circle. "You like her. You care about her. You want her to succeed. We all know it. We get it. But we'll celebrate with her later. For now, she has a job to do and so do we. Shake it off, Blackstone."

With the physical shake of my head, I try my best to calm my nerves or at least push them to the back of my mind and continue our warm-up. Before both teams are formally introduced and the national anthem is played, the team forms a wide circle at center ice as we were instructed to do and the spotlight shines between us all inside the center circle. The announcer, Jim Stabler, states that our long-time mascot, or rather the man behind the mask, Kingston Stockler, is retiring. A video plays on the jumbotron above our heads of several of Astro's greatest moments and then Marlee Remington brings Kingston to the ice to wave his final goodbyes. The crowd goes wild cheering for him and then our head coach, Chris Hicks, gifts him with the hockey stick he used as part of his costume. We all clap and cheer for him as he walks around and gives each of us a hearty handshake and a hug and then Marlee hands Kingston another stick-shaped package wrapped in sparkly paper that he doesn't open, but instead, holds in his hands in front of him.

From his post among the suites, Jim Stabler announces that with the retirement of Kingston comes the introduction of a brand-new team mascot. A song is blasted through the arena that I've heard before, but only because it's one Ella has listened to in the apartment several times. It's Chappell Roan's "Hot To Go" and the crowd is on their feet as the spotlights move across the ice as if they're searching for our newest mascot. Finally, Stabler's voice rings out over the music.

"Introducing the newest member of the Anaheim Stars hockey franchise, let's all put our hands together and give a starry Anaheim welcome tooooo LUUUUUUUMIN!"

I don't know how the hell she does it without skates, but dressed in her full furry costume, Ella slides her way onto the ice like Tom Cruise in *Risky Business* and comes to a stop smack dab in the middle of our circle just as Chappell's song reaches the chorus. Clearly the fans are already familiar with the song because many of them are doing the dance moves right along with our most adorable new mascot. They all slap and clap and touch their toes and chant H-O-T-T-O-G-O and I am all smiles watching my best friend perform in front of us all.

She's fucking amazing and the feeling of pride that hits my chest is almost overwhelming.

She's really doing it.

When the music stops, Ella doesn't. She practically floats around the circle giving a high five to each of us as we all smile and welcome her to the team, but she doesn't stop there. Once all the way around the circle, she gives Coach Hicks a huge hug and as she turns, she catches sight of her tail. With a sparkly star tipping her tail, she pretends to chase it around and around as she turns in circles entertaining the crowd and when she finally catches it, she jumps for joy as everyone claps for her. Stabler declares today as Lumin's birthday and tells Lumin that the team has a special gift just for her as the retiring mascot, Kingston, approaches her on the ice and hands her the stick shaped gift.

Ella, I mean Lumin, pretends to be surprised and then excitedly tears off the wrapping paper of her new gift. She jumps up and down and spins in a circle when she sees her gift is her very own specialized hockey stick complete with sparkly tassels at the top and light up stars that appear at the bottom when she moves it. She takes a few seconds to spin around, moving her stick to show off how much it glows and sparkles, and then does a final wave to the audience blowing kisses to the crowd before she heads off the ice with Kingston and Marlee.

Fuck, I'm so proud of her. And I can't wait to celebrate with her after the game, but until then, we've got a job to do.

"THAT FLIP you did on the ice during first period break was amazing, Ella!" Ledger tells her. "I think my back hurts just thinking about it."

Griffin laughs. "Right? And how the hell did you do that in costume?"

I pull out the chair next to me so Ella has a place to sit and hand her a beer which she quickly tosses back.

"About an hour of practice earlier today," she says, wiping her mouth with the back of her hand while she giggles. "I had to figure out how to flip fast enough that my head would stay on. Thankfully, it didn't take long to perfect but I don't think I'll be doing that all the time. And probably never on skates unless I have a death wish."

Ledger offers her a fist bump. "Well for what it's worth, you were great today."

"Thank you so much. It was a rush of a lifetime," she says. "I'm not sure I'll ever be used to that feeling."

"Welcome to our lives," Oliver adds as he and Scarlett take the seats across from us. "Ella I'd like to introduce you to my fiancée, Scarlett Dayne. Scarlett, this is Ella Montgomery, our new mascot."

Scarlett beams back at her and offers her hand. "It's a pleasure to meet you, Ella. And I have to agree with the guys. You were amazing out there today."

Ella's jaw drops and she looks to me and then back to Scarlett and then back to me before giving me a solid whack to my upper arm.

"Dude! You did NOT tell me Oliver's fiancée was Scarlett Dayne!"

"I didn't?"

She shakes her head. "No! You didn't. But oh, my gosh, it's a pleasure to meet you as well, Scarlett. Small confession obviously, but I feel like I've known you for so long because I started following you on social media a year or so ago when you went to that boutique with the really cute jumpers that were super colorful. I totally bought three of them after seeing you there."

Scarlett's eyes grow large as she slides into her seat and leans over the table to get closer to Ella. "Oh, my gosh! You just made my day! And weren't those jumpers the cutest things ever? I think I could wear those things every single day of my life!"

"Right?" Ella nods emphatically. "And that nail salon that does the funky nail art. What was that girl's name?"

"Alexis!"

"Yes! Alexis! Love her!"

"Isn't she so amazing?"

"Yes! I seriously need to consider making an appointment with her someday just to see what she can do."

"Girl let's do it! You and me both!" Scarlett offers.

Ella's excitement just ramped up another ten degrees. "Really?"

Scarlett giggles. "Yes, really! It's fall so we can get our pumpkin spice vibes on with super cute nails or you could do something with stars to match your costume."

"That sounds like so much fun! I would love that."

"Well, it sounds like we're best friends now then."

Ella laughs. "Absolutely! I could use a best friend out here."

Scarlett gives Ella a high five and for just the teensiest moment, I feel a stab of jealousy in my chest.

She's *my* best friend.

And I don't want to share.

"Hey." I gesture to myself. "What do you mean you could use a best friend? What the heck am I then?"

Ella cocks her head and gives me a sympathetic look. "Aww, I'm sorry, Auggie. That's not what I meant. I guess I should've said I could use a best *girl*friend out here. You know, someone to go bra shopping with and talk about boys with and go to the salon with."

I scoff playfully. "And you don't think I would do those things? I'd go bra shopping with you. Anytime any place."

If it means I have an excuse to look at your boobs, I'll do it happily.

"But also, what's wrong with going braless?"

Griffin clears his throat with his hand over his mouth and mumbles to me, "Abort, August. Abort. You've already failed at the bra and boobies discussion. Abort, my friend."

Scarlett grins. "Uh oh, this sounds like something I must've missed."

For a moment, my asshole puckers and I fear I'm about to relive my huge mistake from the other night all over again, but to my surprise, Ella waves it off.

"Oh, August just a had a stupid douche nozzle moment a couple nights ago and said something he shouldn't have, but it's all good. He saved me from the nasty scary earthquake so all is forgiven."

And she gave me monster morning wood.

I want to say we're even because I was so uncomfortable all night with her in my arms but in reality, I was on cloud nine with her in my arms and in my bed. It's a confusing feeling when we haven't allowed ourselves to ever cross that line of friendship, but fuck, I liked every minute of having her near me. I guess that means we're not even and I owe her big time for giving me the permanent feels and visuals I now have stored inside my personal spank bank.

Thanks to Oliver and his sister, Charlee, at least I have a few ideas of how I might repay her. Maybe if I'm lucky I can put my plan into action tonight when we get home.

"Oh! I love this song!" Ella jumps from her seat when Walk the Moon's "Shut Up and Dance" plays overhead. "Scarlett, you want to come dance with me?"

"Sure! Let's do it," Scarlett says, giving Oliver a quick kiss before skipping off with my girl.

Okay, she's not my girl, but dammit I can't get the thought of making her mine out of my head. The more I think about it, the more I wonder what life would be like if we were to be more than the friends we already are.

"What are you thinking about over there, Blackstone?" Bear asks from the end of the table. "The wheels turning inside your head are very loud and squeaky."

"I'll tell you what he's thinking," Griffin offers. "He's thinking about our newest team mascot and how he can level up that special bond they seem to have."

I sulk in my chair with a sigh, never truly taking my eyes off Ella as she and Scarlett chat together while they dance. "Am I that obvious?"

"He says with stalker eyes towards the girl of his wet dreams," Ledger says with a laugh. "Yeah, a little bit obvious."

Finally steeling myself to look away, I pick up my beer and take a hefty swig. "Ugh, I can't get her out of my fucking mind."

"Good." Oliver nods. "You've got your plan, right?"

I nod. "Yeah. I'm going to try something tonight and see if I can gauge her reaction."

"Perfect."

I take another sip of my beer and allow my eyes to wander back to Ella and Scarlett only this time, rage fuels in the pit of my stomach. "What the fuck?"

The guys all follow my gaze to see a couple of guys talking to the ladies. Ella touches the arm of one of the guys who hands her a napkin. She looks at it and smiles before folding it up and pushing it into her pocket.

"What the hell was that?" I ask, feeling a bit of panic shoot through me. "What did he just hand her?"

"Don't know man," Oliver says with a shake of his head, but when the song ends and the girls rejoin us at the table, Ella is squealing with excitement.

"Why so starry eyed, Miss Lumin?" Ledger asks so I don't have to.

She pulls the napkin from her pocket and I swear all the blood leaves my face as she unfolds it and announces to the group, "That hot guy over there gave me his number!"

CHAPTER TWELVE

ELLA

My first official two weeks of the hockey season are complete and they have been so much fun! I wasn't sure what to think of how the Anaheim crowds might take to a new team mascot after well over thirty years of having Astro on board, but these last couple of weeks have been a dream come true! I literally have the world's coolest job.

After tonight's win in Vancouver Oliver invited everyone to their suite for a more relaxed hangout rather than the hotel bar where there are never-ending fans.

And a plethora of puck bunnies.

I like to think he made that decision for me because if all the guys were to grab a fuckbuddy for the night, I would be left all alone. Or maybe he doesn't want August hooking up with one to spare my feelings. Either way, I'm silently grateful. I mean, August is free to sleep with whomever he wants and though I'm fairly certain he hasn't been with anyone since before I moved here, I certainly wouldn't blame him if he needed the release.

It would hurt somewhere in my heart, but we're not a couple so I have no right to cock block him.

"You all have your drink of choice?" Scarlett asks everyone seated in the suite.

The guys all nod and wrap their hands around either their beer bottles or glasses filled with their liquor of choice. Tequila has always been my liquor of choice so that's what August and I are using.

"Alright here, goes." Scarlett pulls the top card from the deck and reads it aloud. "Never have I ever hooked up with a boss or supervisor." Everyone glances around the room waiting for someone to drink.

Just when I think the first question might be a dud, Ledger picks up his glass and shoots back the amber liquid inside. When he brings his glass back to the table, he smiles and says, "They don't call it fast food for nothing. Plus, I was nineteen." He shrugs. "I had no self-control at the time."

The group chuckles at Ledger's expense as the deck moves to Harrison who picks up the next card and reads it aloud. "Never have I ever had sex in a car."

I don't even have to glance around the room to see every single player pick up their glass and take a drink. My jaw drops and I shake my head with a laugh. "Wow guys. Way to keep it classy."

"You telling me you've never had sex in a car, Montgomery?" Harrison asks me, wiping his mouth with the back of his hand.

"For your information, no. I have not." I glance at August and curl my lips. "And that's why I didn't want to drive your car to my interview."

"Wait." He laughs. "What?"

"Yeah. I sat down and then immediately thought ew, what if he's had loads of sex in this car and now I'm driving it?" I shake my head. "Everything was immediately sticky so I couldn't do it."

"Sticky!" Griffin belly laughs. "She said sticky!"

"My car isn't sticky, El," August says to me, but I turn toward him with a raised brow. "Have you had sex in that car?"

He bites his bottom lip and doesn't want to answer.

"Uh huh. That's what I thought. I hold fast to the word sticky. Also, ew! I rest my case."

"Come on, you're making it sound like I come uncontrollably all over the dashboard."

I stick my fingers in my ears and squeeze my eyes closed. "I don't want to hear about your messy sexcapades Auggie!"

"Alright, alright, next question." Ledger pulls the deck toward him and takes the top card. "Never have I ever regretted sleeping with someone."

Without thought I lift my drink to my mouth and shoot it down my throat...only to find out I'm the only one drinking.

"What?" I scoff. "You mean to tell me not one of you regrets a puck bunny decision?"

The guys all shake their heads and Scarlett chuckles. "The thing you have to know about these guys, is that they're all whores."

"It's true though," Griffin adds. "Well, unless you're Magallan over there," he says, gesturing to Oliver and Scarlett. "Scarlett's no dumpster."

"Fucking right she's not," Oliver agrees adamantly.

Scarlett leans over and kisses her fiancé. "Aww, thank you, baby."

My jaw drops again. "That's what you call them? Dumpsters?"

How insulting!

Ledger speaks up next, saying, "I don't usually call them at all." His comment earns a few high-fives and a few laughs before August nudges me with his shoulder.

"But who do you regret sleeping with? Don't I know about all your partners?"

You think you do.

But I don't tell you everything.

I didn't tell you about this one.

"Wait, let me guess." He narrows his eyes and stares at me like he can see into my mind and then snaps his fingers. "Was it that guy? The one you met at that ping pong tournament back in college?"

Nope.

No.

Not that guy.

"Yeah." I nod. "It was totally him. He had the ping pong balls but his paddle wasn't excessively big if you know what I mean."

"Aww man," Harrison laughs. "Sucks to be that guy."

"Yeah."

"Pfft! Oh, come on, that's not true."

"What isn't?"

"This article on Cosmo's website," I tell August as I continue to scroll on my phone so I can keep reading. Our second night in Vancouver has us both exhausted so we opted for a quiet night hanging out together after having a late dinner with the team. And since August has the better hotel room, and being without him feels weird now that we're living together, I asked if I could sneak in and stay with him.

Thankfully, he said yes.

"Why? What does it say?"

"It says a man should always make his partner come before he does."

August slides his hands behind his head as he lies next to me, further expanding the amount of space he takes up in the bed. "Yeah. That's true. What's wrong with that?"

I drop my phone to my chest. "Really? You really feel that way?"

He turns his head so he can look at me, an amused look on his face. "Of course. Don't you?"

"Not…" I frown, questioning my own preferences. "Not necessarily." I roll my body so I can face him. "Why can't I make you come first?"

August grins. "Babe, if we were really talking about you and me, I would allow it if it's really what you wanted but only because I know I have more in the tank for you. But not all guys are like me."

"By that you mean once they come they can't come twice?"

"Correct." He nods but then stops. "Well, correction. They can come twice. Or three times or however many. But it might take anywhere from a few minutes to a few hours to be able to make things happen again. I'm sure that's why most guys want their girl to go first. But for me it's all about pleasure."

My interest piqued; I narrow my eyes. "Explain."

He's quiet for a moment, and I wonder if I've made him uncomfortable especially when he asks, "Are we really talking about this?"

"Yeah." I shrug with a smirk. "Why not? It's just me. And we've talked about sex loads of times before."

Maybe not lying next to each other in bed but…

"Alright." He inhales a deep breath and quietly exhales. "I guess for me, I get off more…err…harder, I mean I enjoy it more knowing that my partner is getting off on what I do to her. I guess in a way it's validation for the way I pleasure her."

"Sooo for you, is it kind of like the more enjoyable of an orgasm she has, the bigger one you have?"

"Sure."

I roll to my back and stare up at the ceiling. My thoughts only add to my confusion.

"Why do you look so perplexed?" August asks, amused.

My brows furrow as I lick my lips and simply tell him what's on my mind. "Because that's never been my experience, so it's weird to hear you explain it like that."

His eyes fixate on mine. "What do you mean it's never been your experience? You're not a virgin."

"No, I'm not a virgin, but…" My voice trails off.

"But what?"

I clear my throat and stare up at the ceiling, my cheeks heating with embarrassment. "You know what? We don't need to talk about this. Never mind."

"No, no, no." He slides his palm tenderly across my stomach before coming to rest on my hip. His touch heats my body even though I know it shouldn't. "You can't leave me hanging like that, El. I'm your best friend, remember? There's nothing we don't tell each other."

I like you.

You got one hundred times hotter over these last two years.

I think about kissing you.

I think about more than kissing you.

I wonder sometimes what it would be like to be your girlfriend.

But I'm way too scared to tell you that.

That's six things I haven't told you.

He tugs on my hip effectively rolling me toward him so I can't ignore him. "You're not a virgin but what? Tell me." His voice is soft, supportive

Taking a deep breath, I look into August's eyes and tell him, "I don't think I've ever had a penetrative orgasm."

His mouth opens as if he's going to say something but then it closes...and then opens again, his blank stare making me feel like he may not have heard what I said until he emphatically asks, "*What*?"

Squeezing my eyes closed, I shake my head and then wave my hand. "Yeah, I'm sorry. I shouldn't have said anything. Really. We don't have to—"

"Yes we do, El," he says, finishing my sentence for me. "Yes, we do. We're talking about this."

"But—"

"What do you mean when you say you've never had a penetrative orgasm?"

"I mean exactly that," I huff and then quickly announce, "I've never had an orgasm brought on by a penis inside me. There. I said it."

"But you've had sex?"

"Yes."

"More than once."

"Yes."

"With more than one person."

I roll my eyes. "Yes."

"And by sex I mean a dick has actually been inside you."

I bulge my eyes and let my jaw hang open before saying, "Wait...the dick really has to go *inside* me?"

He gives me an unreadable stare before wiping his hand down his face as if he can't believe what he's hearing but then I pat his arm and giggle. "Relax Auggie. That was a joke. And yes, I've had a dick inside me on more than one occasion."

"Then how the hell is that possible?" he nearly shouts and then sees that his tone disturbs me and takes a deep breath softening his voice. "I mean is that just a personal preference thing for you? Are you not on birth control or do you have a condom allergy or something?"

"Nooo." I laugh nervously. "I've been on birth control since freshman year of college, remember? My mom made me have that mega don't-have-sex-until-you're-thirty talk but put me on the pill in case I got assaulted at school."

"Riiiight. I do remember that."

I can't believe we're having this conversation.

I can't believe I started this.

I can't believe I'm about to tell him about my sexual history.

"It's just that, well, most of the guys I've slept with haven't lasted more than a minute or two once they're inside me and then once they've, you know, started, they can't stop or slow down so they just plow through until they're spent."

"Wait." He shakes his head in disbelief. "Do you mean to tell me you've never had an orgasm at all?"

"No. Of course I have."

"So how do you get off when they've blown their load after two minutes?"

I shrug innocently. "If they get me off at all, it's usually with their fingers or maybe a toy if we're at my place."

"So, you don't even get off every time?" Auggie's eyes widen and his mouth hangs open.

Christ, this is embarrassing.

"Not always, no."

August rolls onto his back and pushes his hands through his hair. "Fucking Christ."

"What?" I ask, propping my head up on my hand. "Why is this the most terrible thing you've ever heard?"

"Because I can't believe you've..." He stops himself and takes a quick steadying breath realizing he's yelling at me again for no reason. With a calmer tone, he rolls back toward me and slips his hand through my hair. He swallows and then softly says to me, "Because you deserve to be pleasured, Ella. And any good man would realize that. Any *good* man would take honest to God pleasure in making you feel good. Any *good* man would have a fervent desire to physically watch you and hear you and...and taste you...as you come."

Taste me.

Good Lord those words give me goosebumps.

"So how are you different then?"

"What do you mean, how?" He scoffs. "I'm one hundred and eighty degrees of different from anything you've ever experienced from what it sounds like."

"I don't know about that." I chuckle. "Sex is pretty cut and dry, August. I mean don't get me wrong, it's fun and feels incredible most of the time."

"Most of the time?" He frowns.

"Yeah. Most of the time." I shrug. "It's a little heavy petting, in and out, wham bam, and its done."

His jaw unhinges and his lips part as he stares at me incredulously. His eyes fall to my lips before climbing back up to find my gaze. "Ella, babe," he says, shaking his head. "Sex is so much more than that. And it should feel fucking fantastic one hundred percent of the time. And if it doesn't, you're doing it with the wrong man."

"Okay then tell me."

"Tell you what?"

"Tell me what you would do," I beg him, my eyes darting between his. "What *do* you do? What makes it so much more enthralling in your mind than what I've experienced before? And what am I doing wrong?"

His brows pinch and he shakes his head. "Whoa. Okay, first of all, Ella, you aren't doing a damn thing wrong." His eyes roam my entire face, my neck, and part of my chest as his fingers twine through my hair. "You're...perfect. Do you hear me? Fucking perfect."

"But—"

"No." He shakes his head calmly. "Listen, every guy is different so I can only speak from my own experiences. And you have to understand my hookups are different because there isn't much emotion to them. It's always been about the physical acts for me. A way to release the adrenaline. I know you don't like that answer but it's the honest truth."

"I get it. So, if you're just there to release why do you bother making sure she's getting pleasured too?"

"Because if she's not enjoying it, then her body...her...pussy won't be ready for me and then I won't enjoy it either. Why waste our time when I can make sure she's loving every minute of it? Then I can be sure she's primed so her body can accommodate me."

"Sounds romantic," I say deadpanned.

He gives a lopsided grin. "I never said anything about it being romantic. If I was in love with my partner, I might do things differently."

"Like how? What makes non emotional sex different from emotional sex?"

"Non emotional sex is straight up fucking," he answers bluntly. "It's carnal. It's a lot of touching, it can be rough if both partners agree with that, and it can be fast. It could be the difference between bending a woman over a bathroom sink and fucking her brains out or taking your slow sweet time pleasuring her."

I'll take option two for a thousand please, Alex.

"Are you saying you've fucked women in bathrooms?"

He nods. "Bathrooms, hotel bedrooms, in a dark alley or my..."

He stops but I know exactly what he was going to say. "Your car."

"If you want me to say I'm not proud of it, I can't do that, Ella. Not that I'm particularly proud of the fact I've fucked numerous women over the years, but it was just sex. A quick fuck and I walk."

"Never a relationship?"

"You knew about the last relationship I had and it didn't last exceptionally long. I just don't have the time to worry about a girl I can't be with all the time, but like I said before, if I were with a girl I loved, sex would be different."

"How so?"

He closes his eyes momentarily and guilt washes over me for even bringing this up in the first place. I'm about to tell him to forget this whole conversation because maybe I don't want to know what he would do with someone he loves, but then his lids lift and the intensity of the look in his eyes captures my attention.

"First of all, if I'm in love with my partner I'm going to have my lips on her body at all times." He rests his hand back on my hip, absentmindedly drawing small circles against my skin with his thumb. "Kissing her. Sucking her. Licking her. Tasting every part of her I can get my mouth on. I would want her to feel how hungry I am for her. How much I desire her." He licks his lips. "I'd probably start with her neck and trail my tongue from the back of her neck to that sensitive spot right behind her ear." He runs his finger up my neck to the spot he's referring to. "Right here." He lightly pinches my earlobe and rubs it between his thumb and forefinger. "Then I'd probably nibble her earlobe or suck it into my mouth while I tease her body with my hands."

"Tease her how?"

Hell, where did that question come from?

He brings his hands back to my exposed hip. "Depends on where she is. Sitting, standing, or in my arms, her back to my chest, I'd probably sneak my hand into her clothing. Up her shirt or maybe play with a few buttons and slide in from the top."

He glides his pointer finger over my bare skin in that spot between the waistband of my shorts and the hem of my sleep shirt. His gaze hasn't left mine since he started talking so I'm not even sure he knows he's doing it.

Also, it might be the slightest touch but it feels amazing and I am going straight to hell for enjoying it.

"Mhmm," I say breathily.

"I'd come so dangerously close to her breasts." He turns his hand and gently swipes his thumb underneath my breast.

Hooooly shit.

"Right here. I'd touch her here and make her body start to ignite from the inside."

Yep. Ignite is the right word.

"And then I'd probably kiss her lips, swirling my tongue with hers so she gets a good taste of me. So, she knows how much I crave her. How much I want to pleasure her," he breathes, his pupils growing in size. "And then I'd palm her breast."

"You would?" I croak and then clear my throat. "I mean, you would."

"Did your partners touch you, Ella? Did they hold your breasts in their hands and knead them, rub them, devour them with their mouths?"

I swallow hard trying to ignore the dull ache forming between my legs and then squeak out a weak, "Yes."

His body stiffens next to me as a flash of anger crosses his face. And I can tell he's clenching his jaw. His eyes drift down my body and then his voice cracks slightly when he asks, "Do they go down on you, El?"

I nod, finding it hard to form words as my mouth has gone completely dry.

"And did you enjoy it?"

"What's not to enjoy?" I give him a faint lift to the corner of my mouth. "Not all my partners would go there but some have."

"Did they make you come? Did you come on their tongues?"

The intensity with which he asks that question draws all the air from my lungs and I shake my head emphatically.

"Never."

August closes his eyes and takes a deep breath exhaling calmly and then pulling my body against his. "Good."

"Good?" I snap my head up, resting my chin in the crook of his neck. "Why is that good?"

He tightens his embrace, his arms enveloping me into his warmth. He smells good, clean, like his coconut scented shower gel. "Because one day you're going to find the right guy for you and you'll know it by the way he eats you."

An odd thing to say. I almost chuckle thinking he's joking but there is nothing about his demeanor that says he's teasing me.

"What do you mean by that?"

"If it was me, and I was going down on the love of my life..." he says, slipping his hand up the back of my shirt and feathering his fingers along my skin like he does it every day.

For the record, he doesn't do it every day.

In fact, he's never done it.

"Fuck, I'd be desperate for her. Desperate to taste her, to hear her pleasured moans. I'd have her wetter for me than she's ever been...fucking glistening...and then I'd part those soft pink lips with my fingers and drag my tongue over her sweet cunt in one long languid stroke."

Oooh, my God.

Yes please!

The only thing that keeps me from breaking out in a lust-filled sweat right now is how cold August keeps whatever room he sleeps in, but no number of cold temperatures can keep my heartrate from rising.

"She'd scream for me and thrust her fingers through my hair guiding me through her pussy while I suck on her clit, flicking it with my tongue, and then I'd pulse my fingers inside her."

Holy fuuuuck.

"I'd let her fuck my face until she can't stand it anymore and her pussy clamps down on my fingers as she comes so hard she can't breathe."

"Wow." The word falls out of my mouth like a kid in a candy store with a million-dollar budget.

"And that's when I would know it's okay for me to come. That's when I would finally thrust inside her and claim her warm tight pussy with my stiff cock."

"August," I sigh against him, wishing I could squeeze my legs together and control the aching throb between them, but somehow while talking, August entwined his legs with mine.

"If she was the love of my life, I'd spend hours making love to her," he says, shifting my thigh over his so he can pull me even closer.

Good God if I get any closer I'll be on top of him. His hand rests over my leg, his fingers tickling the back of my thigh. He's dangerously close to parts of me he's never touched before and for the first time in my life, I'm aching for him to do it.

To make me feel everything he's describing.

"We'd spend all night exploring each other's bodies, fucking until my balls ache," he continues. "But she has to come first so I know she's been pleasured, spoiled, and she's happy, but then you better believe I'll make her come again with my cock. And then if I'm lucky, she'll let me do it to her all over again."

He's silent for a minute. I'm unsure of what to say because

my pulse is booming inside my body. His pulse has quickened too. I can hear his heartbeat. And I can definitely feel how turned on he is with our bodies this close together.

Holy hell, the size of that thing.

When he doesn't say anything else, I pull back from him enough that I can see his face, but his hands never leave my body, his fingers tightening around my skin. He's so close to my pussy I can practically feel them there anyway.

My words come out in a strangled whisper. "The future love of your life will be a very lucky girl, August."

He slides his hand painstakingly slowly up my body until his fingers are tangled with my hair and his eyes drop to my lips.

Oh my God, I think he's going to kiss me!

I press my hand against his chest, the sinews of his torso at my fingertips.

I watch his Adam's apple bob up and down as he swallows.

He's really going to do it.

Do I want this?

Yeah, I want this!

I've wanted this for a long time.

His lips separate and he moistens them with his tongue.

I do the same.

This is it!

After all this time we're crossing the line.

It's what we both want now.

This couldn't be more perfect.

I angle my head up to meet his lips, close my eyes, and inhale a silent breath.

And then his lips connect with my...forehead as he places a sweet kiss there before mumbling, "Good night, El."

Wait...

What?

That's it?

I can feel that he's turned on and I...

Fuck, there's a raging horny beast inside me desperately wanting to escape and experience everything that is August Blackstone.

I want everything he just described to me. And I want to give it all back to him.

But he doesn't want me...

I squeeze my eyes closed and tell myself over and over again,

Do not cry.

Do not cry.

Don't you dare cry.

He opened himself up to you because you asked him to.

Holding myself together I conjure up the strength to finally say, "Good night Auggie."

There is a line with August I can never cross and this is it.

I know that.

I've aways known it.

CHAPTER THIRTEEN

AUGUST

Knock, knock, knock.

"Dude, Griff, be home because I fucking need to talk to you!" I shout at his door as I stand outside his apartment sans patience. I think I might be going crazy.

Everything is fine.

It's going to be fine.

I just need a plan.

Everything will be just fine.

"Yeah, no. Affirmations aren't doing it for me," I mumble and then knock on the door again." Why isn't he fucking answering?"

I rap on the door three more times but still no answer. "Dammit! Where are you?"

"I'm right here, dumbass." I turn where I'm standing to find Griffin and Ledger walking toward me from the stairwell, both a sweaty mess with towels around their necks.

"Where the hell have you been?" I scowl.

Griffin cocks his head and gives me an amused look. "Sorry...Mom. We were downstairs in the gym. Why?"

"Then why didn't you take the elevator?"

Ledger laughs. "Did you not read the sign?" He gestures to the large white paper taped to the elevator doors. "It's being serviced this evening."

"Dude, what is wrong with you?" Griffin asks with a shake of his head.

My lungs feel like they've closed up entirely as I struggle to take a steady breath. "I...I... "

God I might throw up.

"Griff he doesn't look good," Ledger says as I bend at the waist and try to steady my breathing. Griffin brushes past me and quickly unlocks his door pushing it open for me.

"Get in here."

He and Ledger toss their gym bags by the door and Griffin heads to his kitchen to grab a couple bottles of water. He offers me one and I gladly accept, twisting off the cap and guzzling nearly the entire bottle. Ledger sits in one of Griffin's bar stools and pulls one up for me as well.

"Sit, Blackstone."

I do as he says and take a seat at the bar looking into Griffin's kitchen.

"You want to tell us what's got you so tied up in knots?" Griffin asks.

"Yeah, man, I don't think I've ever seen you this way. Pissed usually, yeah, but you look like you're about to fall apart."

My mouth is so fucking dry. Like I haven't had a drop of liquid in weeks. I take another swig of my water and swish it around in my mouth before swallowing it down and finally saying, "I fucked up."

"You fucked up," Griffin repeats, deadpanned.

"Yeah. I fucked up."

A silence falls over us before Ledger chuckles and says, "Bro, we're going to need a little more than just 'I fucked up.' How did you fuck up? What happened?"

"She's on a date," I finally spit out.

"Who's on a date?"

"Ella!"

"Oooh," Ledger says, his features softening.

"That doesn't make sense," Griffin adds, his eyes narrowing. "What does that have to do with you fucking up? Did you say something to her?"

"No. I think it's what I didn't say to her."

He crosses his arms over her chest. "Alright. Explain."

"Last week, in Vancouver," I start. "She slept with me."

Griffin's eyes bulge and an excited grin spreads across his face. "DUDE! You didn't tell us th—"

"No, not like that. I mean she slept with me. Like we've done at home a few times. Just sleeping. That's all."

His face falls and his brows furrow. "Oh."

"Except it wasn't just sleeping. It was...fucking weird but not fucking weird at the same time and then it was fucking awkward and—"

"Whoa." Ledger holds his hands up in front of him. "Slow down. Take a deep breath and tell us what happened."

"She was reading this article on her phone. Something about guys needing to make their partners orgasm before they do."

Ledger smirks. "That girl's got some kink. I like it."

"It was just Cosmo magazine. Nothing out of the ordinary, but when she brought it up I told her I agreed with those men."

"As you should because duh."

"Right. But then it came out that she's never had an orgasm brought on by a dick."

Ledger blinks.

Griffin blinks.

"I'm sorry, what?" he asks.

"You heard me."

"She's never had an orgasm by dick?"

"Correct."

Ledger clears his throat. "Is she a virgin?"

"Nope."

"More than one partner?"

"That's what I asked her. And she said yes. And it's not like we've never talked about sex over the years so I know she's had sexual partners but the minute she told me that the men in her life have basically used her as a goddamn dumpster I..." I shake my head. "Well, it was two-fold. One, I immediately felt bad for every woman I ever fucked in a public bathroom stall or alley behind the bar."

The guys chuckle but give me an understanding nod.

"And two, I was blown away and fucking pissed for Ella. That someone...no, multiple men would treat her that way makes me want to fucking punch someone."

"I get it." Griffin nods. "You care a lot about her. Of course, that news would shock you."

"So, then she asks me what she's been doing wrong all these years which broke my fucking heart for her and then asked me what I do with women that makes it so much better than what she was describing."

"Oh boy." Griffin shakes his head with a knowing smile. "Tell me you didn't."

I toss up my hands. "How could I not tell her? She wanted to know!"

"Okay," Ledger says, watching me. "But how detailed did you get?"

"Pretty fucking detailed. And she was right there in my bed and I had my hands on her skin and we just kept getting closer and closer and I didn't know if I was doing that or if it was her but by the time I was done describing everything to her, my hands were dangerously close to places they shouldn't have been but want so badly to go, our pulses were racing, and she looked up at me with these sweet but sexy eyes like she wanted it. Like she was asking for it. Like my kissing her would've been the perfect way to end the night and she would've allowed it!"

"So, you fucked up by kissing her," Griffin says matter of factly.

"No! I fucked up by *not* kissing her!"

"Oh shit," Ledger says. "So, she was expecting a kiss and you didn't go for it."

"Yes."

"Why not?"

"I don't know!" I slap my hand down on the bar in front of me. "Because I'm a fucking scared pansy ass idiot when it comes to her. Because I'm so fucking scared of crossing a line we've never crossed that I talked myself out of it but believe me I wanted too. I wanted her so badly and I had her right fucking there! I could've done it. I could've touched her. I could've kissed her. I could've rolled her over and shown her all the ways I would pleasure her. But I didn't. Because I'm a goddamn fucking chicken."

Griffin finally comes around the bar from his kitchen and pulls up a stool next to me. "Do you want my advice or do you just want to vent?"

"If you have advice, I'll gladly take it."

"You're in love with your best friend, August."

"I'm not in —"

"Bro," he tells me with a cock of his head. "You're so head over heels for her it's not even funny. We all see it. You're the only one who doesn't see it...except that I think somewhere down deep you do see it. You feel it. Otherwise, none of this would've ever happened the way you just explained it and you wouldn't give two shits. You haven't even as much as thought about seeking out another woman since before Ella moved to

Anaheim. The August we know...or knew...wouldn't have cared if someone was living with him or not. If he wanted to get laid, he would've gotten himself laid."

I glance at Ledger who nods in agreement. "He's right, man."

"But you haven't even thought about it," Griffin continues. "Because Ella means something to you. She means enough that you've changed your lifestyle because of her. And that's not a terrible thing. But if you don't just go for it and see what happens, you're going to resent her for the decisions you're making and that's not fair to her. If you want her, tell her. If you want to kiss her, ask her fucking permission first and then kiss her. See what happens." He shrugs. "It's not like you two haven't ever kissed before."

"That was a long time ago. We were kids."

He shrugs. "And now you're adults. Big deal. Either it's going to work or it's not, but how will you ever know if you don't try? Just be man enough to respect her feelings in the end. Even if you try and things don't work out. Because she's on our team now and she's not going away. And we protect what's ours at all costs."

Even though it causes me nearly crippling fear to think about Ella and I not working out, I also can't fathom a time in my life past, present, or future, where I wouldn't want her around. Ella Montgomery is my life. She's my home. She always has been and she always will be.

My heart rate finally comes down the longer we sit here. Chatting with some of the guys whose opinions matter most to me helps me feel less anxious. "What about this date she's on?"

"You don't have anything to worry about," Griffin assures me.

"Are you sure."

Ledger scowls. "Nah. Fuck that guy. He's not the one."

I chuckle at his curt response. "What makes you so certain?"

"Because the one for her is sitting right in front of me. She just doesn't know it yet."

MUCH CALMER NOW AFTER A WORKOUT, a long hot shower, and a few beers, I slip on my pair of gray sweatpants reminding myself that just because my best friend is out on a date tonight doesn't mean I can't look like the sexy mother fucker I know I can be when she gets home.

If she comes home.

Recalling her words as we argued her first night here, I cringe at the thought that I upset her and wish I could take it all back.

"Sleep with whoever you want. It's none of my business but—"

"That's right. It's none of your business, but alright. I'll play by your rules, August. So, just so you know, when I don't come home one night it's because I'm obviously out having the best fuck of my life."

Ugh. The fact she might not walk through those doors tonight has me nauseous. I can feel the anxiety creeping up my body, but I shake it off as best I can.

"She's coming home tonight," I tell myself. "She's coming home to me."

I take a look at my reflection in the bedroom mirror noting all the parts of me that I know ladies check out. And I know this because some women have no shame hiding behind their keyboards on the internet.

Sculpted chest? Check.

Abs for days? Check.

That special V that points to my junk? Yep.

Happy trail? Got that too.

No underwear? Fucking better believe it.

Eat your heart out ladies.

With the night off from a game, and knowing Ella was going on a date, I had originally planned to hang out at home to watch the Red Tails play Seattle since they come to us next week; however, after my small meltdown with Griff and Ledger earlier, they insisted we all watch the game together upstairs in the Clubroom. Something about making sure I don't drink myself into oblivion when I'm all up in my feelings.

"Like I would do that," I mumble, slipping a t-shirt over my head before grabbing my phone, my keys, and another bottle of beer and then heading upstairs.

"Blackstone," Harrison nods as I open the Clubhouse door and step inside. "Nice of you to show up."

"And looking so fucking hot, might I add." Griffin winks at me knowing damn well why I chose the outfit I'm wearing.

"Don't hate me for being the hottest one on the team."

"Pfft." I glance across the room at an amused Bear. "Don't flatter yourself pretty boy."

"Hey Bear." I gesture to the oversized television screen attached to the wall where Zeke Miller, goalie for the Chicago Red Tails, is warming up. "How come when you do that groin warm up, it's not as sexy as when Zeke Miller does it?"

Bear flips me off and grins proudly. "Is it laundry day, Blackstone?" he asks me.

"No. Why?"

"Well, I couldn't help but notice a certain article of clothing is missing. Thought maybe all your tighty-whities were in the wash."

"Mesmerized by my dick, eh Cunningham?" I pass him a wink and a few air kisses. "I'll give you my secret but don't tell anyone." Bringing my hand up to my mouth like I'm telling a secret, I say, "If you yank on it a few times a day, it will grow for you."

"Thanks. I'll keep that in mind."

He grabs a slice of pizza from the box on the table along with a beer and joins Harrison on the couch.

"Where's Magallan?" I ask the group.

"Out to a late dinner with Scarlett. He'll be a little late but he said he was coming. Don't know if Scarlett will be with him or not."

We watch as the Red Tails start their first period against the Seattle Sea Brawlers driving the puck down the ice, passing with prowess, and defending their goal with intensity.

"They look good," Harrison says. "Dex Foster is one fast mother fucker."

"Yep." I nod. "Can't wait to push his buttons and have some fun when it's our turn."

At the end of the first period, I find myself checking my phone for any word from Ella, but my screen is blank. She's been radio silent all evening. I know that's how it's supposed to be when she's on a date, but there have been dates in the past where the guy is a dud and she's secretly texting me the play by play until she can jump ship and leave. Before I moved away from Indigo Bay I was the one she ran home to after a date, good or bad. It's always been me and I'm hopeful it'll be me again tonight. But the fact she hasn't texted me tells me she's most likely enjoying herself. And that's not good for my psyche at all.

"So," Ledger says with a nudge to my shoulder while passing me another beer. "How you doing since we last saw you?"

I lift my beer up and give him a smile. "I'm six beers in so I'd say I'm feeling pretty good."

"Yeah, I figured. But how are you really?"

"I'm fine," I lie. "I'll be fine. It might suck right now but I'll figure my shit out eventually."

"I know you will." He takes a sip of his beer and I do the same. "What are you going to do when she comes home? You going to talk to her?"

"I'm not going to ignore her, if that's what you're asking, but also," I say lifting my bottle again, "I've had too much to drink to consider having any kind of mature conversation tonight. And that's if she even comes home."

She better fucking come home.

"Is she a one-night stand kind of girl?"

I shake my head. "Nope. But if she likes the guy, it wouldn't be a one-night stand, would it? It'll just be the first among many."

"Hmm. I suppose you have a point." He claps me on the shoulder. "Let's hope it doesn't come to that."

"Yeah."

Please God, don't let it come to that.

I could maybe stomach knowing she has a boyfriend while she's living with me, but knowing and-or hearing her fucking someone? Yeah, just shoot me now because I can't handle that.

At the end of the second period the Red Tails are up three to two and I'm another three beers in. If I even make it downstairs, I'll probably just lock myself in my room so I'm not a bother to Ella. Or maybe I'll just conk out right here on the Clubroom couch for the night.

Wouldn't be the first time.

Probably wouldn't be the last.

A few minutes pass and we're watching the third period when the door to the Clubhouse opens and Oliver walks through accompanied by his fiancée. The guys all say their hellos and greetings but he seems to only have eyes for me. The worried expression on his face tells me I'm not going to like whatever it is he has to tell me.

"Fuck, did someone touch my car again?" I ask him knowing they just came up from the garage.

He shakes his head. "No man. It's Ella."

I shoot up from the couch so fast forgetting I've had too much to drink and nearly fall face first into the coffee table full of pizza, chips, and everyone else's beers.

"Whoa. You good?" Griffin asks, grabbing my shoulder to steady me.

"Yeah. Sorry." I turn back to Oliver. "Where is she? What happened? Is she alright?"

"She's downstairs," he says. I sprint for the door immediately, but Oliver calls out to me. "August!"

"Yeah?"

"She's been crying."

"Fuck!"

CHAPTER FOURTEEN

ELLA

"Never in a million years..." I mumble to myself through the onslaught of sniffles. "Mother fucking asshole. What do you mean, am I a prude? I'm not a fucking prude you...you...shitty ass cum bubble." I grab a beer from the fridge and pull open one of the drawers to grab the bottle opener but it's not in there.

Fuck.

Where's the bottle opener?

"Don't tell me I'm a bad kisser," I murmur, opening another drawer and slamming it shut. "I'm not a bad kisser. You're a bad kisser."

Sniffle.

Open another drawer.

Slam it shut.

Sniffle.

"Kissing you is like kissing a fucking dog. No, maybe even a cow."

Sniffle.

Open the last drawer.

Slam it shut.

Sniffle.

"Goddammit! Where is the fucking—"

The door to the apartment is shoved open and August runs through it, coming to a halt in the middle of the living room. "Ella?"

"WHAT?" I shout a little too loudly, tears streaming down my face in frustration.

His eyes are like saucers as he stares at me, taken aback by my less than cheery demeanor. "Are you okay?"

"Do I LOOK okay to you?" I cry.

"What happened?"

Sniffle.

Sniffle.

"WHERE is the fucking bottle opener?"

He nods with a lift of his chin. "On the counter by the stove."

"You know it would be nice if you would fucking put things away when you're done using them so I'm not spending all hours of the fucking night looking for a damn bottle opener that was supposed to be in the first drawer to the left in the first place!"

Yep, I'm aware that came out a little strong but I'm on a pissy roll. Can't stop now.

Huffing out a breath, I grab the opener that's been sitting in front of my face this whole time and roughly pop off the cap to my beer and then take a long well-deserved swig.

"Ella?"

Sniffle.

"I am not a prude!" I snap.

I notice the slightest narrowing of Auggie's brow before he cocks his head. "Okay."

"And I'm not a bad kisser either." I pull open the kitchen

drawer where the bottle opener is supposed to go and throw it inside, slamming the drawer with my hip.

Because that's what decent people do!

They put things away!

"That mother fucker can fuck all the way off and go straight to Hell. That's what he can do! How dare he think I'm not good enough for him? I can kiss! I'm fucking good at it." My heart pounds in my chest as heat flushes through my body. My eyes are already a puffy mess from crying I'm sure. I'm not proud of it, but it's who I am.

I cry when I'm mad.

I cry when I'm sad.

I cry when I'm happy.

I'm a fucking crier.

And while I'm at it, let's just add a super red throwing-a-tantrum face too because that's...pretty.

"Did he hurt you, Ella?" August asks me with a mixture of sincere concern and malice to his voice. "Because I swear to God if he hurt you, I'll kill him."

Staring at my best friend from across the room, I find it increasingly difficult to hold back my tears. I grab for a tissue and blow my nose while shaking my head to let him know that no, Heath didn't hurt me.

Well, he hurt my ego, but physically, I'm fine.

"What happened? Tell me what he said."

Sniffle.

Sniffle.

"We were having a great time together," I start. "Dinner was good. He was great at conversation. Knew his manners and was a perfect gentleman."

"Alright."

"And then we went to play mini golf and we had a great time there too," I say tearfully, my voice breaking. "And then since I drove myself he wanted to give me a goodnight kiss in the parking lot after golf and I said yes and so he kissed me and...and...why do these things always seem to happen to me?"

"What? What happened?" August hasn't moved an inch since he walked through the door and stopped in the middle of the room. His stare has been a mixture of horror, confusion, and curiosity as I replay my night but because this night has been so shitty I can't help but look at him and see the man who had me in his bed just a few nights ago. His hands on my body and my lips so close to his but then chose not to kiss me.

What happened?

You didn't choose me.

And neither did Heath.

"He kissed me, Auggie. And it was like kissing a fucking wet sloppy dog."

"Oo...kay..." He tries his best not to react but I know he's wondering what the hell is going on.

"But then he had the audacity to question *my* kissing ability."

"He what?"

"Yeah! He pulled away and tipped his head and said, 'hmm interesting.' And I asked what he meant by that and he actually fucking said to me, 'Well, it's not like that was awful but it just wasn't...what I was expecting.' And so, I asked what he was expecting and he said he expected a whole lot more tongue because he likes his women wet and spitty and that wasn't quite enough for him but then maybe he could train me to give him what he wanted."

Auggie's face contorts. "The fuck?"

"RIGHT? That's what I said! And then he fucking asked me if I was a prude! So, I slapped his face and told him to fuck all the way off and got in my car and came home."

"Fucking right you did," he says with a proud smirk.

"But...but..." My chin trembles and tears fall from my eyes all over again as I sob to my best friend. "But I've never had a guy tell me I'm a bad kisser before and he was essentially telling me I wasn't good enough at it for him and then you didn't kiss me the other night either and I thought you were going to but then you didn't so now I'm not good enough for you and I'm not good enough for Heath and I've clearly never been good enough for any of the guys I've been with or else I wouldn't have had to tell you that I've never had a goddamn orgasm without the help of a finger or toy!" I finally inhale, but then blurt, "And I tried to be all brave and strong in front of him, but dammit, sometimes enough is enough!" I stomp my foot. "What's a girl got to do to find a guy who will treat them the way they deserve to be treated? And how the hell is it so easy for you and it's not for me?"

August doesn't respond.

He merely stares at me from ten feet away.

His shoulders rise and fall with each of his breaths and I watch his Adam's apple bob as he swallows. I have no idea what he's thinking but I see his jaw tick once, and then twice, and then he's moving.

He's moving toward me.

"I'm sorry," I tell him, casting my eyes down to my hand that's still around the neck of my beer bottle. "I know I'm just being an emotional girl and I didn't mean to—"

"Shut up," he says.

I lift my head to find him much closer to me, his body moving with purpose, the expression on his face one of resolve.

"But—"

It's the only word I get out of my mouth before August is right in front of me, sliding his hand into my hair, cupping my face with his other hand, and crashing his lips to mine.

What the...

Catching me off guard, I nearly fall backwards against the cabinet but he steadies both of us with a wrap of his strong arm around my waist and then backs us up so I'm effectively trapped against the kitchen counter. The bottle slips from my hand and tips over on the counter but August is quick to push it into the sink, his other hand never leaving my body.. I brace my hands against his rock-hard chest, letting them slide down his abdomen until I'm clutching the fabric of his soft t-shirt.

His lips move against mine hungry at first, like he needs every breath I have inside me. I willingly part my lips for him and he softens, moaning against my mouth.

He. Just. Moaned. Against. My. Mouth.

This is really fucking happening.

August Blackstone is kissing me.

With his thumb on my chin, he repositions my head to the side and takes full advantage of the better access, dipping his tongue into my welcoming mouth. I swipe my tongue against his and he moans again.

And suddenly I'm not so sure this is a pity kiss.

Because he's not stopping.

And he's using tongue.

Oh, my God, August's tongue.

Finally letting myself take a little of what I've wanted for a long time, I tighten my grip on his shirt and kiss him back with a little more fervor and a lot more desire. And every moment of it is the most amazing thing I've ever experienced.

He tastes like beer and pizza and I don't even know if this is real anymore or if I'm dreaming all this but just in case it is a dream, I take advantage of the moment while I can. I sneak a hand up the back of his t-shirt, gripping his muscled back, and he responds by pulling me closer against him. Close enough that I can feel his growing length beneath his sweats.

Dear Jesus...how did I not know just how big my best friend is?

What I wouldn't give to touch it.

To give it a squeeze.

To see it with my own two eyes.

His lips are so soft as he moves against mine, sucking in my bottom lip, caressing my tongue with his, and holding me to him as if I might really be his.

The feeling is remarkable and one I wish so badly I could revel in.

I wish I could be his.

After all these years spent as best friends, August knows me inside and out.

He knows everything about me.

And I know everything about him.

It's like we were meant to be together but have denied ourselves all this time.

This kiss gives me hope.

Hope that maybe crossing the line from friends to lovers wouldn't be the end of the world.

Scary? Yes.

Doable? Perhaps.

"Fuck," he mutters, pulling himself from me just as swiftly as he started, his forehead resting against mine. His breaths fast and sharp as his chest heaves. He bites his top lip as he stares at the ground, refusing to look at me. And he doesn't say a word more.

Yeah that's what I thought.

Too good to be true.

He doesn't want this.

He doesn't want me.

He didn't mean any of it.

I guess it really was just a dream.

And then without warning he nods and mumbles something that sounds like "Yeah, okay" and then wraps his arms around my thighs. He lifts me up and then sets me on the kitchen counter. He opens my legs and steps in between them, cups my face in his hands, and kisses me all over again, but this time he's soft and slow, less demanding, like he's getting to know my lips, my tongue, and my mouth for the very first time. Like this kiss means something to him.

Enjoying the persuasive touch of his lips, I groan against him wishing he would do so much more than kiss me. Blood pounds my brain and my body ignites with every swipe of his tongue inside my mouth as I envision him pleasuring me the way he described in bed a few nights ago.

"Fuck, I'd be desperate for her. Desperate to taste her, to hear her pleasured moans. I'd have her wetter for me than she's ever been... fucking glistening...and then I'd part those soft pink lips with my fingers and drag my tongue over her sweet cunt in one long languid stroke."

Moisture pools between my legs as I sigh into his kiss. I'm aching for relief but can't even rub my legs together for a little friction because of where August is standing.

Trying to gain some sort of pressure, I wrap my legs around August's waist, pulling him tightly against the bottom cabinets and hooking my heels together at my ankles. His hand tugging lightly on my hair, he brings his other hand to the small of my back and then down to my ass holding me against him.

Holy shit.

I can feel him.

His erection presses against my center and I moan into his mouth, reveling in the pressure.

Knowing exactly what I need, he wastes no time sneaking a hand underneath my dress, his fingers playing with the hem of my pink satin panties.

My drenched pink satin panties.

"Tell me to stop, Ella."

I hear his plea but his touch feels so good and I don't have the willpower to say no to him.

"Ella..."

When I don't push him away or tell him no, he slides his hand over my thigh, a feathered touch as he inches higher and higher.

"I mean it, El," he breathes. "I need you to tell me to stop."

I shake my head slowly, my heart pounding inside my chest, and whisper, "I can't do that."

He watches my face as his hand cups my warm wet pussy and I sigh audibly, biting down on my lower lip when he slides a finger through my arousal.

"August!"

"Shhh." He places a finger over my lips and then kisses them for good measure. He backs away from me but only enough to lift my leg and position my foot onto his shoulder. "You didn't tell me to stop."

Silently, I shake my head one more time, internally pleading with him to continue.

"You know I'm not done," he says. "I'm so far from done."

Again, I say nothing so he has zero reason to stop or walk away. He slowly spreads my legs farther apart and then peppers lazy lingering kisses up my thigh. He lifts my other leg, positioning my foot against his right shoulder and then peers down at my soaking wet pink panties. Hooking his thumb inside them, he moves them aside and licks his lips at the vision before him.

"Fucking Christ, you're beautiful."

And then his tongue is swiping through me, first in one long languid stroke just like he described, but then he goes back for more, trailing his tongue through my arousal, licking me, tasting me, pleasuring me. And I am dead.

I've died and gone to heaven.

Heaven is August Blackstone devouring my pussy.

Heaven is August's tongue dipping inside me, lapping at my arousal, and then swirling around my clit over and over and over again until I've lost all ability to form coherent thoughts.

Heaven is the relentless flicking of August's tongue against my clit while his fingers curl inside me.

Heaven is a white-hot heat spreading through my entire body until I'm coming so hard I damn near pass out.

Heaven is August holding my legs and kissing my neck, my cheeks, my forehead, and my lips before saying, "You are the furthest thing from a bad kisser, Ella Montgomery. And I'll be damned if a man ever treats you like that again because from here on out, the only person you'll be kissing...the only person who will be anywhere close to the sweetest pussy I've ever eaten in my whole goddamn life, will be me."

Heaven is August Blackstone carrying me to his room, stripping me down, and pulling one of his shirts over my head and then snuggling me in his bed for the rest of the night.

CHAPTER FIFTEEN

AUGUST

God only knows what time it is, but my eyes lazily open as I recall the sexiest dream I think I've had in a long time. Ella on my kitchen counter, her legs hoisted up to my shoulders, her breathy gasps as I made her come on my tongue.

Fuck, did she taste amazing.

And her body...

Perfection.

Best damn dream of my life.

And then movement brings my attention to the person lying next to me in my bed. The woman whose head rests on my chest. The one sleeping in my t-shirt. Visions of my stripping Ella down and sliding my t-shirt over her head before slipping into bed with her replay through my mind and suddenly my heart starts racing and my body heats.

It wasn't a dream.

Last night happened.

Ella crying...

Ella shouting...

Ella crying some more...

I kissed her...

Fuck, did I kiss her.

And then I...

"Fuuuuck," I silently whisper, shoving my hands through my hair trying to remember everything we said to one another. Everything I did to her.

"The only person who will be anywhere close to the sweetest pussy I've ever eaten in my whole goddamn life, will be me."

Oh God.

What have I done?

I crossed the line.

I crossed the line big time.

She may have seemed okay with it, but did I even give her a fucking choice?

My pulse thunders inside my chest and I wonder how it hasn't yet woken up Ella who continues to sleep peacefully using my chest as her pillow. Now that I'm keenly aware that her head is on my chest, I'm finding it difficult to catch my breath. My chest is tightening like I can't seem to get enough oxygen.

Is my hand going numb?

I wiggle my fingers and toes and all seems to be in fine working order.

Fuck, it's hot in here.

Am I going crazy?

Is that what's happening?

I kissed my best friend...no, I more than kissed her. I finger fucked her, and now I'm going bat shit crazy?

I squeeze my eyes shut and tell myself that everything is fine. This is all fine. She'll wake up and be blissfully happy and we'll figure something out.

It's fine.

Totally fine.

Alright, worst-case scenario.

No. I don't want to think about the worst case.

Shit. But now I can't stop thinking about it.

I need the guys.

I need them to tell me I did the right thing and everything is going to work out fine.

Quietly picking up my phone from my bedside table, I send a message to our group text chat.

ME

MAYDAY! MAYDAY!

ME

MAY FUCKING DAY!

ME

PLEASE LET THIS BE A DAY WHERE YOU ARE ALL UP EARLY!

BEAR

Well, I wasn't but the incessant dings on my phone have now woken me up.

HARRISON

😳 Moving a little slow, but I'm up. What's going on?

LEDGER

I'm up watching sports tv. Did you guys hear about Bodhi Roche? The kid scored every goal for his team last night.

OLIVER

This better be good Blackstone. I'm giving up morning head for this.

GRIFFIN

Dude, we can't see you, Magallan. If you need morning head, get it! What's going on Auggie? 😒

ME

I kissed Ella.

BEAR

That's your mayday? 😔

GRIFFIN

DUDE! That's huge! Way to go soldier!

LEDGER

Yeah man! You made the move. Congrats!

OLIVER

What brought that on? When Scarlett and I saw her, she was crying.

ME

Date gone wrong. The son of a bitch told her she was a bad kisser.

HARRISON

Ouch. What a douche.

GRIFFIN

Bastard. Who is this guy. I'd like to kick his ass for her.

ME

Yeah. She was in one of those moods where she was just ranting about this guy and then brought up the other night in Vancouver when I was telling her about pleasuring my partners and how she thought I was going to kiss her but then I didn't kiss her and then she said I didn't want her either and she felt like the biggest loser and I couldn't fucking help myself. She looked so fucking sad and me not wanting her is the farthest thing from the truth.

BEAR

So, you kissed her instead of talking to her.

ME

Yeah. And I may have done more than kiss her.

GRIFFIN

What's that supposed to mean?

LEDGER

I mean are we talking like you kissed her and then made her a sandwich after or...?

BEAR

Did you take her to Pound Town but the gate was locked and you couldn't gain access?

LEDGER

LOL @Bear! Yeah, did you get lost looking for the Pussy District?

ME

I, in fact, found the Pussy District, thank you very much. And it was...everything.

HARRISON

You fucked her?

ME

I...Not with my dick if that means anything.

OLIVER

It doesn't. You still crossed that line.

ME

Yeah.

OLIVER

Aaaand? What did she say?

ME

I didn't let her say much of anything. I just felt it in my soul and did what I thought felt right. She wasn't complaining nor did she ask me to stop. So I did my thing and then told her the only person who goes near her pussy from here on out is me.

GRIFFIN

Aaaand??

ME

And then I took her to my room, helped her out of her clothes, slipped one of my t-shirts over her head, and cuddled her for the night. She wanted to talk about it but I told her to just relax for the night and that we'd talk about it in the morning.

OLIVER

For what it's worth Scarlett just said "Awwwww." 🤍

GRIFFIN

So, you finally made the move. You went for it and she didn't deny you.

BEAR

Right. So, what's the mayday again?

ME

What if I'm making a huge fucking mistake? What if she doesn't want this? I didn't just cross the line with her. I fucking erased the line altogether. The line no longer exists.

LEDGER

Alright let's play worst case scenario. What's the very worst that could happen?

ME

She could wake up and tell me I've ruined any resemblance of a friendship we once had and that she doesn't want me and move out of my life for good.

GRIFFIN

That's highly unlikely. What else?

ME

She could tell me last night meant nothing and didn't feel good at all and that she faked the orgasm I gave her.

GRIFFIN

Bro, you either tongue fucked her or finger fucked her so some part of you was inside her when she came. You'd know if she faked it. Did she fake it?

ME

No.

GRIFFIN

So that scenario is out too. Next?

ME

She could tell me she loves me and then rip my heart out six weeks or six months or even six years from now.

HARRISON

That one is always the risk my friend. She could do exactly those things. But then so could you.

ME

Never. I'd never do that to her. I'd never hurt her. Not intentionally anyway.

BEAR

Best case scenario?

ME

She loves me. Falls in love with me and we get married one day and have the best sex of our lives that creates a future brood of Blackstones and we live out our days together for the rest of our lives.

GRIFFIN

Not that he's given this any thought whatsoever! LOL 😄

OLIVER

August, I think you're going to be fine and I think you can take a deep breath. You can't take back what happened last night, but you said it felt right and she wasn't saying no so...it sounds like you're all good.

HARRISON

Right. Now you two need to talk it out. This part isn't something we can solve for you. It's up to the two of you.

GRIFFIN

Where is Ella now?

ME

Laying on my chest sound asleep.

GRIFFIN

Then put the phone down, asshat, and hold on to her because she's the best thing to ever happen to you.

I peer down at the beautiful woman resting next to me and huff out a soft and quiet laugh.

GRIFFIN

And I swear to God if you let her get away or do something stupid to lose her, I'm going to be pissed as hell.

LEDGER

Same.

HARRISON

Yep.

OLIVER

Scarlett agrees.

I read Griffin's last message to myself no less than three

times, each time calming myself down a little more until his words sink in.

This is fine.

I did the right thing.

This can be okay.

I glance down at Ella whose breathing remains even and calm and then send a quick reply to my friends.

My family.

ME

Thanks guys. I really needed this.

GRIFFIN

We're family. That's what we're here for.

I lay my phone back down and then wrap my arm around Ella's warm body. She shuffles a bit and then says, "Are you done freaking out yet?"

My body stiffens. "Uh, What?"

She giggles silently against my body. "You were texting the guys."

"You saw that?"

"When you're holding your phone out in front of you, all I had to do was open my eyes and I could read everything. Pussy District, huh?"

Oh, fuck me.

I can't believe she read that.

My cheeks heat and there's an emptiness in the pit of my stomach that does not feel good. My mouth goes dry and I'm not sure what to say next so I blurt out the first thing that comes to my mind.

"Let me hear ya say heeeyyyyyy! We want some pussaaaaaay." I even wave my hands in the air like I just don't care. And all I get is a blank stare followed by Ella's burst of laughter that thankfully breaks the ice and makes her smile.

"You are...unbelievable!" She cackles. "Throwing me some 2 Live Crew this early in the morning?"

I rub my hand down my face and laugh a little with her. "Honestly, it was just the first thing to come to my mind, but I'm glad I could give you something to laugh at. Laughter looks so much better on you than sadness."

Her smile fades a bit and she tips her head to look at me, her thumb rubbing against my bare skin. I won't lie, the physical contact is nice.

"I guess now is as good a time as any, huh?"

"For what?"

"To talk about last night," she says through the crackle of her morning voice. "You know, rip off the band aid and all."

"We don't have to talk about it if you don't want to."

Wrong answer, dumbass.

You should talk about it.

You need to talk about it.

"You kissed me, Auggie," she states matter-of-factly, as if she's telling me the sky is blue or that the Pope is Catholic.

"Yeah...uh...about that."

Her hand stops moving and she rests her palm on my stomach. "Auggie?"

"Yeah?"

"I'm going to need you to consider what you're about to say next because like it or not, I'm dangerously close to your penis right now so your next sentence could end in one of two ways."

Shit. I think I love this girl.

She doesn't beat around the bush.

And even though last night was a bit of a cluster fuck of emotions, she still has space in her heart to have a sense of humor.

"My dick is yours for the taking, Ella," I tell her. Reaching down to her chin, I tip her head up so I can see her eyes. "But what I was going to say was that last night was one of the best nights of my life and I don't regret a damn thing."

Her eyes grow and her brows lift. "You don't?"

I shake my head. "No. Why, do you?"

On the outside I'm the coolest, calmest person I can be for my best friend, but on the inside, fuck. I'm a nervous fucking wreck.

"No Auggie," she says shaking her head as well.

Thank Christ.

"I'm sorry I yelled about the bottle opener though."

Her apology causes me to laugh. "Babe, I don't give a damn about the bottle opener. It was my fault it was left out. I may have had a few too many beers last night waiting for you."

"You waited for me?"

I shrug. "I may or may not have panicked about you being on a date last night."

She pulls her body up to a sitting position next to me and lays her hand on my thigh connecting us with the slightest touch. "Oh no! You did?"

I nod.

"Auggie, why didn't you say something?"

I fiddle with a few strands of her hair, winding them around my finger, feeling the softness against my skin. "Because it's not my place to tell you how to live your life and you were so excited to be going on a date. I wasn't going to be the one to ruin that for you."

"But you didn't want me to go?"

"Pfft." I chuckle. "Are you kidding me? Ella, I would've given my left nut for you to not go."

"Hey, let's not go too far now, okay?" She pats my thigh lovingly. "Your nuts are valuable. But..." She shakes her head, her brows furrowing. "I guess I just don't understand. I thought..." She pauses for a moment. "I thought you didn't want me?"

Passing her a shy smile, I ask, "Whatever gave you that idea?"

"Oh, I don't know. Maybe it was the unattractive tits remark a while back coupled with the other night in Vancouver when you didn't kiss me. I really thought you were going to kiss me."

Fuck.

She's right.

I've given her reason to doubt any kind of attraction I have for her.

"Come here," I tell her, patting my lap. She turns herself toward me and swings a leg over my lap so she's straddling me. Fuck, it's nice. Really nice. I reach up and smooth her hair away from her face.

"Ella, if I'm being honest, I've thought about kissing you since the first fucking day you moved in here."

"You have?"

"Mhmm. But then I put my foot in my damn mouth that first night and we sort of argued. And I hated that I hurt you and figured there was no way in hell you would be interested and plus there was no way I was going to risk our friendship just because I hadn't gotten laid in a while and was a little horny."

She lifts a brow, questioning my words, but I continue.

"But then I realized I wasn't just horny. I had feelings. Real honest to God feelings. So, when I saw how sad you were last night after your date and that I had even an inkling to do with that sadness, I threw caution to the wind and did what I should've done a long time ago."

"You ate me out on your kitchen counter," she states. "That's what you should've done a long time ago?" The corner of her mouth turns up and fuck if she isn't the most adorable person on the planet.

"Well, I meant I should've kissed you a long time ago. Eating you on my kitchen counter wasn't planned, but I needed to make you feel good. I wanted to make you feel good." I cup her face in my hands and angle her head so she sees the sincerity in my eyes. "And I meant what I said when I told you it was the sweetest pussy I've ever eaten in my whole goddamn life."

She stops me with her palm to my chest. "I don't want to know about any of the other pussies you've eaten, alright? Can we just pretend mine is the only one?"

"As far as I'm concerned, babe, yours is the only one I'll ever remember. The first one I've ever wholly enjoyed and the last one I'll ever lick for the first time."

She gives me a shy smile and her cheeks pinken as I stare back at her.

"Auggie?"

"Yeah?"

"What if I told you I slept better last night than I've ever slept in my entire life?"

"You did?"

"Mhmm."

"Me too. I literally thought I was dreaming about last night until I woke up and you were in my arms."

She glances down at her hands and then returns my gaze. "So where do we go from here? We kind of crossed a big line last night."

I inhale a deep breath and release it with an understanding nod. "We did. *I* did."

"We did," she corrects me, nodding.

"How does that make you feel?"

"Is it weird if I say it's a little bit scary but feels a whole lot right?"

I shake my head. "Not weird at all. Hence my panic text with the guys," I tell her, passing her a resigned smile. "The feelings I've had for you these last several weeks have been making me feel confused as hell. You're my best friend, Ella. I didn't think this would ever be a place we would come to."

"Me either," she says. "But I think somewhere in my heart and in my mind, I kind of always hoped we would. But also, I'm scared, Auggie. If this gets messed up..."

"It won't," I answer, smoothing my thumb across her cheek and down her jawline. "I'll never hurt you, Ella. You mean too much to me."

"So, this is it then?" she asks. "You and me. Me and you."

"There's nobody else, Ella. I think it's always been you and me. Me and you. We just had to stop denying ourselves. I don't think I can be your friend anymore. I see you as so much more than that."

She takes a deep breath and lets out an audible sigh and then smiles at me. "So, you're breaking up with me now?"

"Yeah." I chuckle. "Our lifelong friendship is officially over. You're my girl. My partner. My lover. And one day my wife if I have anything to say about it."

Whoa.

I just called Ella my wife and I didn't flinch, gag, or even get nauseous.

And neither did she.

She leans forward and kisses my lips softly and then pulls back. "Deal. What's next?"

"We go where we want to go, El. We're adults. There's nobody to tell us we can't or shouldn't feel the way we feel or that we can't or shouldn't do whatever we want to do."

"And what is it you want to do, exactly?" She teasingly climbs my chest with her fingers and doesn't meet my gaze. Watching her movements as her touch climbs my body I say the one thing that's been on my mind I'm certain will grab her attention.

"What if I told you I want to give you the biggest orgasm of your life with my dick so you know how great sex is supposed to feel? And that I want to do it again, and again, and again, until you can't walk straight."

The smile that spreads across her face makes me smile in response.

Like I said, I knew that would grab her attention.

She pats my chest with her hands three times and then says, "And what if I told you that after a strong cup of coffee and perhaps brushing my teeth I'll nibble on your dick like a rat does cheese?"

I burst out laughing at her 2 Live Crew reference and then wrap my arms around her body and roll us until I have her on her back. I kiss her one more time and then smile at her, rubbing my nose against hers. "I like a girl who can talk dirty to me."

CHAPTER SIXTEEN

ELLA

I hear Scarlett outside my dressing room door. "She's in here. Come on, I'll introduce you."

There's a knock on my door followed by a "Ella! It's Scarlett along with several friends! Okay if we come in?"

"Absolutely! Come on in!" I turn just in time to see Scarlett step inside along with six other women all dressed in Chicago Red Tails jerseys. My eyes grow, as does my smile, as I welcome them all. "Hi ladies! Wow I think I can venture a fairly good guess who you all are given your attire this evening."

We all have a quick laugh before one of the women steps from the group of them and shakes my hand. "Hi. I'm Carissa Nelson, Social Media Marketing Director for the Red Tails aaaand team captain, Colby Nelson's wife. It's a pleasure to meet you."

"The pleasure is all mine," I tell her with a friendly smile. "I'm Ella Montgomery, official mascot of the Anaheim Stars."

"Oh, we've heard a lot about you," she says with a wink.

Wait, seriously?

"You have?"

"Of course! We knew Astro when he was the mascot of the

team, so for the Stars to introduce a new mascot, that's a big deal! In fact, I was kind of hoping you might be willing to do a few social media posts with our Remi before the game."

I beam back at my new friend. "Of course! That would be so much fun!"

"Great! I'll catch up with you sometime within the hour after I've met with Marlee upstairs. I'll find you."

I nod. "Perfect."

Carissa sees herself out since she has pregame responsibilities, but the rest of the ladies hang back with Scarlett.

"Okay so now I can introduce you to the rest of the gang, and I'm going to do it quick because girl, I know you have some tea and I need you to spill it so I can hear all the juicy stuff!" Scarlett says smiling.

"Oooh juicy gossip?" one of the women says. "Did we walk in here just in time or what?"

Scarlett laughs. "Yeah you did! I have it on particularly good authority that our girl, Ella here, reeled herself in some August Blackstone and I am HERE. FOR. IT! So, Ella," she says, gesturing to one of the women to her left. "This is Charlee *Magallan* Landric." She over-emphasizes Charlee's maiden name to be sure I catch on, which I do.

"Right! Oliver's sister!"

The woman nods. "Yep. That's me."

"And my soon to be sister-in-law!" Scarlett beams as she jumps up and down and claps her hands. "Sorry, I might be a little excited about that. It's not every day you gain a sister."

"Girl, it's not just me," Charlee says. "You marrying Oliver means you get all these wonderful ladies too."

Scarlett pumps her fist. "YAASS!"

"Ella it's nice to meet you. And it just so happens, I know a little about you and August so I'm equally as eager to hear what's been happening with you too."

"Okay, okay, we all clearly need to hear what's going on." One of the girls with dark hair steps forward. "So, hiiii! I'm Rory Foster Malone. Sister to Dex Foster but wife to Hawken Malone."

The blonde woman next to her steps forward. "I'm Tate Foster, Dex Foster's wife."

"Pleasure to meet you," I tell them both.

The next woman wears a camera around her neck as she shakes my hand. "I'm Kinsley Shay, Quinton Shay is my hubby."

"And I'm Ada Miller. Zeke Miller's wife."

"Wow." I smile at them, shaking my head in bewilderment. "It's so wonderful to meet you all."

Scarlett waves her hand dismissing my pleasantries. "Yeah, yeah. They're all great and we're all going to hang out together after the game. Get to the good stuff, babe! How are things with you and Blackstone?"

"Well, I had this terrible date with a guy who I actually thought was nice and fun and all that jazz, but then he told me I was a bad kisser because I wasn't spitty enough. So then—"

"Wait." Rory raises her hand. "I'm sorry, but did you say you weren't spitty enough?"

I nod. "Yeah. Spitty. That was the word he used."

Her face contorts as does Tate's and Ada's. Kinsley just laughs. "Oh, my God, that's so gross."

"Right? I agree. So, I slapped him and drove myself home and then broke down in the solace of my apartment which is where Auggie came in."

"Auggie," Charlee coos. "You call him Auggie? That's so cute!"

"Yeah. We've literally been the very best of friends since we knew how to walk. We were neighbors growing up and he was just that kid I was always with. So, anyway, he walks in and I'm a sobbing mess and he asks what happened and I told him everything, including how the few nights previous to that in Vancouver, when we were chatting, I felt sure he was going to kiss me but he didn't and I think I was more messed up by that than I thought and then before I knew it he was walking towards me and told me to shut up and then he kissed me." I shrug like it's no big deal even though it's a super big deal.

To me, anyway.

"Eeeeek!" Scarlett squeals, clapping her hands excitedly.

Charlee's eyes grow in excitement. "Way to go August!"

"Was it one of those super romantic devour you kind of kisses?" Tate asks, wagging her brows. "Or was it one of those slow sweet I-love-you type kisses."

"It was definitely a devour kiss at first and then he stopped and I thought maybe he was regretting his decision to kiss me in the first place. But then he lifted me up and put me down on the kitchen counter and kissed me again and that time was slower. Softer." I smile. "Definitely more meaningful."

Scarlett brings a hand to her chest. "Be still my heart. It's so great to see August Blackstone smitten for someone. It's so freaking cute."

Rory leans in with a smirk on her lips and asks, "So what's it like?"

"What's what like?" I ask her.

"It's a thing. We all talk about it in our friend circle so I'll just pass our little tradition on to you and Scarlett. You have to talk about the dick. What's the dick like? Is it like…" she uses hand gestures, "long and lean or bulbous and weighty?"

"Yeah, oooh or is he pierced?" Tate winks. "My husband is pierced and it is…" She fans herself. "Phew! It's hot. Not gonna lie."

The ladies are all giggling and I join in with them but with reddening cheeks, I have to answer, "Honestly, I can't answer that question. We haven't had sex yet."

They stare at me blankly.

"I mean, I've, you know." I smile, bobbing my head. "I've felt it when he's close to me and I know it's an impressive size, but I haven't like...felt it, felt it. It's only been a week or so since we decided to move from friends to..."

"Lovers?" Charlee says with a seductive tone to her voice.

"Yes. Lovers."

She pats me on the shoulder. "Perfectly understandable. But girl, you get that dick and then you make sure you tell us all about it because we will be dying to know! We're here to support you always!"

"That's right," Ada says with a nod. "Us hockey gals have to stick together."

Scarlett nudges me with her elbow and gestures to the ladies with her head. "Hear that, Ella? We have a tribe!"

"Alright, we should probably let you get yourself ready for the game. But we'll be cheering for you, Ella," Tate says with a smile. "It was so amazing to get to meet you!"

Scarlett reminds me that they'll all be at her and Oliver's place tonight to hang out after the game and then we say our goodbyes. In the next fifteen minutes I'm in costume and ready to go. Marlee and Carissa stop in to get me and I'm off to make a few social media videos with Remi Red Tail before tonight's game.

CHAPTER SEVENTEEN

AUGUST

Ella's already on the ice by the time the team hits the tunnel. It seems Lumin is giving Remi Red Tail a run for his money as he chases her down the ice. The crowd cheers "LUMIN! LUMIN! LUMIN!" as she glides across the ice with her glowing hockey stick.

I'm so proud of her every time I see her do her thing.

"Look at her go, man!" Ledger says, hitching his thumb behind him from the tunnel. "That girl is fast."

"Tell me about it. She used to kick my ass when I'd make her race me when we were kids. It pissed me off every time until I finally realized she was helping me get faster. By the time I hit high school I was the fastest one on the team."

"Think you can outskate her now?" Griffin asks.

I shake my head and chuckle. "Hell, I'd like to think so but watching her out there now...I'm not so sure."

"Guess we'll have to put you both to the test sometime, huh?" Harrison laughs.

Oliver motions for us to huddle up before we take the ice for warm up. "Alright guys. I'm not losing to my brother-in-law in our house, you got that? Watch their defense. Foster and

Malone are strong and Miller isn't going to let much through if he can help it. We've got work ahead of us with these birds but let's show them who's boss in Anaheim."

Just as we turn in line to make our way to the ice, Ella is coming off clapping her hands and raising her fists in victory. The guys congratulate her on a job well done before we take the ice one by one.

"Way to go Lumin!"

"Hey great job out there!"

"That's our girl, Lumin!"

"You're a beast out there, Lumin."

"Think you'd give Blackstone here a run for his money!"

"Nice job out there, babe. Knew you'd kick his ass." I offer her a fist bump with my glove which she meets but she surprises me when she slaps my ass right before I take the ice.

And I can't lie. That little gesture just gave me the extra zip I needed to want to play a hard and fast game.

We go through our normal warm-up routine and then we're called to center ice for the playing of our national anthem. From there, our dance with the birds begins.

Landric and Magallan face off, smirking at each other under their helmets. The puck is dropped and Landric comes out on top with Magallan right on his heels. Landric passes to Quinton Shay but Ledger intercepts and takes it down the ice to Red Tails territory. He's unable to get it past Dex Foster who shifts it to Colby Nelson. Colby takes possession and works the puck out of their defensive zone sending it to Landric but I'm there just in time to check him into the glass.

"Sorry Landric. The puck is mine," I shout as I pass him a quick wink.

Ledger, Oliver, and I work together to get the puck back into the scoring zone, working the puck in front of the net. I shoot my shot but Miller is too quick and blocks it with his knee as he slides left.

"Don't fucking think so brother!" Miller says as we fight to regain a hold on the puck. The crowd boos as the puck makes its way into Anaheim territory but when Landric tries to score, Bear refuses to let it pass.

No goal.

"Come on, Stars," I mutter to myself. "These birds are not beating us today."

Harrison is able to work in a hit but it's deflected by Quinton Shay and pushed back into the Anaheim zone. Shay is jacked into the boards by Griffin and the puck is back in the Stars' possession. Griffin tries to move the puck and succeeds, getting it to Oliver who shifts to Ledger.

Ledger moves into scoring range and tries to shoot this time but the puck hits Miller's other knee pad and ricochets right into Coby Nelson's grasp.

"Dammit," I mutter. "Give it back Nelson."

Colby laughs. "In your dreams Black—ah, fuck!" Harrison sneaks in for the steal and throws it back to me as I laugh at Colby.

All in good fun of course. These guys are a blast to play. A hard solid team, for sure, but a good game is great fun.

I curl behind the net refusing to stop moving while I maneuver the puck back and forth with my stick, waiting for my moment, and when I finally see it, I waste no time taking the shot. Miller sinks to the ground, his knees butterflied, but by the grace of God, it slides just past his leg and into the net and the sirens go off as my arms go up.

"SCOOOOORE! HELL YEAH!"

The crowd erupts and it's hard to hear any train of thought, but the guys all swarm around me, patting my helmet and hugging me.

"That'a boy, Blackstone!"

"Damn, that was fast, Auggie!" Harrison says with a smile. "Proud of you!"

"Great start, Blackstone!"

The first period ends with the Stars leading 1-0.

During the first intermission my face is glued to the television in the locker room as I watch Ella do her thing. She happily makes her way through the crowd until she finds two people she can tell are there together and places her fur-covered paw on each of their heads forcing them to turn toward each other. The crowd cheers for the couple to kiss and when they do, Lumin claps and cheers and then pats them both on the head. She does this for four or five more couples and then makes her way to the t-shirt cannon in the corner of the arena. With each blow of the cannon, she pretends to almost fall backward and then proceeds to shoot t-shirt after t-shirt into the excited crowd.

"Aww, look at our boy Blackstone," Griffin says as we're all seated in the dressing room in various stages of undress. "Pussy-whipped and in love. He hasn't taken his eyes off that screen."

"She's a hell of a lot prettier than you are, Ollenberg," I tell him as I wipe my sweat-soaked face with my towel.

"Touché, my friend."

"And you're right. I'm fucking proud of her." I gesture to the screen. "Look at her out there doing her thing for the team. She's amazing. If that means I'm pussy-whipped, then so be it."

"You really care about her," Oliver says with a smile. "We can all tell that."

"Hell yeah, I care about her. She's..."

Everything.

"She's my home. She's always been my home. And if I play my cards right, she'll always be my home."

"Wow," Harrison chuckles. "Talking a little fast aren't we? That's a huge turnaround from the man you were before Ella came along."

I shake my head. "Not fast at all. I'm thirty years old and we've known each other since we were two. Twenty-eight years is a fucking long time to build a relationship. We just finally got to the point where we didn't need to deny our feelings for one another anymore."

"Have you consummated this new phase of your relationship yet, Blackstone?" Ledger asks from the other side of the room.

"Trust me, it's not that I don't want to," I tell him, grabbing my water bottle and twisting it open. "I'm just putting the ball in her court. I don't want to force her into doing anything she doesn't want to do."

"Do you think she doesn't want to?"

"Nah, I just think the timing hasn't been right. You guys know what our schedule is like."

Bear stands and adjusts his pads in preparation for the second period. Then he pats my shoulder and gruffly says, "Tonight is the night then."

I laugh. "Okay, Bear. And when exactly should that happen? While we have game night with the Red Tails at Oliver's?"

"Hey!" Oliver admonishes. "Don't knock game night. Charlee says it's a fucking fun time and she can't believe we don't have routine game nights."

Ledger pipes in. "So, what are we playing tonight? Spin the bottle?"

"Fuck no," I say with a stern shake of my head. "And risk someone else kissing my girl in front me? That's a hard pass."

"Oh, I imagine the guys or gals from the Red Tails will have something in mind. From what Charlee says, their game nights are always hella inappropriate and top-notch fun."

"THAT WAS AN AMAZING WIN!" Ella throws her arms around my neck when I stop in her dressing room after the game. "And you scored! Oh, my God, I thought I was going to pee my pants from cheering so hard!"

I kiss the side of her neck and chuckle as I hold her against me. "They're a hard team to beat, that's for sure. For a while there, I wasn't sure we were going to come out on top, but once Harrison scored at the end of the third I felt rather good about it."

"As you should have. And the crowd was electric tonight. You can tell they were really excited about a solid game."

"Those are the games we love playing. When the crowd is as into it as we are." I pat her ass lovingly. "You looked magnificent out there as well, you know. Watching you kick Remi's ass before the game was hot. Reminded me of old times."

She winks and gives me a chaste kiss to my lips. "You mean those days where I cleaned your clock on the ice."

"Yep. You had no idea at the time, but I was crushing on you so fucking hard back then."

She pushes off my chest. "What?"

"Your tight little ass always looked hot in those leggings you would wear. I enjoyed chasing after you very much."

"Is that so?" Her voice is less incredulous and a little more seductive.

"Yep."

"Hmm. Well maybe if you're really lucky, I'll let you place your hands on this tight little ass later and take your best shot."

I palm both of her ass cheeks and pull her tightly against my body. "You're such a tease."

She laughs. "In all the best ways, babe. I've got to give you something to think about while we're playing games with the birds tonight."

I lean in and connect my lips with hers, tasting the cotton candy I know she had earlier. "Babe, you just guaranteed that's all I'll be thinking about for the rest of the night."

She cocks her head and gives me her best fake sympathetic look. "Aww, you poor thing."

"Yeah, yeah. Keep that up and I'll be spanking that tight little ass tonight."

Her eyes grow wide and playful and her smile widens. "Ooh, don't make promises you don't intend to keep, Auggie."

"Ella Montgomery, I have every intention of keeping that promise."

"BODHI ROCHE?" Colby asks when his name is brought up in conversation. "Yeah we've been watching him too."

We're all seated around Oliver and Scarlett's backyard enjoying the warm weather of a California evening in November. Knowing both teams have tomorrow off from game play, Oliver and Scarlett invited the Red Tails to hang with us for the night and Oliver's sister, Charlee, brought up the idea of game night. Apparently this is something the Red Tails do often, which I think is kind of rad as I gaze around the room at these big burly men about to play games.

Although if I'm being honest, the only real thing on my mind right now is what's coming later tonight when I get Ella home. I don't even care if it's not straight up sex because I know whatever we get ourselves into, it's going to be out of this world. Every now and then she gives me a look that says she's thinking about it too which will make a few hours from now that much hotter. Anticipation is everything.

"He's garnered quite the following on social media," Carissa says. "Apparently he's quite the player."

"Probably in all senses of the word." I roll my eyes. "We've heard he's a bit of a pompous little dick. You guys can have him if they move him up to the big boy leagues."

"I don't think it's a question of if," Zeke adds. "More like when."

"I thought I heard somewhere that the Bay Scrapers were looking into grabbing him," Milo says before taking a sip of the beer in his hand.

"I heard maybe the Grizzlies." Harrison shrugs. "So, I guess only time will tell."

"Okay so teams!" Charlee announces, wanting to steer the conversation away from hockey for the night. She holds up her game night cheat sheet. "Team one will be Dex, Barrett, Ella, Rory, and Zeke. Team two is Tate, Kinsley, Harrison, Milo and Scarlett. Team three is Quinton, Carissa, Ledger, Hawken, and Griffin. And Team four will be Colby, August, Ada, myself, and Oliver."

Ella gives me a swift kiss on my cheek and whispers, "You're going down, Blackstone."

I merely smirk back at her and lick my lips before saying, "Damn right I am."

I give her a pat on the ass like she did me earlier tonight and then watch proudly as her cheeks pinken immediately. Then I simply smile and enjoy the sway of her ass as she walks away from me to join her group.

Yep.

Flirting with her is going to be fun.

"We're going to play Mad Gab, completely NSFW addition

and we're going to make up our own phrases because I don't really have the game with me. So, everyone takes a couple slips of paper and a sharpie. You want to write the actual phrase on one side and then on the opposite side, you'll write out that phrase by using other words or word-soundings. So, for example if you were saying 'a paper jam' you might write 'ape ape purge am.' Get it?"

Everyone nods and passes around the paper and markers. After a few minutes of subtle and not so subtle chuckling, because of course most of us are in our middle school boy eras right now, Charlee collects the folded phrases and mixes them up in her black bag.

Shaking the bag as she speaks, she explains, "So, one of us will pull the phrases out of this bag and someone from each of your teams will say them out loud. You'll get one minute to get your team to figure out as many sayings as possible and the team with the most phrases completed wins."

"Easy peasy," Dex says, rubbing his hands together and fist bumping Ella. "We've got this in the bag."

I pass him my most mischievous smile and tell him, "Yeah that's probably what you said before tonight's game."

CHAPTER EIGHTEEN

AUGUST

"Thumb max chicks dick. Thumb max chicks dick. Thuuumbmaaaaxchicksdick. Oh my gosh! The Magic Stick!" Rory exclaims. She and Ella give each other a high five and clap their hands excitedly.

"Yay! Next one!" Ella says as Tate flips over the next card to show them.

Zeke furrows his brow and mumbles, "Ace. Crow. Dumb."

Dex repeats, "Aaaace crooow dumb."

"A scrotum," Bear answers easily to their group's delight. "Next."

Tate holds up the next card and Ella reads it aloud. "Ta hit sand as. Ta hit sand as."

The most adorable smile spreads across her face and I can tell the moment she hears what's she's saying. Pointing to her tits, she proclaims, "Tits and ass!"

"Yes!" Dex and Rory shout in tandem. "Great job!"

"And that's time," Tate announces, looking at the stopwatch feature on her phone. "Alright, who's next?"

"We'll go next," I say, raising my hand. I give a fist bump to

Oliver, Charlee, Ada, and Colby as we prepare to out play team one.

Quinton takes the bag of phrases and holds up the first one for us. Colby gives it a try.

"Add hooch beg."

"A douche bag!" Ada jumps up and down clapping.

Quinton's eyes grow and he smiles. "Damn that was fast. Okay next!"

The next card goes to Oliver to read. "Spain come mead had dee" His brows furrow as he says the phrase again. "Spain come mead had dee."

Charlee gasps and asks Oliver to say it one more time to be sure.

"Spain come mead had dee."

She laughs. "Spank me, daddy!"

Oliver cracks up. "What the fuck? How did you hear that? I couldn't figure that out for the life of me!"

"Next one! Next one!" Quinton holds the next phrase up quickly and I point to it eagerly saying it out loud.

"We ewe haunts om puss sea."

Griffin, Ledger, Hawken, and Milo crack up laughing obviously knowing exactly what I'm saying, but I have to say it again because hell if I've figured it out yet."

"Pussy something," I hear Charlee mumble next to me.

"We ewe haunts om puss sea."

"You haunt pussy?" Colby guesses but Quinton shakes his head.

Oliver rubs his hands together. "Okay say it again but slower."

"Weeeee ewe haunts om pusssssea"

Ada squeals and throws her hands up in the air. "Let me here ya say HEY! We want some pussy!"

Everyone laughs at the 2 Live Crew song reference and Ella

glances at me. When my eyes finally meet hers, she bursts out laughing again and nearly falls off the stool she's sitting on. I can't help but laugh right along with her because there's no way in hell that was a coincidence.

"You got me, babe," I tell her with a defeated shake of my head and a smirk on my face. "You got me on that one."

"I can NOT believe you didn't catch that one!" She cackles.

"Uh oh," Scarlett laughs. "Is there a story behind that one that we need to know about?"

"Nope!" I shake my head adamantly, feeling my cheeks heat. "Nothing anyone needs to know."

"Okay then our group is going next! This has been too funny to watch."

Quinton hands the bag of phrases off to Dex who giggles like a little punk and pulls out the first phrase.

"Go for it Milo," Harrison tells him.

Milo reads the phrase, "Ache um duh mister."

"What?" Tate frowns.

"Ache um duh mister."

"A cum dumpster?" Kinsley asks.

Dex nods and gives her a wink. "Right on Kink!"

"Kink?" I ask. I thought her name was—"

"Long story," everyone says in tandem.

"Okay next one!" Dex pulls the next phrase from the bag.

"Ear wreck tiled his funk shin."

"Erectile Disfunction!" Tate shouts. "That was too easy."

Dex giggles at the next one. "Okay next!"

Scarlett cocks her head as she reads, "Chick ago win det un nail."

"What the fuck?" Harrison murmurs. "You might have to say that again."

"Chick ago win det un nail."

Milo shakes his head in confusion. "Maybe say it really fast this time?"

"Chickagowindetunnail."

Tate's face deadpans as the answer comes to her. "Oh my God, Dex. You didn't."

Dex giggles and all too excitedly says, "Yes I fucking did."

She palms her forehead, embarrassingly amused as Dex requests that Scarlett say it again for everyone nice and slow this time.

"Chick aaaagooo wiiin det uuunnn nail."

Harrison turns to Milo and asks, "Is she saying Chicago wind tunnel?"

"Oh fuck. Dex!" Milo bursts out laughing. "Yeah that's exactly what she's saying."

"I don't get it." Bear shrugs. "What's a Chicago wind tunnel?"

Dex smirks and says, "It's when—"

Tate throws her hand over Dex's mouth and glances at Bear. "Urban Dictionary, my new friend. You can learn all you need to know from Urban Dictionary. And I'll ask you to kindly excuse the oddity that is my teenage boy of a husband."

It's late when Ella and I make it back to the apartment. Letting me know she has to pee she excuses herself to her room so she can use the bathroom, so I do the same and then brush my teeth so I'm ready for bed. Ella has slept with me almost every night since the earthquake and definitely every night since I kissed her, so I see no reason tonight would be any different.

Except I hope it's a little different.

I hope tonight she comes to bed naked.

I take a quick minute to make sure the apartment door is locked and then shuffle back to my room turning off lights as I go. I unbutton my shirt and pull it off, tossing it in the laundry basket just outside the bathroom, and when I turn back around Ella is standing in the doorway of my bedroom. Dressed in nothing but one of my t-shirts, her soft coffee brown hair hangs over her shoulders. She's absolutely breathtaking and she doesn't even know it.

"Have I ever told you how sexy you look when you're wearing my t-shirt?" I ask her as I wrap an arm around her and pull her inside my room.

She smiles but shakes her head. "No actually, I don't believe you have."

"Well, you look exceptionally sexy tonight." I press my lips to hers in a sweet kiss and then slide my hands down her body until my hands are on her ass. I even give it a squeeze for good measure. "Now I believe earlier tonight we were discussing this tight little ass of yours and how much I'm dying to play with it."

"You're right. And I said if you play your cards right, you might just get a reward."

What?

Is she denying me?

I catch her gaze and bring a hand up to cup her face. "Have I done something to upset you? Are you okay?"

"I'm perfectly fine, Auggie," she tells me with a seductive smile. "But I have a little game to play with you tonight."

My brows raise. "Ooh. I'm intrigued. What did you have in mind?"

"Our own little mad gab game." She smirks and shows me a few note cards in her hand.

"If you can figure out the sayings on these cards, you get the reward," she says. "And if you can't figure them out..." She shakes her head sadly. "Then no reward for you I'm afraid."

Oh.

My girl likes to play.

I like it.

"Alright. You're on, Montgomery. But maybe I should make my own set of cards."

She giggles at the suggestion and holds up a few blank notecards and a pen. "I figured you would say that."

I huff out a laugh. "You know me so well."

"I know how competitive you can be is all." While I jot a few key phrases down on the notecards she gave me, Ella has a seat on the edge of my bed and waits patiently.

"Alright, I'm ready," I tell her a moment later. "Who's going first?"

"You are." She holds up her first card for me to read.

"Tay cough York loathes"

I grin knowing exactly what this card says. "Take off your clothes, El."

"Oh, this old thing?" She wags her brow and then slowly slips my t-shirt up and over her head.

Fuuuck me.

She isn't wearing a bra.

Her tits...

I gaze at them intense appreciation.

"Ella," I whisper, stepping back and covering my mouth in disbelief. For once I'm a man of few words when a nearly naked woman is standing in front of me. "You're stunning." I reach out to touch one of her breasts but she backs up and shakes her head.

"Uh, uh, uh," she says, wagging her finger and then holding up another card. "You'll have to earn the next move."

"Playing hard ball, huh?"

She merely shrugs.

Amused at her lack of response, I read the words on the next card aloud. "Sock come eyed ick."

Her left brow rises as mine furrows. This one is slightly trickier. "Sock come eyed ick. Sock come eyed ick. Sooock-comeyedick. My dick. Sock come my dick."

Oh shit.

My eyes meet hers. "Suck my dick."

With a wink and a seductive lick of her lips, she drops to her knees. "Thought you'd never ask."

She makes quick work of the dress pants I had on after the game tonight, unbuckling my belt and pulling it though the loops in one smooth movement. She unzips my pants and lets them fall to the ground where I carefully step out of them. I refuse to take my eyes off her even though she's only focused on one thing.

My stiff cock.

Oh my God she's serious about this.

This is really happening.

She's never even seen my cock let alone held it in her hand, but the moment she releases me from my boxer briefs and wraps a hand around my shaft, I suck in a gasping breath.

"Jesus fucking Christ."

Her eyes never stray from my crotch as she squeezes me. "You alright up there?"

"Never fucking better, babe." I tip my head down and steal a glance at her. "You know you don't have to do this if you— fuuuuuuuuck me," I gasp, throwing my head back and squeezing my eyes closed. She wastes no time sheathing her soft warm lips over the head of my cock and flicking the crown with her tongue as I shudder.

"Shhhhiiiit, Ella." I slide my hand through her hair,

clutching it between my fingers as she stretches her lips to take me in until I'm hitting the back of her throat.

Jesus.

"Such a fucking good girl, El. Your lips feel amazing."

With one hand squeezing the base of my cock, she pumps my shaft with the other hand as she pulls off of me and then sucks me back in again.

I watch her suck me for a few silent but wonderful lengthy seconds before I tell her, "I've never seen anything sexier than this in my whole goddamn life." If it were any other woman sucking my cock right now, my eyes would be closed and I'd be reveling in the feeling of pleasure. Delighted in the act of fucking a warm mouth without a care in the world. But this time, the warm mouth is Ella and I'll be damned if I can look away from this sight.

She's so fucking beautiful.

She looks up at me with a pair of the most gorgeous fuck-me eyes and I nearly come on the spot. She swirls her tongue around my tip once, twice, three times, and then sucks me into her mouth until I'm hitting the back of her throat again. Her hand slides down to my balls where she rubs them between her fingers and my legs are instantly weak.

"Ella," I murmur, loving every single fucking second of this. "That's it baby. You take me so perfectly. God, I'm in so deep."

She moans with me inside her as her gifted tongue tickles the underside of my shaft.

"Shit, babe, I'm almost there," I tell her, my breathing ragged as my body begins to shake. She sucks on me harder this time, moving her head forward and back as I hold her hair back. The slurping noises coming from her mouth are so fucking hot and before I can warn her again, my balls are tightening, my insides are spiraling, and I'm coming down her throat.

She swallows like the champion goddess she is and smiles up at me. "Looks like I made the man come first."

I pull her up from her knees and kiss her so hard she almost loses her balance and falls over. "What if I told you that was single-handedly the hottest thing I've ever seen and by far the best blow job I have ever had the pleasure of experiencing in my life?"

She wipes her mouth with the back of her hand and grins. "I would say I'm glad I could be of service."

"Yeah well, I hope you're ready for your turn."

CHAPTER NINETEEN

ELLA

Auggie stands behind me, my back to his chest, and holds a card out in front of me to read. "Tut chim might it ees."

He leans down close to my ear and murmurs, "I'm sorry, what's that babe? I didn't quite hear you."

"Tutchimmightitees."

My titties.

Got that part.

Touch.

Oh.

"Touch my titties."

"With pleasure," he says, bringing a hand down over my shoulder to cup my breast. My head falls back against his chest and I arch my back at the overwhelming pleasure of his hand on my body. This is the very first time August has ever touched my breasts and to say it's far exceeding every expectation I ever had is an understatement.

"August..."

Teasing my nipple between his fingers, he chuckles and says, "Next card babe."

With his other hand, he holds the next card up for me to

read. "Sell eyed dior han deb beet tween mile eggs. Oh hell, that's a long one."

"Say it again and I'll help you out."

Pronouncing each word a little slower, I say, "Sellleyed dior hannnn deb beeettweeeen mile eggs."

"That's it," August murmurs, trailing his hand from my breast down my sternum and past my belly button. His fingers play with the waistline of my panties and then push just past them.

Good God, his hand on my body is causing heat to spread everywhere. "Do you need to say it one more time?"

"Alright," I breathe. "Sell eyed...slide dior hand..."

He moves his hand down through my lace panties.

I got it!

"Slide your hand between my legs."

"Yes ma'am," he says. He reaches down just a bit more until he's at the heated apex of my thighs and drags his fingers through my very wet and wanting pussy.

Oh, my God!

Reaching behind me, I grab his thighs with each of my hands as I gasp loudly. "Oh, shit! August!"

"Hmmm. So wet for me, El." He feathers his fingers through my arousal. "Is this all for me?"

"Mhmm."

"I'm going to need you to say it."

"Yes, August," I gasp. "It's all for you. I've been nothing but wet for you since the day I moved here."

He kisses my neck, my jaw, and that spot behind my ear before sucking my earlobe between his lips. And then with the gentlest pressure, he pushes himself against my ass so I feel how hard he is again. "And you've made me so fucking hard by simply existing that I've had to jack off in the shower on a daily basis. Read the next card."

SUSAN RENEE

"Another one?" I ask, assuming he was going to toss the cards and fuck me already.

"You didn't think I would give in that easily, did you?"

With a grin, I shake my head. "You? Of course not. Bring it on big boy."

He holds up the next card and I try to focus on it as his finger circles my clit.

"Ben demi oaf her."

That's an easy one.

"Bend me over, August."

With his hand on my back, he turns me toward the bed and bends me over so my chest is pressed against the mattress. But do his fingers ever stray from between my legs?

No.

No, they do not.

He tosses another card to the bed for me to read and then rips through my lace panties, tossing the shredded material to the floor.

"What if those were my favorite?" I tease.

"I'll buy you ten more in every color I can find," he promises, kneading my bare ass with his free hand. "Now read the card."

"Bye tim eye as sand spaying kim me...August..." My voice trembles and I whimper at his unforgiving touch.

"You can do it, Ella. One more and I promise I'll give you anything you want."

I try to focus my eyes on the card in front of me. "Bye tim eye as sand spaying kim me."

"Bite my ass..."

He doesn't wait for further instruction. As I try to work out the rest of the card he leans down and bites my ass cheek, and then licks my skin to soothe away the pain.

"Oooh myyyy God. August, please!"

"The card babe..."

"Bite my ass and...and..."

Spaying kim me

"Spank me! Bite my ass and spank me!"

Oh God, he's going to spank me too?

Yes please!

"That's my girl!" He rubs at my ass, kneading my cheeks with his strong hands and then spanks me right between my legs. I cry out at the sting to my pussy surprised at how wet I feel I response.

"Yes! August! Yes! Oh, my God! Again!"

"My girl likes to be spanked?"

Wiggling my ass in front of him, I nod. "Apparently yes."

He kneads and rubs again and then spanks me a second time, sending me into a euphoric bliss. "Fuuuuuck me! August! I need you!"

"Do you want my cock, Ella?"

"Yes! Please!"

"You're sure?" he asks. "Because once I thrust inside you, there's no going back. You're mine and I'm yours. There's never anyone else again."

"Never anyone else," I repeat. "Please August! God! I'm so fucking drenched for you."

"Stay right here while I grab a condom."

"No condoms!"

"What?"

"August you know I'm on the pill. I've been on the pill for years. And besides, if something were to happen, there's nobody else on this Earth I would rather have as the father to my children."

"Fuck, Ella. You can't say things like that."

"I'm sorry."

"Don't be sorry, babe," he chuckles leaning over me to kiss my back. "Hearing you say things like that just made my dick even harder." I feel him take his cock into his own hand behind me and line himself up with my entrance and then he sinks inside me. If my eyeballs could roll right out of my head, they would have at the deliciously full feeling his cock gives me.

"Sweet Jesus Christ. Ella." He gasps. "Fuck, you're so damn tight."

"I feel so...God I'm so full. I need to feel you fuck me, August. I want to feel you."

He brings his hands to my hips and pulls nearly all the way out and then thrusts back in. "Mother fucker. If I continue this way, I may not last long. It's too damn good. Your pussy is fucking magic."

His pace picks up as he rocks into me, my ass slapping against his taught body with every thrust. The only sound between us is his grunts and my groans and then suddenly he disconnects our bodies.

I lift my head to ask what happened but he doesn't give me the chance. He lifts me into his arms and wraps my legs around his waist before sitting himself down on the bed. He scoots back enough that he has the view he wants and then says, "Ride me, El. I want to watch you ride me." He kisses my lips and gives me one of the cutest smiles I've seen in a long time. "You're so fucking pretty and I have to watch you come apart on my dick before I can allow myself to let go. Please, Ella."

He doesn't have to tell me twice.

I would do anything for this man.

My best friend.

My lover.

Lifting myself slightly off his lap, I take his hard wet cock in my hands and line him up before lowering myself on top of him, taking him inside me inch by glorious inch.

"Yessss," August says, closing his eyes for a moment. "Just like that. Ride me, baby."

Moving against him, I slide forward and back, forward and back as he slides in and out, in and out. He leans forward and takes one of my nipples into his mouth and my lips part and I lose the ability to breathe.

"Oh!"

"Oh God!"

"Oh God! Yes!"

One breast in his mouth, he palms my left breast and pinches my nipple. "You're perfect like this, Ella," he says. "So, fucking perfect. Your pussy is..." He gasps. "It's incredible. It's like I can feel every last inch of you. I think you were made for me."

His words.

The way he looks at me with the eyes of a man madly in love.

The way his hands feel on my body. Possessive and strong but tender and warm. It's enough to send me over the edge into an oblivion I don't think I've ever experienced so intensely before.

"August! I think...I think...

"Fuuuuck, Ella."

"I think I'm going to come!"

"Go for it, baby. Ride me harder. You won't break me. Fucking take my cock all the way."

The overstimulation throughout my body is too much to bear. He circles his tongue around my nipple one last time and I'm screaming his name and wrapping my arms around his neck as my orgasm rips through me so hard my body convulses.

"Oh fuck! Ella! You're fucking milking me with your...*fuuuuucking* hell." August holds me tightly against his chest as he explodes inside me. With one hand on my back, his other hand palms the back of my head. He buries his face in my neck as we both breathe through our shattering orgasms.

"August..." I pant, barely able to make a sound. "That was..."

"I know, El. I know."

We both know. It's like we've both been waiting our whole lives for this very moment. This very grouping of minutes between us when we would be able to let the world wash away and spend the time together, just the two of us, raw, naked, explorative, and wanting.

And every single second of it was more memorable than I could have ever imagined.

"Sweet Jesus Christ. Ella." He gasps. *"Fuck, you're so damn tight."*

Relaxed and lounging in the oversized bathtub in Auggie's bathroom, my hand rests at the base of my neck as I recall some of what he said to me last night in the throes of passion.

"You've made me so fucking hard by simply existing..."

"You're perfect like this, Ella."

"I think you were made for me."

Everything about last night was magical.

The sense of humor he had in agreeing to play my game.

The way he touched me with a gentle need.

The sincerity with which he spoke to me.

August made me feel special.

Like I really meant something to him.

He didn't make me feel cheap or like I was just another wet and willing woman.

I was his.

And he was mine.

And I don' think I've been able to wipe the smile from my

face ever since. My phone dings where it sits on the shelf by the tub so I reach for it, wondering who could be writing me this late in the morning.

PAIGE

Bran is itching to set a date, but I just can't decide! Do I want a spring wedding because it's such a pretty time of year with all the flowers and pastel colors? Or do I want a fall wedding because Tuft Swallow in the fall is so beautiful now that I've lived here through the season and can attest to its beauty? I don't know what to do!

ME

Just don't have a winter wedding because New England in the winter has the potential to be brutal. I vote fall. You're right. All of upper New England is beautiful in the fall.

PAIGE

👀 But then we have to wait a whole other year to get married! And depending on the timing, I have to make sure you can be there. I need you as my maid of honor!

ME

Aww, girl you know I'll be there no matter what! But if you do it in the spring, then that doesn't leave you a ton of time to dress shop or venue shop and all that jazz.

PAIGE

Oh, that's easy. The wedding is going to be on Bran's farm. It's gorgeous out here. And as for the dress, I'm thinking of finding an antique dress and revamping it a bit. What do you think?

ME

I think as someone who lives and breathes antiques, it's the perfect idea for you. You should fly out here and come shopping with me! I bet you'll find some real showstoppers!

PAIGE

Hmm ok! Perhaps it'll be late spring. Let me talk to Bran and then we'll have to look at your hockey schedule so I know you can be there.

ME

Sounds good to me!

PAIGE

Ok tell me about you! What's new?

A wide smile fans across my face as I type out my response to her question.

ME

Oh, you know. Not much. Hockey stuff. Had sex with Auggie. Working like crazy. That's about it.

PAIGE

Wait.

PAIGE

Wait.

My phone rings in my hand and I laugh out loud as I swipe across my screen to accept the call. She doesn't even give me the chance to say hello before she screams, "WHAAAAAAAAAAAAAAAT???"

"Well hello to you too," I greet with a chuckle.

"Bitch, back that text the fuck up! I just had to reread it three fucking times to make sure I was reading it correctly! OMG you had sex with Auggie?"

I close one eye and cringe as I nod. "I totally had sex with Auggie."

"GIRL!" she shouts and then her tone completely changes as she softly and curiously asks, "How was it? Was it everything you've ever imagined it would be?"

"And sooo much more, Paige. So much more."

She gasps and then sighs audibly. "Oh my God! Tell me everything! How did it happen? Did he make the first move or was it you?" Her voice lowers. "Is he good? Like goooood good? I bet he's amazing. Oh, my God, I bet you had the best night of your whole fucking life!"

I spend the next several minutes explaining to my other best friend how amazing my night with August was in as much detail as she can handle. She laughs when I tell her about the game we played to get us where we wanted to go but swoons when I tell her about our snuggling afterwards and how Auggie said I was made for him.

"Holy shit, El. I am so freaking happy for you guys. I feel like you've waited so long for this and it's finally happening."

"Yeah. It's weird because it honestly wasn't something that crossed my mind when I planned to move out here to California, but on the other hand, moving out here to live with him felt completely normal. Like, of course I would move here and of course I would live with Auggie. Then things started happening and my thoughts would stray to those forbidden places, you know?"

"Yeah I know that feeling," she says. "I felt them with Bran. Like I had no business having sexual feelings for the quiet guy with the goat but then I couldn't stop myself."

"Yes! That's how I feel with Auggie."

"Well, for what it's worth I think the two of you are perfect for each other. I've always thought that. And one day when you're Mrs. August Blackstone, I'll be able to say I knew you two were destined to be together way before either of you did."

"Well, I suppose if that day comes, you'll have plenty to talk about during your maid of honor speech."

"Eeeek! You know I will! Years of memories to tell everyone." A bell dings on her end of the line. "Oh, I've got customers. Gotta run. I love you Ella! Let's talk again soon, okay?"

"Absolutely. Have a wonderful day, friend!"

"You too!"

CHAPTER TWENTY

AUGUST

"Get ready to shoot! Aim right for the five-hole!" I shout at Ella as she slowly maneuvers the puck toward Bear who is standing with his legs spread in front of the net. The rest of us are standing along the wall giving her pointers as she uses her special light-up hockey stick to shoot her shot. The puck goes straight through Bear's still legs and slides into the net.

"YES!" Ella pumps her fist.

"That was great, Ella!" Oliver calls from the wall. "But let's try it with him moving a little. You have to be able to anticipate where he's going to move. Which way he's going to move, and then shoot the other direction."

"Oh God, that sounds super hard."

"Nah, don't worry about it. Remember these mascots aren't players either. They can skate but they're no better at this than you are."

"I mean they're a little better than me in that they've been doing this tournament for years."

"Yeah, but you trained me for hockey for years," I remind her. "Don't forget that. You learned the skills just as much as I did. And I venture a bet you could skate rings around them."

"I sure hope so," she says as she skates back to the center of the ice and prepares to go again. This time Bear skates a little sporadically back and forth in front of the net as she moves the puck down the ice. Trying to calculate which way he'll slide so she can shoot, she's too focused on what she's doing and not keeping her eye on the puck.

"Ella look up!"

Too late.

She ends up skating right into Bear, loses her balance, and falls right in front of him. He just laughs and lends her a hand to help her up.

"Might want to try sinking the puck next time, Montgomery," he says, smiling down at her.

Wiping her brow with the back of her furry Lumin glove she gives him a cheesy smile. "Sorry about that! This is harder than I thought! How the heck do you keep your eye on the puck and watch where you're going while skating at a fast rate of speed?"

"Practice," Ledger says with an understanding nod. "Lots of practice."

"Ah. That's fair. I'd say you all deserve a raise but you get paid an ass load so I think you're good."

The guys laugh as she gets herself back to the starting point and tries shooting a goal three more times. Twice, Bear doesn't let her in, but the third time, he takes pity on her and allows the puck to slide between his legs.

"Thanks for the pity goal, Bear." She laughs and gives him a high five. "I'll take it."

"You're alright, Montgomery," he says, putting an arm around her shoulders. "You don't look too bad out there."

"You'll be the cutest pussy on the ice that's for sure," Griffin announces with a smirk.

"Watch it, Ollenberg," I say to Griffin who's standing on the ice in his blue pajama pants with pink bunnies all over them, but he only laughs and shrugs a shoulder. "What? She'll be wearing a damn cat costume and she's literally the only female mascot in the league. I'm not wrong."

He's not.

And she'll be the cutest pussy on the ice in every sense of the word.

"Come on, El. Let's get some lunch."

TODAY'S THE DAY.

Ella's big Tournament of Mascots debut.

The entire team is seated in the stands to cheer on Ella as she shines among the western conference's mascots. Our friends, the Chicago Red Tails are also in attendance tonight to cheer on their mascot, Remi Red Tail.

"What the hell are you wearing?" Dex asks from behind us as Griffin plops down beside me with a beer and a box of popcorn.

He glances at the pajama pants he chose for today's event.

"You like them? I had them custom made." He grins and lifts his jersey enough for us all to see his bubble butt of an ass. He's sporting dark blue pajama pants with yellow stars on them along with our team logo up and down each leg. "This is the inaugural wearing of these pants," he adds. "Thought today would be the perfect day for them."

Dex leans over to Colby Nelson and asks, "Why don't we have cool pants like that?"

"Because clearly Anaheim is the superior team."

Griffin points to Colby with a mouthful of popcorn. "You heard it here first folks! Fuckin' right we're the superior team."

"That was sarcasm, dumbass."

"Doesn't matter. You said it out loud mother fuckaaaa!"

"I approve of the pants, Griff," Ledger says with a laugh. "Because team spirit and all."

He leans over to Ledger and asks, "Hey. Do you know who else thought these pants were amazing?

"Who?"

He smiles and tosses a piece of popcorn into his mouth. "Marlee Remington."

We all know Ledger has had a thing for Marlee Remington for some time now but he's never done anything about it. At this point, it's just plain fun to razz him.

Ledger looks around the general area of where we're seated but Griffin chuckles. "She's not here, asshat. I saw her earlier when I came in this morning. She said I had nice pants and thinks we should have them made for the team shop. Pretty sure she tossed me an air kiss too."

Ledger smacks Griffin's arm, causing him to drop some of his popcorn. "Shut up, turd. She didn't blow you anything."

"Nah, you're right. She didn't. But maybe one day she'll blow *me* riiiiight up."

Ledger's cheeks heat and he flips Griffin the bird. "I hate you right now."

"No, you don't. You love me. Also why don't you just ask her out already?"

"Oooh who are we asking out?" Milo Landric asks. "Spill the tea back here, buddy."

Ledger's about to answer when the music fades and Jim Stabler, our team announcer, introduces today's players.

"Goooooooooood evening hockey fans! Welcome to the thirty-second annual Mascot Tournament! Tonight, we welcome our beloved mascots from the hockey league's Western Conference and celebrate our love of hockey with them as we raise funds for an incredible charity. Let's put our hands together for St. Jude's Research Hospital!"

The crowd goes wild as a video is played on the jumbotron advertising St. Jude's and the many families they have helped over the years. And then Jim continues, "Let us cheer on our favorite team mascots as I bring them to the ice starting with our very first ever female mascot, LUUUUUUUMIN!"

I pop up from my seat to cheer on my girl and the guys follow suit, each of them clapping their hands and shouting for her as she skates into the arena. As she twirls onto the ice chasing her tail and then showing off her light-up hockey stick, I notice they not only put her in our team jersey but added a sparkly blue tutu as well.

She's so damn cute out there.

I'm so proud of her.

Lumin remains on the ice giving high fives, fist bumps, and hugs to the rest of the mascots as each of them is called to center ice. In attendance tonight is Chicago's Remi Red Tail, Vancouver's Wally Wolf, Minnesota's Grizzy, Seattle's Bracken Brawler, Boulder's Yensen Yetti, Milwaukee's Pete the Parrot, L.A.'s Flip the Dolphin, Kansas City's Growler, Wyoming's Bucko Bronco, Alberta's Icer, and Portland's Ozzie Osprey.

"We'll start our Tournament tonight with the Mascot Skills test," Jim announces. "Where each of our mascots will dribble the puck from center ice to the net and take one shot. Each mascot to get their puck into the net will score one point. ARE WE READY MASCOTS?"

The crowd cheers around us as we watch on.

"Who do you think has the best skill out of all of them?" Hawken Malone asks from behind us.

The entire row of Stars players seated with me answers in tandem, "Lumin."

The Red Tails laugh, Milo clapping my shoulders. "Nothing like true love, eh, Blackstone? You've trained your team well."

True love...

I haven't really given much thought to being in love with Ella. I mean sure, I've always loved her. I've always had feelings for her whether I wanted to acknowledge them or not, but true love? Like the fairy tale stuff?

I think Milo could be on to something.

I love Ella.

But I also think I'm in love with Ella.

No. I don't think. I know.

I'm in love with Ella.

"Dude, I'd marry her right fucking now if she wanted to."

Our row goes silent and I can feel every eye on me from the guys seated around me. I get it. They've never heard me talk like this before. They know I've had the hots for Ella but it's so much more than that. This isn't one of those situations where we have to figure out if we can do life together because we've been doing life together since we could walk and talk. Really, we just had to get to the point where we could let our real feelings be known and then of course...the sex.

Had the sex been bad, it may have been bad for the stability of our relationship, but sex with Ella is any fucking thing but bad.

It's mind blowing.

Earth shattering.

Adventurous.

Satiating.

Damn. Fucking Ella is straight up fun.

She's all I've ever needed in my life.

She's all I'll ever want.

"That's right, I said it," I tell them without looking at my teammates. I only have eyes for Ella right now. "I'm that in love with her. I don't need or want anyone else. She's it for me. So yeah, if she came up here right fucking now and asked me to marry her I'd say hell yes and fly her to Vegas right now."

"That's a big step, bro." Griffin pats my shoulder. "I'm really proud of you."

"Thanks."

"But also, don't make her ask you. Give her the big grand gesture and the girly proposal." He looks out onto the ice. "Ella's a cool girl. She comes across as the type who would like that sort of thing."

I huff out a laugh. "You're not wrong. She's definitely the hearts and flowers and romance kind of girl."

"Hey speaking of Ella," Zeke Miller asks. "Do you guys know what this mysterious plan is for Remi and Lumin today?"

The guys turn to look at Zeke and then glance back at me like I'm the keeper of secrets but I shrug my shoulders in response. "What do you mean mysterious plan?"

"I don't know," he says. "But Jonah mentioned this morning that he had this plan for today's showdown and he was going to ask Ella to be a part of it."

I shake my head. "She didn't say a word about it, so whatever it is, it's also a mystery to me."

Hawken chuckles and reaches over Griffin's shoulders to grab some popcorn from his box. "I have no doubt whatever shenanigans Jonah is up to, Ella will fit in perfectly with his plan and it'll be amazing."

With mascot Grizzy acting as goalie, each of the mascots take their turn dribbling the puck and taking their shot. The first four don't make it in, but Yenson Yetti does and so does Remi Red Tail. Pete the Parrot tries to dribble down the ice but loses control of it when he hits it with his stick too hard and ends up flying after it only to fall flat on his face.

Griffin laughs. "That guy's nuts."

"I want to be him when I grow up," Harrison adds with a chuckle.

Flip, Growler, and Bucko Bronco all miss their shots when their pucks are blocked by Grizzy. The only mascots left to go are Icer and Lumin. Icer decides on a last minute slapshot that hits Grizzy in the stomach. The puck falls to the ice as does Grizzy after he grabs his stomach and bends at the waist pretending to be hurt.

"Bad form!" Dex shouts to the amusement of all of us. "Lower your weight and bend your knees next time!"

"Alright, Ella's up," I tell everyone as if they don't already know.

Come on, Babe.

You can do this.

There's a flutter in my stomach that wasn't there ten minutes ago and a tense feeling in my chest. Hell, I think I'm nervous for her.

Kind of wish I had a cinnamon roll to stuff in my face.

Ledger claps me on the shoulder. "Relax Buddy, she's got this. She's Ella."

"Yeah." I nod. "I know."

Griffin stands up and starts a slow clap as he shouts, "LU-MIN! LU-MIN! LU-MIN!"

I immediately stand up and join him as do all of us on the team. And before she even begins to dribble the puck, there's a solid chant around the arena. We watch excitedly as she pushes the button on her stick that makes it sparkle and then she kicks off with her skate down the ice. Keeping the puck in good control, she works her way closer to the net. Grizzy widens his stance and lowers his center of balance so he can move in either direction. The crowd continues to chant for Ella as she picks up speed. She's thirty feet from the net, twenty, ten...and then suddenly she spins in place, twirling with her stick in hand.

"What is she doing?" I laugh, a goofy smile on my face. She twirls once, twice, three times which confounds Grizzy. He stands up tall not understanding what's going on and that's when my girl takes her shot.

Fucking genius.

"AND IT'S IN! SCOOOOORE FOR LUMIN!" Jim announces to a crowd gone wild.

"HELL YEAH!" I shout with my fist in the air and a wide smile on my face. "THAT'A GIRL LUMIN!"

"Damn, that girl's got skill," Quinton says behind us.

Colby nods. "Carissa did something kind of like that when I taught her how to play the game." He shakes his head with a smirk. "Women and their creative ideas."

"She's a goddamn genius," I tell them.

And I love her for it.

"Alright mascots, you know what it's time for!" Stabler announces to the crowd. "It's time for round two of this Mascot Tournament of Champions as we test our dancing skills in this year's MASCOT DANCE OOOOOOOFF!"

"Oh Hell, this ought to be good." Griffin laughs and flags down a drink carrier for another beer.

"Up first to show us his boot scootin' moves, give it up for BUCKOOO BRONCO!"

With the red carpets laid out on the ice now, Bucko Bronco enters the arena as the sounds of "Cotton Eyed Joe" fill the room. He hops and jumps around like a wild stallion and then performs his line dance flawlessly as the crowd claps to the beat of the music. When his part is done he waves to the crowd and takes a bow as everyone cheers for his efforts.

"Our next performance is a group of three of our mascot favorites who just want toooo PUSH IT! Let's hear it for Pete the Parrot, Wally Wolf, aaaand Yensin Yetti!" The three crazy mascots strut into the arena wearing their sunglasses causing laughter to sound through the crowd but nothing is better than watching these three dance to Salt-N-Pepa's "Push It"! They try to perform some type of choreographed dance but no way in hell are they getting it right.

"Oh shit!" Dex laughs. "I think even I could teach them a thing or two about dancing."

Griffin snorts. "Right? I mean it's all in the pelvis, but damn, they make it look painful."

We sit through a few more dances that include a twerking dolphin, Grizzy leaping like a ballerina, Bracken Brawler moon-walking to some Michael Jackson, Ozzie Osprey dancing to "I'm a Little Tea Pot", and Icer doing the "Electric Slide". When Growler takes his turn on the ice, "I Want to Dance With Some-body" is played across the arena and the whole crowd is on their feet joining him as the rest of the mascots dance along as well. When the song ends, the stage managers come out to the ice and pull up the red carpet making us all wonder—

"Where the hell are Remi and Lumin?"

Ledger asks what we're all wondering but then the mascots scatter to the outer walls of the ice as the lights go down and the spotlight shines in the center. I can't hold back my grin knowing that whatever is going on, it's going to be epic. As soon as the tune starts to play in the arena the crowd goes absolutely wild knowing exactly what's about to happen.

"Now I've...had...the time of my life..."

"Oh shit!" Bear straight up belly laughs. "Are they for real?"

Just as the song begins, Remi steps on the ice in his skates and floats to the center of the arena followed by an unusually sparkly Lumin.

"Yep," I say with a nod. "I think they're for real." I look on in wonderment and awe as my girl dances to the ever-famous *Dirty Dancing* song with Remi, only mildly jealous that it's not me down there dancing with her.

Holy shit, she's going to skate this.

They skate their hearts out and when it comes time for the couple's famous lift, my eyes grow huge as Ella skates to the opposite end of the ice from Remi and he motions for her to skate to him. She lets herself go and flies to the other end as fast as she can and just as the two of them meet, Remi drops to his knees and lifts Ella up over his fluffy bird head to the amazement of the crowd.

"Fuck me!" I shout above the sound of the music. "She's amazing! They're amazing!"

Milo and Colby laugh behind me, clapping me on the shoulder as Milo nods. "She is definitely made for this job. It's cool that she and Remi get along so well. They can have a lot of fun together. Jonah's a good guy. He'll never disappoint."

"Ella and I were just watching his video not too long ago. Of that day when he asked out the Zamboni driver. Sorry, I forget her name."

"Giana!" Colby answers. "Oh, my God, that was a fucking fun day. When Jonah asked our wives about helping him they wouldn't stop squealing for hours. They loved being a part of it."

"Yeah." Milo nods. "And now Jonah and Giana are married! Talk about hockey love, huh?"

"Yeah." I smile. "That's really awesome."

Turning back to watch Lumin and Remi take their bows I consider the fact Ella and I aren't too much unlike Jonah and Giana. If someone would have told me I would find the love of my life in a hockey arena, I would have laughed in their face. But here she is, the mascot of our team.

Telling her about that job might very well be the best thing I have ever done. Better than any goal I've ever made or game I've ever won.

I got the girl of my dreams and I couldn't be happier.

CHAPTER TWENTY-ONE

ELLA

CHARLEE LANDRIC

GIIIIIRL! You KILLED it out there!
Congratulations on your huge mascot win!
Seriously, we were all watching online. You
were magnificent!

RORY MALONE

OMG Totally agree! And that Dirty Dancing
performing was *chef's kiss*!!!

SCARLETT

That's my girl! 😊 Did you love every second
of it?

ME

I really did! The dodgeball game is a little tough
to play in costume but the dancing and the
skills test were so much fun!

KINSLEY SHAY

Girl don't sell yourself short! You took those
guys by the balls!

ADA

Kins is right. You managed those balls better than a lot of them. And they certainly didn't mind throwing balls at a girl. LOL!

ME

Right? Geesh! To be fair, I did have a few of them ask before we went out there if it was ok. They didn't want to hurt me and they did feel bad throwing balls at me but I told them fair is fair and besides, I had a huge furry face to soften the blow. LOL 😂

RORY

Well pat yourself on the back and then take a nice hot bath. You totally deserve it!

ME

ha-ha funny you say that as I'm currently sitting in Auggie's bathtub.

CHARLEE

👀 Uh oh! Don't let us interrupt anything! #ballplayofadifferentsort

ME

BAAHAHAHAHA I promise you're not. Auggie went to the gym downstairs for his evening workout so it's just me and some music and some candles.

KINSLEY

Sounds like heaven! Nutsack never lets me get a bath with candles. He's why I can't have nice things.

ME

Nutsack. Is that what you call Quinton these days? 😏

KINSLEY

LOL! No. Nutsack is my cat. He's a hairless cat and he's nothing but trouble.

ADA

Don't you knock on my little nutsack, Kinsley!
He's an adorable little man.

KINSLEY

Oh, I don't disagree. He's lucky he's cute!

ME

You know next time I see Auggie's nutsack I'm
going to look at it as if it's an adorable little
man, right? Don't think I can unsee that now.

KINSLEY

smiles You're welcome!

CHARLEE

Well, enjoy your bath, Ella. Have a wonderfully
peaceful soak and enjoy the peace and quiet. I
imagine once Auggie gets home, it won't be
quiet for long. 😊

ME

Don't mind if I do and I think it's possible you
might be right. He was one proud boyfriend
after today.

SCARLETT

You deserve it girl! Let's chat later! Lunch this
week?

ME

Yep sounds good! Text me your schedule!

SCARLETT

Will do!

B efore I put my phone down and enjoy my soak, I scroll
through the pictures I took throughout the day today as
well as the selfies I took of Auggie and me after the game. I
choose a few and post them to my social media thanking
everyone for an incredible day filled with love and laughter and

helping to raise lots of money for charity. As I finish my post and lay my phone down on the shelf above the tub, August walks in sweaty from his workout.

"Hey beautiful. What are you up to in here?"

I give him a relaxed smile as I move some of the mounds of soap suds around in the water. "Oh, just soaking my sore muscles in the hot soapy water. I don't think I've had to work as hard as I did today in a long time."

"I believe it." He smiles. "You amazed me today..." His voice trails and his brow furrows and I feel like there's a 'but' in there somewhere.

"What's with the face?"

He gestures to me covered in soap suds. "There's too much soap in that tub, El. I can't see your tits in the water."

I snort out a laugh. "That's why they call it a bubble bath, Auggie. You weren't here so I didn't know I needed to take a peep show bath."

"Hmm, well if I can't see 'em, maybe I can touch them. Can I join you in there?"

Cocking my head I narrow my eyes and tell him, "Only if you add more hot water and maybe rub my shoulders while you're in here."

He steps over to the edge of the tub and turns on the hot water. "Babe, I'll rub more than just your shoulders if it means I get to put my hands on your body. Scoot up a bit." He pulls off his muscle-shirt and yanks down his shorts and there he is in all his naked glory.

"You could just...stand there like that for a while if you want to," I tell him, completely ogling him from head to toe.

He grins. "You like what you see, Montgomery?"

I nod lazily, completely relaxed. "Mhmm."

Slowly sliding into the huge tub behind me, Auggie wraps a gentle arm around me and pulls me against his body. "Come here." He brings his other hand around my waist as well and kisses the back of my neck. "You smell nice. Like vanilla and berries."

"That would be all this soap."

"I like it. Makes me want to eat you, El."

"Eat away," I tease, letting my head fall back against is shoulder. "This tub might be the best part of your entire apartment. Well, except for you, of course. It just helps me feel completely relaxed."

"I'm glad to hear it," he says, placing his strong hands on my shoulders and gently kneading away any tension. "Want to know a secret?"

"Yes. Of course."

"What if I told you I've soaked in this tub after a long day and jacked off to thoughts of you being in here with me?"

His question brings a smile to my face. "You have?"

"Mhmm. On more than one occasion. Many times right after our Tuesday night chats."

"And what do you think about when you're in here jacking off to thoughts of me?"

He nibbles my earlobe and then kisses just behind my ear. "I think about you sitting with me just like this."

"Mhmm...what else?"

He brings his warm wet hands to my breasts. "I think about having these babies in my hands while you relax against me just like you are now. So, I can roll them or knead them or just hold them in my hands."

"I'm not going to lie, Aug, your hands on my breasts is Heaven."

He murmurs softly in my ear. "How about you reach up there and turn the hot water off and then I'll spend some time helping you relax."

That sounds like a fair deal to me.

I do as he asks and then slide back between August's legs, my knees bent as we share the tub space. Gently he slides his hand between my knees separating them and bringing his feet to the inside of my ankles so my legs are effectively pinned wide open for him. Then he brings his hands back to my breasts, holding them like two precious globes and feathering his thumbs over my nipples.

"You have gorgeous breasts, Ella."

"Oh, now you think they're nice? Nice enough to turn you on?" I tease. "Because a couple of months ago you said—"

"Fuck what I said a couple of months ago. I was wrong. The fact of the matter is, I wanted you then too. I was just too much of a coward to say it."

"Auggie..."

He brings one hand up my neck and palms my throat. "But you're mine now, babe. And I'll be damned if I don't spend the rest of our days together letting you know just how much you affect me."

"Yeah?"

"Mhmm."

His hold on my throat turns me on more than I ever expected it would. I can feel the weight of his hand when I swallow. "And how are you going to do that?"

He kisses behind my ear one more time and murmurs, "First I'm going to make you come with my hand. And then I'm going to make you come again on my cock, right here in this tub."

Oh, my God. Yes!

"Well, you've got me by the throat, August. So, I'm not going anywhere."

"Damn right you're not," he chuckles behind me as he slides his hand down my wet body right between my legs. "Not until I've visited and made a mess of the Pussy District... Twice."

He feathers his fingers over my pussy and even though I'm

sitting in a bathtub filled with warm water, I can still feel that I'm wet for him. I whimper when he touches me, the tenderness of his contact making me ache for more.

"August..."

"I know, babe, but I can't help myself. I enjoy touching you too much," he explains as he pushes one finger and then another inside me. "It's like I'm finally making up for all the years that I kept my feelings for you buried deep inside."

"You didn't have to do that," I tell him as I arch my back against him, the pressure of his fingers filling me, bringing me to life. "You could have told me."

"I couldn't tell you, El. I was too chicken to tell you. I didn't want to lose you, but I have you now."

"Fuck, Aug, you sooo have me now. Please, make me come."

He works his mouth around my neck as he curls his fingers inside me and flicks my clit with his thumb. My mouth falls open as I jerk up but he holds me still, his hand gripping my throat with just enough pressure.

"You going to fall apart on my fingers, El?"

"If you don't cut that out, I most certainly am!" I gasp. "God! You feel good."

He turns my head so my lips meet his and dips his tongue into my mouth, kissing me with force as his fingers continue to move inside me. With nowhere to brace myself except for Auggie's legs, I push against his knees to try to get any type of leverage but he's got me pinned. I have no choice but to take the onslaught of pleasure as his fingers work my pussy.

"Jesus, Auggie, I'm so close already."

"Good. I want to hear you come." He flicks my clit with added pressure from his thumb and pinches one of my nipples, twisting it in his fingers as he bites my bottom lip.

"Fuck! Auggie! I'm going to...oh God..."

My eyes squeeze shut and my mouth falls open once again

only this time it's my voice ringing out from inside it as I groan so loud I wonder if Auggie's neighbors hear me. When I come back to my senses, Auggie wraps his arms around me and kisses me once, twice, three times around my neck.

"Sit up just a smidge for me."

I hold on to the sides of the tub and raise myself up, watching behind me as he grips his large cock and strokes it from root to tip. He moans to himself and then swings a hand around my waist once again.

"Alright I'm ready, babe. Have a seat on my cock." He guides me back down lining himself up with my entrance and then without warning thrusts his pelvis upwards and slams me down on him.

"Oh, my God!" I groan as he stretches me, filling me with his girth.

"Fuuuck," he moans. "So goddamn tight." He takes a few deep breaths and blows them out. "You're incredible, El. Fucking incredible." He pulls me back against him so my back rests against his chest and then pulls his knees up so I'm basically cradled in his lap. He palms both of my breasts, squeezing my nipples, and then pushes his pelvis up again impaling me with his cock.

I gasp. "Oh fuck! August!"

"Babe, your pussy is so tight like this." He grunts against my ear. "I'm sorry that I won't last long because you feel so fucking good." He thrusts up again and then again creating a pounding rhythm of penetration that has me at the precipice in a matter of seconds. Water sloshes around us as his movement creates crashing waves. It spills out onto the bathroom floor but we pay it no mind. The messier the better.

"Yes! August!" I shout. "It's sooo fucking good. Please... please don't stop."

He palms my tits and thrusts into me, the sound of his

grunts turning me on more than I ever could have thought possible. "Fuck, El. I'm almost there."

"Harder, Auggie. More!" I cry. "I need you."

His hold on my tits is strong and unrelenting as he pumps into me and pulls my body down over him. I give him whatever help I can but I can't move much in this position. Our skin slaps together as our bodies connect and it is music to my ears. To finally have the ability to connect to August like this, skin to skin, is euphoric. He reaches down between my spread legs and rubs my clit with his finger as he fucks me and that's all I need to reach the edge of the cliff and jump fearlessly right off. My body shakes and my stomach hollows and then I'm screaming his name once again.

"August! Oh God! Fuck! I'm coming, August!"

My pussy spasms and clamps like a vise around his cock as I come. He gasps and grunts loudly in my ear. "Shit! It's so...fucking...tight!" He grips my hips and holds me still as he pumps harder and faster a few more times and then he explodes inside me. "Ahh, shit. Fucking Hell..."

His cock still inside me, he lightens his hold on me, his touch now soft and tender. He kisses my shoulder and then nuzzles his chin into the crook of my neck hugging me to him and holding me for a few calm, warm moments while we come down from our highs.

"What if I told you I want to get a tattoo?" he murmurs a few minutes later.

"I would say let's go!" I turn my head slightly so I can see him. "What kind of tattoo?"

"A tree."

"A tree?"

"Mhmm."

"Why a tree?"

He slides his warm wet hand over my left breast, his fingers tracing the small owl tattoo I have there. "Because the owl needs a tree."

His answer takes my breath away.

The owl needs a tree.

"That might be one of the most meaningful things anyone has ever said to me, Auggie." I swallow back tears because I don't want to make too much of his comment but also, I think I just fell a little harder for this man.

My best friend.

My home.

"What if I told you I never knew sex with someone I love could be so powerful?" he asks.

His question makes me smile. I place my hands over his, rubbing them slowly up and down his arms. "Aww, you love me?" I tease, knowing all too well that we've always loved each other.

"Let me rephrase," he says, huffing out a soft chuckle. "What if I told you sex with someone I'm so madly in love with I can't think straight half the time, could be so fucking powerful that I can't remember what my life was like before she got here?"

Oh.

Okay.

That's a little different.

The owl needs a tree...

He's not just saying he loves me.

He's saying...

I go quiet for a moment replaying his words in my mind a few times as if they're affirmations I'm forcing myself to remember. "You're in love with me?"

"Ella, I'm so far gone I don't even know what to do with myself anymore," he tells me, grasping my hands in his. "I love you so damn much it hurts sometimes. Like, it physically hurts when you're not with me. When I can't see you. Or talk to you."

I smirk playfully. "Well, when you put it that way it sounds more like an obsession."

"Then I'm unapologetically obsessed with you," he says, placing a kiss on the side of my face. "Since the day I watched you ride the escalator down the stairs at the airport wearing my old hockey sweater I knew something was different. I knew something had changed about the way I saw you. You were stunning and if I could've held you for hours that day right there in the airport I would have. Being near you makes me feel...whole."

I don't like that he's saying all these wonderful things to me and I can't see his face because of the way we're sitting, so I stand up and step out of the tub. His eyes are on me the whole time and I'm certain he's confused as to why I haven't said much. Grabbing a towel, I wrap it around myself and then hold one open for him. With a curious smile on his face, he steps out of the tub and pulls the chain to let it drain and then allows me to cover him with the towel I have for him.

"Ella?"

Without responding, I take his hand and lead him into his bedroom where I tug open his towel, letting it fall to the floor, and gesture for him to have a seat on the edge of the bed. I drop my towel as well and then gently climb into his lap, wrapping my legs around his waist and my arms around his neck. His body, though still wet from our bath is warm and comfortable. I stare into his eyes for several long seconds, taking in the whole of this man, my best friend who makes me feel like the most loved woman on this planet.

He opens his mouth to speak but I stop him, bringing my finger to his lips. Then I cup his face in my hands, my fingers splaying over the scruff of trimmed beard, and press my lips to his. When I gently pull back his eyes are trying to read mine, so I smile and finally tell him,

"August Blackstone I couldn't be more in love with another human being if I tried."

The air leaves his lungs in one long sigh as if he's been holding his breath this whole time. He closes his eyes for a second, but when I thread my fingers through his wet locks and smooth my thumb down his cheek he opens them again and gazes at me with an expression of pure joy. Pure love. Pure adoration.

"I knew I loved you before I ever got on that plane," I tell him, my eyes never leaving his. "I've wanted you for years but we never went down that road and I wasn't about to be the one to mess everything up between us. I was content to always be your best friend. But being here with you has been better than anything I could have ever imagined."

His strong hands wrap around my ass. He pulls me as tightly against him as he can and feathers his hands down my back, causing goosebumps to appear on my skin.

"You make me feel safe. You make me feel like I can do literally anything I ever want to do. You make me whole, August."

"I'm sorry, El," he says. "I'm sorry I wasn't strong enough to tell you soon—"

"Neither of us was strong enough back then, Auggie." I shake my head. "There is nobody to blame here and nothing to blame anyone for. We're here now. Together. You and me."

"Forever?" His brows raise and I see the hopeful glint in his eyes. Though there's a flutter in my stomach, there's also a lightness in my chest that makes my response so amazingly simple.

"Forever."

"I love you, Ella."

"I love you, Auggie."

CHAPTER TWENTY-TWO

AUGUST

It's the game I've been dreading all season.

Anaheim verses the New Orleans Gators.

Any other game we play during the season doesn't affect me. It's just another game. Another team. But the New Orleans Gators aren't just another team. Not to me. The Gators is the team my childhood rival, Jeff Furbling, was playing for when I ended his career. By all means it shouldn't be a big deal now. It's been seven years since that day. Almost eight. But that doesn't mean I don't think about what happened every single time I play against this team. To him, I'm positive it's a huge deal. It doesn't help that in past years Furbling would ramp up his social media bashing of me during the week leading up to the game. Oddly enough though, this past week has been relatively silent.

Does that make me feel any better about this game?

Not even a little.

It's the guilt.

The whole idea that not only did I land the crushing blow that resulted in the end of another player's career, but that it was Jeff fucking Furbling. He was someone I knew. He was someone I trained with. Someone who went through everything I had gone through to get where we are. Well, were. We were friends way back when, before we became rivals. Before we really knew what competition was. Before we had to compete against each other to prove we were the best. Now he's not on the ice anymore and that's all because of me. Now every time we play the Gators that same sinking feeling comes back like a punch to the gut. I know it wasn't my fault directly. I know I didn't walk into that game planning to hurt anyone let alone end someone's career, but the fact of the matter is it happened.

It all fucking happened.

And as much as I sort of despise the guy now, the guilt of what I did still sits with me.

"Hey." Ella nudges my shoulder at dinner before the game, her brows pinched with worry. "What's going on with you?"

"Huh?"

"Why are you all up in your head today?"

"What do you mean?"

She cocks her head and gives me that don't-shit-me look. "Auggie, you forget I know you inside and out. Not to mention your ice practice this morning sucked. You missed six out of thirteen shots and that's not like you at all."

"You watched practice this morning?"

"Yeah." She shrugs. "I had a meeting with Marlee and then some promo videos to make so I figured I would pop down and watch a bit when I was done. You were kind of sluggish. Even Hicks called you out about it."

"Yeah. He did." I nod not wanting to recount Coach's reprimand.

"So, what's going on?" she asks me, rubbing my back gently. "Do you need to talk about it?"

"Nah." I shake my head. "Just my stupid past punching me in the stomach again."

Realization hits her and she cringes. "Oooh, the Gators." She palms her forehead. "I'm so sorry, Auggie. I was so busy this week I didn't even consider what team we were playing tonight."

"It's okay."

"It's also okay that it bothers you still," she tells me.

"It pisses me off that it still bothers me," I finally confess. "It's been years. What happened, happened. I can't do anything to change it. I've apologized over the years. I've sent gifts, I've donated to charities. Anything I could do to get him the fuck off my back."

"Has it been bad again this year? I honestly don't remember seeing much of anything about it on social media."

"Actually, it's been eerily calm," I tell her.

A relieved smile appears on her face and she pats my forearm. "Well maybe that's a good thing then! Maybe he's finally realized he's been a complete douchebag to you over the years and you don't deserve it. Maybe he's decided to fuck all the way off and leave you alone because his words fall on deaf ears anyway."

"Deaf ears?" I scoff. "Ella, his words are heard by every fan out there."

"And those fans have watched you play your heart out for the past six years," she reminds me adamantly. "They've watched you grow up and become a man. They've supported you through all your growth and encouraged you along the way. They've cheered for you and loved you and they encourage you and love you now. Need I remind you that last year when he started in with all his bullshit several fans came to your defense?"

She's right.

That did happen.

And it felt damn good.

"I guess you're right."

"I know I'm right." She smiles that smile that melts me every time. The smile that makes me want to lift her up and squeeze her against me. The one that makes me want to take her home and do all I can to hear those little sighs and moans and screams of pleasure that turn me the fuck on.

Because she's my safe space.

She calms the storms in my head.

She's my home.

"So maybe instead of sitting here washed in your own self-loathing, you turn the attitude around and tell yourself it wasn't your fault. Injuries are part of the game. You're not without injuries in your career either, Auggie. You've just been able to recover from yours. You've grown from them and you've become a better, stronger player because of them. You don't let shit get you down. You're August fucking Blackstone."

I am August fucking Blackstone.

"Have I told you lately how much I love you?"

She shrugs and smiles at me again. "I mean, maybe not since this morning when we went opposite directions after walking into this building."

I cup her face in my hands and kiss her soft lips and then rest my forehead against hers. "I love you, Ella Montgomery. And I have no idea where the hell I would be in this life without you by my side."

"I love you too, Auggie. And it feels so good to finally say those words and mean them in the way I've meant them for a long time."

"Ditto."

I slip my hand behind her head and bring her lips to mine. I explore her mouth as her tender lips float against mine and we both sink into this kiss. Fuck, what I wouldn't give to be able to take her behind closed doors somewhere in this arena so we can fu—

"Hey! Get a room!" A balled-up napkin hits my face and falls to my plate. I don't even have to look to know it was Griffin, but nevertheless I glance in that direction anyway and there he sits, with an ornery smirk on his face a couple tables away. Dressed in pair of pajama pants with hot dogs all over them and an Oscar Meyer Weiner t-shirt, he gives us a cheesy wave with the flit of his fingers and we both laugh.

"He's such a doof," Ella says softly.

I couldn't agree more.

SOMETHING FEELS OFF.

I felt the tension on the ice during warmup in the way a few of the Gators would look our way but there was nothing I could do. Sometimes we get a vibe from the visiting team that they didn't come to play. They came angry and that's the vibe I'm getting from the Gators.

But what the fuck do they have to be mad about?

"You feel that too?" Ledger asks as he skates past me and swirls back around the net to where I am. "It's odd, right?"

I nod. "Yeah. I can't pinpoint it and I don't like it. I have a feeling this is going to be a rough one tonight."

"I think you may be right. Guess we better bring our A-game, yeah?" He nudges my arm and then skates off.

Yeah.

A-game.

I let my body take over the rest of our warmup, going

through the motions and doing what always needs to be done, but all the while I search the ice and glance through the stands for anything out of the ordinary that might give me a clue as to what the hell has me on edge. It's not like Jeff Furbling is back on the ice and it's not like I haven't played against the Gators numerous times since that day. Sure, they have some new team members just like we do but that's nothing to be stressed about. It happens with every team every season. I catch sight of Lumin in the stands being interviewed by a member of the press team and feel better knowing she's safe in the hands of team staffers.

That's my girl up there doing her thing.

She's my rock.

My safe place.

The one I get to sleep next to at the end of this night.

Reminding myself that regardless of how this game turns out, in a few short hours, I'll have Ella in my arms again and with any luck my cock buried deep inside her makes all the tension dissipate from my body.

Let's just get this fucking game over with.

We get through the pregame ceremonies with no problems but the game itself starts out with a flurry of drama. Oliver faces off against the Gators' center, Mickey Fyte. Oliver wins the puck but breaks his stick on the draw. Harrison gets an early touch on the puck and keeps possession long enough to get it passed to Ollenberg who's off to a good start. We're able to keep the puck under an Anaheim hold for a solid thirty seconds of game play before we lose it to the Gators. Bear blocks their first shot attempt and sends the puck back to Ollenberg who shoots it down the ice. I'm able to sweep in for the take, but without warning, I'm checked by Homer Offerston from the Gators, hit hard behind the net. It quickly becomes three on one and they refuse to let up, each one of them crashing into me as if it's all legal game play.

What the ever-loving fuck?

I lose my balance and fall but not before I hear, "Furbling says hello Blackstone." Offerston sneers and I swear I hear him mumble something like, "Punk ass Rumpleforeskin."

"What the fuck are you doing?" Harrison shouts at Offerston with Griffin and Ledger right behind him.

With a swing of a fist Garrison adds, "That was completely uncalled for, you potato face humpty bitch!"

Fists fly and words are shouted and a couple helmets are knocked off as six of us fight on the ice. I land a few solid punches to Offerston and one of his comrades who I don't recognize and one of them grabs my jersey before landing an uppercut to my chin. "We played with Furbling back in the day, fuck nut," the guy says to me. "We saw what you did."

Son of a fucking bitch, so this is how it's happening now?

Instead of social media posts he's resulted to letting former teammates fight it out for him?

"You don't know shit," I spit back at him. "So, fuck off limp dick!" I get a few more hits in before the referee breaks us up, but now I'm revved up and ready to kick some Gator ass.

"You okay Blackstone?"

"Never better," I tell him, feeling the heat of anger boiling up inside me already. I fix my helmet and look up at the jumbotron to see we're only a little over a minute into the first period of the game.

Seriously?

A fight in the first minute of the game is not a good omen.

But fuck the Gators.

Karma's a bitch and all is fair in the game of hockey.

And fuck Furbling.

If he wants to fight, he can fucking show up and do it himself.

Homer is called to the penalty box and I'm off to the bench

to get cleaned up. Quite sure I'm cut above my eye because there's blood on my glove. The team has a two-minute power-play, but a second stringer takes my place on the ice.

"What the hell was that about?" Anthony, our team medic, asks me while taking a quick look at me eye.

"Nothing important."

"Hey Blackstone!" a fan calls from behind the glass. "I heard you were the worst player on the last team too."

I pay no attention to the stupid cunt in the stands. Most of our fans who pay enough to sit this close to the ice are damn near drunk by game time anyway.

"It doesn't look bad. I'm just going to steri-strip it and put a band-aid over it for now. We'll revisit it after the game unless it gets worse." Anthony dabs the wound with alcohol and cleans it up before covering it with the appropriate bandages and then sends me on my way. I'm ready to get myself back in the game.

Because Offerston's got it coming.

"Hey Blackstone, you're definitely not pregnant because this period is slamming you!"

"Yeah? Then you can suck my bloody dick asshole," I mumble right before jumping the wall and reentering the game.

The Gators finally get the puck into our territory and Bear has to be fast on his feet. He blocks a shot and sends it back down the ice but it's rebounded and shot at him again, this time banking off the net. I loop around as the puck slides right to me and pass it off to Ledger until I can get out from behind the net. Once I'm back in the open, Griffin dribbles the puck down the ice with me out in front clearing his path. The crowd gets louder the closer to the net we get. Griffin looks at me and smiles with a wicked grin that tells me he's about to do something stupid and then he comes to a screeching halt, looks at Findley, the goalie for the Gators, and says, "Hey man. How many wieners do you think I can deep throat at one time?"

And then without even looking he passes the puck to me, and I shoot it into Findley's five hole to score the first goal of the game. The siren blows and the crowd erupts and all I can do is laugh as the guys crowd around me and give me celebratory hugs.

"Well done Blackstone, but what the fuck was that?" Oliver asks with a laugh as he collides into me, slapping my helmet.

I'm laughing right along with him as I shrug. "Hell, if I know! Griffin was being Griffin!"

"What did you say to Findley?" Harrison asks when Griffin approaches. "And what the hell were you doing? That wasn't the play."

"Yeah, I know," he says with a smirk. "I took a page out of Ella's fake-out playbook but I didn't think I could twirl the way she did, so I just asked him how many wieners he thought I could deep throat at one time."

Harrison, Ledger, Oliver, and I crack up laughing. "You are something else, Ollenberg," I tell Griffin as I give the guy a hug.

"I thought you deserved a little revenge since they came after you so fucking early tonight."

"Thanks, man. I owe ya one."

"Nah. That's what friends are for."

Griffin and I set off to the other side of the ice to sit out this next shift. I grab my water bottle and take a few long chugs when I hear a fan from somewhere behind us yell, "Hey Blackstone! Don't be such a pansy next time. You've got to want it if you're going to survive!"

"Yeah okay fuckhead," I mumble, not bothering to look behind me. Fans heckle us all the time, it's nothing new.

Griffin chuckles and then nudges me with his elbow. "Yeah Blackstone. Pansy ass mother fucker. You've got to want it."

"What do I want?" I ask him with a smirk.

He shrugs. "I don't know. To knock that guy's teeth out maybe? He was trying to give me shit earlier too."

"Drunk ass bitch most likely."

"Without a doubt."

"Hey Blackstone!" the guy shouts again. "Tell your girl to stop changing her lipstick color! My dick looks like a rainbow!"

A few fans get a hearty laugh out of the heckles being tossed my way and as much as I usually let them roll off my back, I'm so not in the mood tonight. Especially when he starts talking about my girl.

Nobody talks about Ella like that and gets away with it. I start to turn around but Griffin grabs my jersey and pulls my attention back to the game. Without looking at me he says, "Don't give them the satisfaction man. It'll only get you in trouble."

"Yeah but they're talking about Ella."

He laughs. "Dude, they don't know who the fuck they're talking about. They probably don't even know who Ella is let alone know that she's across the ice in the stands leaving a little sparkle everywhere she fucking goes. They're drunk. Let them be drunk. They're not hurting anyone."

They're pissing me off.

But I suppose he's right.

I get paid millions of dollars to play the game I love and they're probably waking up every day and going to a job they can't stand. I suppose I can take their drunk heckles without taking it personally. He rolls his eyes and shakes his head before he takes a huge gulp of water. "Stupid fucking drunks." He tosses his water bottle and gestures to me. "Ready?"

"Yep."

THE STARS ARE UP three to two nearing the end of the third period when I come off the ice for my last shift break, this time with Ledger by my side.

"Tough game," Ledger says, handing me a water bottle as he's also handed one for himself.

"Bunch of mother fucking assholes if you ask me."

"Aww." Ledger cocks his head. "Is someone salty because he got his pretty little face nicked up?" He laughs and pats my head as someone shouts from behind us.

"Hey Blackstone! You got any naked pictures of your girl-friend?" When I don't answer him after a second or two, he adds, "Want me to send you some?"

"Fucking son of a bitch." I stand up to finally say something to the asshole fan behind us but Ledger grabs my arm and yanks me back down.

"Not a chance, Blackstone."

I stare at him incredulously and he merely shrugs in response with an annoyed laugh. "We need you in the game. And the next game. Don't go getting yourself ejected because of some stupid fan. The game's almost over anyway then he'll be out of your hair."

"Just one good hit. Come on," I whine.

"Sorry, son." Ledger smiles. "Take it out on the punching bag in the gym later."

I'd really like to take it out on that heckler's face.

"Going to Jay's after the game?"

"I imagine so," I tell him with a nod. "Unless Ella's not up for it, but otherwise count us in."

"That's the spirit." He stands and throws his leg over the wall. "Let's go kick some Gator ass."

We're about to retake the ice when the same heckling fan shouts at me one more time. "Hey Blackstone! You finally got your sweet little pussy to this side of the country, huh?"

My brows furrow and my body stiffens at the mention of my girl being on this side of the country.

"Are you just fucking her or are you fucking her over like you did me?"

My veins turn ice cold as my body freezes. I squeeze my eyes closed and try to take a calming breath and then I bravely turn around only for my eyes to land on the one person I never wanted to have to see again.

Jeff Furbling.

"Don't," Ledger says to me, trying to get me to refocus my energy. "Leave it on the ice August. He's a nobody. And he's just trying to get under your skin."

"Yeah well, he fucking succeeded. And he's not a nobody."

"Who is he?"

Jeff stands up and cups his hands around his mouth so he knows I'll hear what he has to say. "You might have her now, Blackstone, but I had her first! And she was a fucking good time!"

"You mother fucking son of a bitch!" I scream, stepping to the far side of the bench and lifting my leg to stand up on it. Whatever I have to do to get to this mother fucker. "Just wait till I—"

"Whoa, whoa, whoa," I'm pulled off the bench as I watch Furbling lick his lips and wave back at me. "Stop! Stop! Just stop, Blackstone. Take a fucking deep breath."

"Don't tell me what the fuck to—"

I finally catch sight of who's talking to me and notice it's

Coach Hicks, but I'm so fucking pissed off I can't even see straight right now.

"I'm sorry, Coach. But—"

"But what? You think you're going to climb this glass and fuck that guy up?" he shouts at me.

I huff, my cheeks red with anger as my blood heats throughout my body. "If you give me the fucking chance, yeah!"

"Who the hell is that guy? Do you know him?"

"Yeah." I huff out a breath again and finally say, "It's Jeff Furbling."

Coach's brow furrows as he repeats the name. "Jeff... Furbling. Furbling...why do I know that name?"

"Because he played for the Gators in his rookie year, sir. When I was playing for North Carolina. But he got checked during a game and I was in that game and I was the last person to run into him. I gave him the crushing blow that ended his career. It was a fucking accident but he hasn't let it go and I get it but what the FUCK am I supposed to do about it now?"

Coach stares at me for a moment, and seeing the frustration and irritation in my whole self asks, "Do you need out, Blackstone? Done for the night?"

"What?" I ask, almost pissed off that he would even offer me the chance to run away.

Like that's happening.

"Fuck no. I want to play. And then I want to kick that guy's fucking ass for good."

Coach's jaw ticks as he looks to me and then up in the stands to Furbling. "He's drunk, August. Anyone can see that. Get out there and finish the game. Fuck that guy."

He doesn't have to tell me twice. The ice is one of the only places where I can focus. My body knows what to do so my brain can figure out what the absolute fuck just happened.

"Blackstone, you good?" Oliver shouts as I rejoin the team for some endgame action.

"I'm fucking fine!"

CHAPTER TWENTY-THREE

AUGUST

I'm so not fine.

Did he mean what he said?

Did he have Ella before I did?

Did they sleep together?

Were they a thing and I didn't know?

Would she have kept that from me?

"I had her first! And she was a fucking good time!"

I want to make myself believe Furbling was lying to get under my skin. In my mind, there's no way anything has happened between him and Ella. I would have known. She would have told me back then. We told each other everything.

But Hell! He certainly knows how to get under my skin.

I wish I could talk to Ella. Ask her. Find out the truth so all the whirling emotions fighting each other in my brain would calm the fuck down. I wish I could just grab her and get the fuck out of here, but I can't yet. We both have responsibilities right after the game. She's busy upstairs getting pictures taken with fans, and Griffin, Barrett, and I are on tap to sign autographs out on the ice.

As soon as the buzzer sounds, the crowd roars and we celebrate another hard-fought win. We shake hands with the other team even though all I want to do is beat the shit out of every last one of them. I don't even make eye contact as I move through the line and then I'm off to the tunnel where I hand our equipment manager my gear and wait for Griffin and Barrett. Bear's the last one off the ice and he looks just as pissy as I feel.

"Let's get this done and get the fuck out of here," he says.

"Don't have to tell me twice."

"Aww, what's the matter, gentlemen?" Griffin says with a hand on each of our shoulders. "Bad night?"

"Fuck off, Ollenberg," Bear says to him as we step back out on the ice.

"Hey what happened back there? With the coach?" Griffin asks.

"I don't want to talk about it right now. I'm pissed off enough."

We skate up to the crowd of people who are in line to have things autographed. Some have t-shirts, some have pictures purchased from the team shop, and some have special personal items they want us to sign. Working our way down the line, I follow Griffin, signing my name to each item held out and saying hello to the fans. I thank them for coming to the game and for their support. Usually this is a fun thing to do after a game but my mind is anywhere but on what I'm doing. This is just a distraction from what I want to be focused on.

All I want to do is find Ella.

And I do.

When a naked picture of her is thrust in front of me.

"Thought you could sign this for me, August. It's one of my favorites."

I snap the picture from his hands before I lift my eyes to see Jeff Furbling standing in front of me with a fucking smirk on his face. My nostrils flare and my face heats as I stare back at his ugly face and then glance down at the photo in my hands. Inside my stomach is churning and every person standing here for an autograph has turned to shadow. I can't focus on anything or anyone.

"Fuck you, Furbling. This isn't even—" I look down at the picture in my hand again and bile rises in my throat. I want so fucking badly for this to be a hoax. I want so badly to beat the shit out of Furbling for even trying to make me believe that he slept with my girl. But this may very well be my very worst nightmare coming true. All the blood drains from my face. My heart pounds, my body tenses, and my stomach hollows at the tiny detail in this picture that tells me it is indeed Ella.

The owl tattoo right above her heart.

"She's a sweet little fuck, isn't she August?" He laughs. "Should we ask her whose cock she likes better?"

That's it.

I can't do this anymore.

Can't be the nice guy.

All.

I.

See.

Is.

Red.

Red everywhere.

Before I know what the fuck I'm doing, I grab Furbling and yank him over the wall. His back hits the ice and he tries to say something but I refuse to give him one more word until I've hit him at least once so I pull my fist back and punch his face.

"Did she know?" I shout at him. "Did she fucking know you took that picture?"

All he does is laugh so I pound into his face with my fist as hard and as fast as I can.

Oh my God he took pictures of her!

"You fucking son of bitch!" Hit number two.

She slept with Jeff?

How could she do this to me?

"You stay the fuck away from her..." Hit three.

"Or I swear to God I will fucking kill you with my own two hands." I get three more hard hits in before Barrett and Griffin grab me from behind and pull me off Furbling who tries to get up and fight back and slips on the ice and falls. With my teammates holding me back and pulling me toward the tunnel, I shout, "You should be glad I didn't slit your fucking throat with my skate!"

"Dude, shut the fuck up!" Griffin says as he strong-arms me into the tunnel. "What the fuck are you doing August?

"You'll be lucky if you don't get yourself thrown in jail for that mess," Barrett warns.

"Do you think I give two shits about that?"

They toss me in an empty room somewhere in the hallway that leads to the locker rooms. When I glance around I can see it's one of the physical therapy rooms. Griffin stands next to me while Bear stands in the doorway, effectively blocking it with his arms folded in front of him.

"Start talking," Griffin commands.

"He slept with Ella."

"Who slept with Ella?" He hitches his thumb toward the door. "That guy?"

"That guy was Jeff Furbling."

Griffin's brows pinch. "Furbling...why do I know that—"

"Because he was the guy who played for the Gators when I was rookie. The guy who had a career ending injury during the game and hasn't played since."

"Ooookay..."

"Because I was the final blow. I played in that game when I was with the Sharks," I tell him, trying to take a deep breath.

"He got checked pretty massively only I didn't see it all happen at the time so when I came in hot and bounded into him again, the crash snapped his body in too many places. He never fucking recovered enough to get back on the ice."

"August, that's so not your fau—"

"He fucking slept with her, Griffin!" I seethe, interrupting what I know he was going to say. "He slept with Ella. Fucked her and then took fucking pictures of her!"

I'm so hot I don't know how I'm not physically exploding right now. My mind is coming up with irrational thoughts, I'm losing any and all ability to think coherently. I'm just so fucking pissed off. It's like the world just tilted and threw everything I've ever known off balance.

"She's been fucking with me this whole damn time!"

"Wait." Barrett's brows furrow and he cocks his head. "What?"

"She told me she loved me, but she slept with..." I shake me head. "She slept with the one person on this earth that I...I can't..."

"AUGGIE?" Her voice rings down the hall as rage builds up inside me. "AUGUST!"

"He's in here," Barrett says, leaning his head out the doorway. I hear her clopping down the hallway, which tells me she's still in her costume. When she rounds the door, she's carrying her mascot head in her hands, her face is red, and she's a little sweaty. She takes one look at me face and is by my side instantly, her hands cupping my face as she assesses my injuries.

"Oh, my God! Auggie! What the hell happened to you?"

Seething with anger I look her square in the eye and say, "You happened to me."

Her expression falls. "What?"

I push her hands away from my face and stand from the

exam table where I was sitting. She flinches as she steps back, her eyes bulging, and her brows furrowed. "Auggie, talk to me." She shakes her head. "I don't understa—"

"You never understand, do you? Because you don't fucking want to. You just waltz into someone's life and assume they'll take care of you and give you everything you could ever want because that's all you do is take, take, take, isn't it?"

"Auggie...?"

"What's the matter Ella? Jeff Furbling didn't do enough for you so you came out here to California to charm me into falling for you?"

"What?" She frowns. "What are you even talking about?"

"You FUCKED him, Ella!" I shout, my voice growing rough. I stare at her intensely so she can see the raw emotion in my eyes. "You spread your legs wide open for that fucking son of a bitch and you asked him to stick his dick inside you. You fucked him."

"I...I didn't..."

"You DID, Ella!" I step into her personal space, towering over her, making myself as huge as possible. "Don't fucking deny it because you know what he showed me today? He showed me a goddamn naked picture of you!" I hold up the picture in my hand and toss it at her. "Did you know he had those? Huh? Did you know he took fucking pictures of you while you slept...NAKED? Or did you actually pose for these?"

A look of horror falls over her face and tears spring to her eyes as they flit to Griffin and Bear but I shake my head. "Don't look at them! Look at ME!" I shout at her. "I'm the one standing RIGHT FUCKING HERE!" I huff. "I'm the one who gave you whatever you wanted! I'm the one who bent over backwards to make sure you were cared for here! I'm the one who gave up my lifestyle when you showed up so you wouldn't feel uncomfortable! I'm the one you seduced with your pretty little tits and walking around my apartment in lingerie, crying to me about the lack of orgasms in your life. But it turns out you're nothing but a whore, isn't that right, Ella?"

"Aug—"

"Shut up, Griffin!"

Ella shakes her head, tears spilling down her cheeks. Her lip trembles and she nearly chokes back a sob when she whimpers, "That's not true, Auggie."

"Stop calling me that. My name is August. Only my best friend gets to call me Auggie and you are certainly not that person."

I step away from her toward the door but I'm so filled with rage that I know I'll regret it if I don't say what's really eating at me, so I turn around and scream as loudly as I can, "BECAUSE MY BEST FRIEND WOULD NEVER SLEEP WITH THE ONE PERSON ON THIS EARTH THAT WOULD HURT ME THE MOST! SHE'D NEVER DO IT! BECAUSE MY BEST FRIEND WOULD HAVE A GODDAMN MODICUM OF RESPECT FOR ME!

"I was lonely, August!" she cries as I'm about to march out of the room. "It wasn't what you think! It was a mistake. All of it. I don't even have a good excuse! You had just left after Christmas and I was missing you so damn much and he...he was there for a game and...it was years ago. I was drunk and he saw me at a bar. He was drunk too and we...he was an asshole, August, and...and you were my life then and now. You still are!"

I push my hand through my sweat soaked hair and then shake my head. "Well, I hope it was fucking worth it, Ella, because I can't even look at you now without seeing him. All this time you could have told me. You knew how I felt about him. You knew the guilt and pain I've gone through for years because of him and yet you never once told me that you've felt his cock inside you and that is something I can't forgive." I sneer. "We're done here. I never should have given you the time of day and I'll be damned if I waste another breath on you."

"Auggie...August, please!"

I don't even listen to her plea anymore. I glare at Barrett until he moves from the doorway and then set off down the hall to the locker room where the rest of the team is sitting quietly. It's evident they could hear my argument with Ella in the way they're all watching me. After I throw my gear around and whip off my jersey I turn to them all and shout, "What the fuck are you all staring at?"

"Do you want to talk about this?" Oliver asks.

I punch my hand into my locker. "DO I FUCKING LOOK LIKE I WANT TO TALK ABOUT IT?"

I don't even bother to shower because I'm that pissed off. I strip out of my uniform and pull on my workout clothes instead of my suit and head for the parking garage so I can get the fuck out of here. I don't head home because I know that's where she will be. She has nowhere else to go. So, I drive myself to a bar. Any bar but the one we usually hang out in so I can drink in peace without anyone bothering me.

I just need to numb the pain.

I need to drink away my anger until I can't feel a goddamn thing.

And then I'll drink one more just because I can.

CHAPTER TWENTY-FOUR

ELLA

I'm utterly and completely stunned.

Burying my face in my hands, I sob uncontrollably. "How did this even happen? How did we get here?"

I slide down the wall of the room Griffin and Barrett and I are still standing in not knowing what I should do next. My best friend in the entire world, the love of my life, just walked out on me and I'm not so sure there's any coming back from that.

"Ella," Griffin says softly, kneeling down in front of me. "Ella, I want to help. I want to be able to talk through this with you because Jeff Furbling was on his case the entire game. He just thought it was a drunk fan. He's pissed off right now. I know. I get it. He's also my best friend and he's already gotten into so much trouble tonight. I need to..." I open my blurred eyes and see him gesture out the door and I nod.

"Yeah. Of course. Please, he needs you, Griffin."

"I'll talk to you soon. I promise."

I simply nod and wipe my eyes with the backs of my hands. Barrett still stands in the doorway unsure of what he should do. I can see the compassion in his eyes for what I just went through, but also the loyalty for his teammates. He wants to be there for August too.

"It's okay, Bear," I murmur. "He needs you more than I do."

Though I'm not sure he'll let you get anywhere near him.

Because that's what August does when he's angry.

I've known that for years.

Because I know him better than anyone.

But clearly he doesn't know me.

Bear heads down the hall too, leaving me alone in the physical therapy room. I allow myself a few solid minutes to cry before I pick myself up and step out of my costume. There's chatter outside in the hallway that I try my best to ignore until one of those voices is close enough to be recognizable. I step out of the room just as she appears outside.

"Scarlett."

Her eyes bulge and her brows furrow at the sight of my tears. "Oh, my God! Ella! What is going on? There's a man down the hall screaming about assault charges and he looks pretty messed up. What is happening and oh, my God, are you okay?" She cups my face in her hands and looks me over assuming I was a part of whatever kind of brawl took place on the ice.

"I'm fine. I'm not hurt," I tell her. "Well, not physically."

More tears stream down my face before I can finally say aloud, "I think August just broke up with me."

She gasps and wraps an arm around me, pulling me into her for a comforting embrace. "Noooo. There's no way. He loves you, Ella."

"I don't think he does anymore."

"That can't be true," she says, leading me out of the room and down the hall. "Come on, let's get your stuff to your dressing room and we can talk there."

As we trudge down the hall I try to tell her about what happened. I tell her about the history between Jeff and August and the fight that took place tonight and how Jeff baited him during the entire game. Of course, August was going to be set off like a rocket with whatever Jeff had to say, but then I told Scarlett about him using me as his bombshell and that in the end, that news is what hurt August the most.

"He'll never forgive me for this, Scarlett. We didn't even sleep together but he thinks we did and he won't hear anything other than what he thinks he knows."

She stops as we reach the door to my dressing room, her arm still draped with mine. "Wait, so you didn't sleep together?"

I shake my head. "No. He was so drunk he couldn't uh...he couldn't..."

"He couldn't get hard?"

"He couldn't stay hard." I nod. "He asked me to give him a minute and in that time I had fallen asleep because I was drunk too." I cry. "I'm not proud of it. That's why I never said anything to August." *Sniffle.* "What was I supposed to say, 'Hey, I almost slept with him but I didn't so just pretend I didn't say anything in the first place'?" *Sniffle.* "Why upset him? I had forgotten all about it because it was a stupid mistake so many years ago. August and I were never a couple. We were never like that with each other." *Sniffle.* "What happened with Jeff and me was so inconsequential, I never gave it another thought. I woke up the next morning and..." *Sniffle.* "He was gone so..." I shrug. "What more was there to do, you know?"

"I get it," Scarlett says, patting my arm. "This wasn't your fault."

"But he thinks it's all my fault, Scarlett. And now I've lost him."

"You haven't lost him," she assures me. "That man loves you and I know he's still in there somewhere. He's just blinded by hurt and rage right now."

"HE FUCKING ASSAULTED ME! OF COURSE I'LL SUE THE SHIT OUT OF HIM. AND THIS ENTIRE FRANCHISE!" The angry words come from just down the hall. The timbre of his voice sends chills down my spine. I want to cower in my room and cry my eyes out until I have no tears left to cry, but at the same time, I love August. He can hate me all he wants, but I'll be damned if I stand by and let this sorry excuse of a man continue to ruin August's life. I grab Scarlett's hand and give it a squeeze.

"Excuse me a moment. There's something I have to do."

Leaving her standing in my dressing room, I step down the hall and into one of the team's medical exam rooms where one of our medical staff members is cleaning up Jeff's face. He sees me in the doorway and smirks. "Guess you made your choice, eh Ella?"

With my head held high I walk into the room and come to a stop right in front of him.

"Yeah, I did."

"Thought you would."

"And I choose August."

His face falls.

"I will always choose August. Even when he hates my guts because he thinks we slept together, I will choose him. And one day soon, when he has calmed down enough from what went on here tonight, I will tell him how your shriveled up little dick wouldn't work for you enough to even get it up for sex in the first place and that nothing ever happened between us. And as for you pressing assault charges against him or anyone in this franchise..." I sneer as I lean closer to his face. "You do that and I will take you for everything you have for not only taking nude pictures of me without my knowledge or consent but for circulating those pictures of me to the public. You are a sad pathetic waste of a man." I shake my head with pity. "You could've been somebody even though you were injured. You could've worked harder. You could've taken any other path to greatness regardless of any disability you may have had but you didn't. You've done nothing but blame August for your shortcomings for years." I give him a disgusted once over and tell him, "Your father should have pulled out and shot you against the wall or let your mother swallow you down the back of her throat." The other adults in the room chuckle at my poignant comment. "You are done here! Do you hear me? You're fucking done! You will not step foot back in this arena ever again. I'll make sure of that and you will not say one word online or in person to or about August Blackstone. Grow the fuck up and get out of our lives for good or I will come after you so fucking hard you'll spend eternity wishing you had."

And for good measure, because I can and because the medical staff in this room know me, I slap Jeff's face so hard my palm stings and then walk out of the room hoping that I will never see or hear from Jeff Furbling again.

CHAPTER TWENTY-FIVE

AUGUST

The sting of alcohol no longer bothers me.

It slides down my throat like ice water on a sweltering day.

There's nothing in my brain anymore.

No thoughts.

No emotions.

Not a fucking care in the world.

I'm right where I want to be.

I know at some point I'll fall asleep and when I wake up, this night will be a blur that will begin to refocus. I know I'll have to deal with the pain and the emotions of earlier at some point but at least I know I get this night to myself. To not think. To not feel. To not give a shit about anyone but myself.

I toss down another shot of tequila and gesture for another.

"You sure, August?"

I don't even have to use my words to answer the man behind the bar. I merely raise my eyes from my glass to his face and he nods in response, filling my shot glass to the brim.

"Rough night?" a voice says next to me.

A voice of the female variety.

"You could say that."

"Me too," she says. Not that I care at all. I don't even glance her way.

"Did your girlfriend betray you too?" I ask her.

She tosses back her drink and then lands her shot glass on the bar. "I walked into my house after a late work meeting to find my husband's dick deep down another woman's throat in the middle of my living room."

Fuck.

I almost laugh.

"Sucks."

"Yep," she says. "She was definitely sucking. Looked like she was sucking his brains out right through his cock."

"Why do the good people in the world get treated like shit?" I ask aloud. "Why do the bad things never happen to the bad people?"

"God, if I had the answer to that question…I've asked myself the same thing more times than I can count."

Tossing back my filled glass, I finally turn my head to look at the woman talking to me. Mahogany brown hair. Oval face. Blue eyes. A little too much lipstick but otherwise she's mildly pretty and doesn't smell like cheap perfume.

She doesn't smell like anything at all.

"I would've taken care of her, you know?" I blurt out, slurring my speech a little. "I would've given her the goddamn world but she decided to sleep with…"

The woman lays her hand on my knee and gives me a sympathetic glance. "Who did she sleep with? You brother?"

"No. I don't have a brother. She picked the one man she knew would hurt me the most."

"I'm sorry she did that to you."

I shrug. "Her choice. I'm done."

"Yeah. I know that feeling." She slides her hand a little farther up my thigh and I jump out of my seat.

"I gotta take a piss."

I climb off my stool and stumble my way to the bathroom and when I come out, the woman I was talking to is waiting for me in the hallway. She corners me and smooths her hands down my chest.

And I don't hate it.

"You want to get out of here? With me?" she boldly asks, placing a kiss on my cheek.

When I don't push her away she moves in and kisses my lips. She tastes of tequila, but maybe I'm just tasting myself as my tongue sweeps through her mouth. Having no thoughts or cares about anything might be just what I need tonight. I have a woman who clearly just wants to get fucked and if I'm being honest with myself, I wouldn't mind getting lost in a wet and willing pussy for the rest of the night. This is how I lived my life before Ella came to town. No reason now why I can't go back to that. I take her by the hand and tell her, "My car is out back."

She smiles and nods and I start to lead us to the door.

"Hey Blackstone?" It's a voice I think I recognize, but when I turn to see who's talking to me all I see is a fist before my world goes black.

—

My head is pounding.
What the fuck is going on?
Where the hell am I?
And how did I get here?

I try to open my eyes but can only easily open one. The other feels as though it's swollen shut, but when I look up I find five other pairs of eyes glaring at me.

Griffin, Ledger, Oliver, Bear, and Harrison are all standing over me with their arms folded across their chests.

"What the fuck are you guys doing here?" I murmur, my voice full of rasp and the pain thumping through my head with every word I say.

"They're with me, dipshit," Griffin says irritated. "You're in my living room."

What am I...

"Why am I here?"

"Do you not remember a damn thing about last night?"

"Not particularly. Why is my eye not opening?" I bring my hand to my face to feel what's going on and wince in pain when my fingers make contact with my left eye.

Griffin scoffs. "Because I had to punch you in the damn face to make sure you didn't make a huge mistake last night."

I frown. "What are you even talk—"

Ella.

Furbling.

The shouting.

The bar.

Tequila.

The mystery woman.

Kissing.

"Oh."

"Yeah, oh," Griffin snarls. "What the fuck were you thinking, man? You're better than that."

"Am I?"

"Griffin told us what happened, August," Oliver starts. "So, we're going to need to talk this out because you're about to mess up your whole fucking life over one man."

I lift my arm and hold up my finger. "Correction. One woman."

"Forget about Ella for a minute. We'll get to her."

"No need." I shake my hand. "I'm done."

Bear laughs. "Dude, you're so far from done. Shut the fuck up and listen."

My cell phone buzzes on the table and Harrison picks it up to answer it.

"What the hell? That's my phone."

"Tom?" Harrison says.

Tom? What's my agent calling for?

"Yeah he's awake...No we're about to find out...yeah...yeah I think so...I'll keep you posted...yeah whatever the cost. Just work it out...yeah. Thanks Tom." Harrison pockets my phone not giving a care in the world that I'm giving him the stink eye.

"What was all that about?" I ask him.

"It was about the assault charges Jeff Furbling is ready to press against you. We've also been in touch with Coach Hicks and Mike Exling."

"The general manager of the team? What for?"

"Because they're questioning if they should even be keeping you on after the stunt you pulled yesterday."

"That wasn't a fucking stunt," I tell them. "That was pure—"

"Anger," Oliver says, nodding. "Yeah we get it. So shut up and listen because we're not about to let you walk away from this."

"Ella told us all about Furbling. She told us what happened all those years ago and she told us that playing the Gators eats at you every single fucking season," Ledger says, shaking his head. "Dude, why did you never say anything? We could have protected you."

"I don't need your protection. And what's there to fucking say?" I ask, trying to sit up. The emptiness in my stomach isn't helping the nausea or the headache. "I ruined a man's life and now he hates me for it so every time we play his old team I feel bad about it?"

"Yeah, dumbass." Bear nods. "That's exactly what you say."

"And why are you talking to Ella anyway? I told you we're over. She slept with the asshole."

"Okay first of all, we're not going to let you say a damn bad thing about Ella."

I whip my face toward Harrison and almost black out when the room spins. "What the hell?"

"She hasn't done a damn thing to you and you know it, August. You're just butt-hurt that she *supposedly* slept with someone you don't like, but guess what? Her life is and never was yours to control. If you didn't want her to sleep with anyone, you should've fucking nutted up and told her how you felt years ago. That was your first mistake. Secondly, you really need to take some time to talk to her because from what she says, that night did not go the way you perceived."

What the fuck?

Why are they suddenly on her side?

"But she—"

"Didn't get a word in edgewise because you never gave her the chance before you fucking walked out on her, *Auggie*." Griffin enunciates my nickname with a piercing stare. "You accused her of your worst fears, threw your hands up, and walked away."

He's right.

That's exactly what I did.

I was just so angry.

And hurt.

Devastated is more like it.

"You guys, I can't look at her or even...think about her without seeing him. Picturing them together. Picturing him fucking her. I can't."

"For the love of mother fucking Christ, August," Oliver blurts out. "She didn't fuck him, alright? They didn't fuck!"

My brows furrow. "What?"

He throws up his arms in frustration. "This is why communication is key, man! She didn't fuck him because he was too drunk to get it up."

Wait.

They didn't...

"But...but the pictures..."

"She passed out drunk! She had no idea the pictures were taken, you stupid ass fuck nut!" Griffin tosses me a water bottle. "We all learned this over the past twelve hours while you've been passed out on this couch. Now would you please drink this so you can help your fucking hangover enough to be coherent? For Christ's sake talking to you is like trying to skate on cement."

I sit up and drink down the entire bottle in one sitting and then wipe my mouth with the back of my hand. "So, you're telling me she didn't sleep with Furbling?"

"Yes!" Ledger nods.

"And she didn't know those pictures were taken?"

"Correct!" He nods again.

Fuck.

"Are there more of them out there?" My brows shoot up and I slide my hands through my hair realizing just how greasy and dirty it is after not showering last night. "There could be any number of pictures of her body out there on the internet."

"Exactly." Ledger nods one more time. "And that's what you should have been thinking about last night instead of letting your fucking ego get in the way."

"Dude," Griffin says, taking the seat next to me on his couch. "You very nearly walked out of that bar with that woman last night. You would've thrown everything between you and Ella away over some tramp who was feeding you line after line just to get to your dick. Had I not been there..."

"How were you there, by the way? Why were you there?"

He cocks his head and gives me an incredulous look. "You didn't think I was going to let you drive out of the arena and spend a night drinking yourself into oblivion without keeping an eye on you did you?"

"But..."

"I followed you dumbass. I grabbed my clothes and shoes from my locker and ran to the garage in my uniform. Most uncomfortable drive of my life but that's what friends are for. Once I saw you walk into the bar I knew I needed to give you a few minutes' worth of shots so I was able to change my clothes at least. You never saw me walk in and I was only sitting a table away. I heard everything. You were going to sleep with that woman."

"But...I was drunk." I shake my head. "I didn't mean—"

"Yeah, just like Ella didn't mean it seven years ago?"

Shit.

"You're right." I hang my head. "You're absolutely right."

"Yeah, I know I am."

"I've made such a mess of things?"

"A little bit, bro. Yeah."

"How am I supposed to get her to talk to me about any of this after all I've done?"

Griffin pats my leg and gives me a half smile. "You start by going to get a shower because you smell like shit." He leans a little closer and adds, "I left my favorite pajama pants and t-shirt for you in the bathroom."

CHAPTER TWENTY-SIX

ELLA

"Wow! That's...a lot." Paige's wide-eyed stare on Facetime comes at no surprise. "I remember that night with Furbling. And by that I mean I remember you telling me you had dodged a huge bullet. And hell, that was so long ago! I can't believe August would just accuse you and hold something against you like that. As if he's never made a fucking mistake in his entire life."

"Yeah. I remember feeling so stupid the next morning. But I was really grateful things didn't, you know, work out." I shrug. "And I'm trying not to blame August too hard until I can really sit down and talk to him again. He was having a really tense day yesterday to begin with because he knew the game itself would be rough. He just didn't expect what happened would happen. So I get it. He was pissed and hurt and his world was sort of knocked off its axis for a bit."

"Yeah but come on. He's done nothing but love you for your entire lives and in mere minutes he was willing to throw that all out the window."

Well, when you say it like that.

My eyes start to glisten as I nod. "I know. And maybe he is done, like he said. Maybe he wants nothing to do with me."

"When was the last time you saw him?"

"Right after the game, when all this was happening."

"Wait, he didn't come home last night?"

I shake my head. "No. But Griffin Ollenberg is with him. I know he is. They're best friends and teammates and I know Griffin would never let anything happen to him. So I'm at least ninety-eight percent sure August is safe and breathing."

"So, he hasn't reached out apparently."

"No."

She scoffs quietly. "God, someone needs to give that guy a swift kick in the nads. You're the best thing that's ever happened to him and he knows it."

I lift my shoulder. "Or I'm the worst thing that's ever happened to him."

"What?" She huffs. "How the hell do you figure that?"

"Maybe I've held on to him too strongly over the years. Maybe I should've let him go, you know? Maybe I'm not who he wanted."

She points to me sternly through the phone. "That's bullshit and you know it, so stop thinking that way. If he didn't want your friendship, he wouldn't have called you over the years. He wouldn't have texted. He wouldn't have stayed in touch. He certainly wouldn't have asked you to move to fucking California to live with him and apply for a job where he fucking works."

"Yeah I guess you could be right."

"Could be right," she mumbles, shaking her head in disbelief. She stares at me for a second trying to get a read on my emotions and then cocks her head. "So, what are you going to do now? Are you moving out?"

I inhale a deep breath considering her question and shake

my head. "I don't know. I don't think so. Not yet anyway. At least not until August tells me himself that's what he wants."

"He didn't say those words last night?"

I shake my head. "No. I mean, I could probably infer from his demeanor that he doesn't expect me to stay here, but he also didn't technically say he wants me out. I guess a part of me is still holding out hope that he'll be a little more rational when he calms down."

Though I could be dead wrong.

"Good for you. Stand your ground."

I want to laugh at her comment but I can't muster the energy. "I'm not sure if I'm standing my ground more than hoping against all hope that I won't have to be out here on my own. It's a big city."

"You can always come back."

I scoff. "And let my mom tell me how right she was about me not being able to make it here? That it's too big of a place for me and I'll get swallowed up and spit out by a city that doesn't care about me? No thank you. But if he wants me to go, I'll leave. I can't stay here and mooch off of him if he doesn't want me around." I breathe in and release a long sigh. "I suppose I should spend some time today at least looking at other places just in case. Not sure what I can really afford with my salary but I know it won't be like what I have now."

A new apartment won't come with the lavish things August can afford.

It won't come with the comfort. The warmth. The strong sense of safety.

And it won't come with August.

The thought of that makes me sad.

"But then what will you do with the job?"

"Keep working," I tell her simply. "It'll be hard as hell, but

I'll have to figure out how to make it work without having to run into him all the time.

Paige sighs. "I hate seeing you like this, friend."

"I know," I tell her, trying not to cry all over again. "I'll be fine. Pain is only temporary, right?"

"Yeah..." She doesn't sound very convincing. "Tell you what, what if I look at plane tickets and come out for a visit? We can stay in a hotel, wedding dress shop a little, and if you need someone to go with you to look at a few places, I'll be there to help you."

"I think seeing you in person would be wonderful, but maybe give me a day or two to figure out what's happening with me and August. I wouldn't want you walking into some stress induced hell."

"Yeah, I get it. Just let me know once you guys have talked rationally."

If we get to talk rationally.

"Okay."

CHAPTER TWENTY-SEVEN

AUGUST

"You spread your legs wide open for that fucking son of a bitch and you asked him to stick his dick inside you. You fucked him."

"You're nothing but a whore, isn't that right, Ella?"

"We're done here. I never should have given you the time of day and I'll be damned if I waste another breath on you."

"Shit." I hang my head in shame and brace myself against the wall with my hand as the hot water rushes over my body.

How the hell did I even get here?

In the past twenty-four hours, I lost my shit and beat a man with my bare hands, I lost my best friend and the woman I loved, lost all my dignity, and quite possibly my job as well.

How do I even begin to come back from this?

I go through the motions finishing in Griffin's shower, grateful that the guys are standing by me to help me through this mess but feeling like the world's biggest fucking loser.

To be honest, I don't care about the job.

Okay, maybe I care a little. Hockey has been my life since I was old enough to skate. But more importantly, the person I love the most in this world is God knows where doing God knows what all because I tore her apart without listening. Without asking questions first. I jumped the gun and reacted instead of putting her best interests in front of my own. The moment I saw that picture of her I reacted with hate for Furbling rather than compassion for Ella.

I was such an idiot.

I know whatever she's thinking, doing, or saying right now, she's crying her eyes out while she does it because that's who she is. She's an emotional crier and I'm gutted thinking about what I've put her through.

I didn't want to hurt her.

But I did.

Fuck, I said some things I can't take back. Words that will undoubtedly stay with her forever and there's not a damn thing I can do about it other than apologize profusely for being the world's biggest piece of shit.

The last thing I want to do is lose her.

Especially over something like my stupid fucking lack of communication skills.

I wouldn't blame her if she doesn't want to forgive me.

"You doing alright in here?" Griffin pushes the door open a smidge as I turn the water off and grab my towel.

"No." I wrap the towel around my waist and step out of the wet shower. "What am I supposed to do now, Griff?" I mumble quietly so this doesn't turn into a team intervention in the bathroom. "How am I supposed to fix this?"

"Well, Oliver spoke with Coach who said Furbling isn't pressing charges."

My brows pinch. "He's not?"

Griffin shakes his head.

"What the fuck? How did that happen? Why not? I beat the shit out of him right there on the rink for everyone to see. I'm certain it's on social media. There's no way I'm getting away with this."

Griffin stares me down and then cocks his head and softly says, "Because Ella got to him last night after you left apparently."

Ella.

All the blood drains from my face.

"Ella. How do you know this? What's going on?"

He gestures out the door. "Scarlett got here a few minutes ago with lunch. She'll tell you everything."

"Scarlett? What does she know about it?"

"Just get dressed and meet us in the living room."

As quickly as I can I towel off and throw on the clean clothes that Griffin left for me, rolling my eyes at the gray pajama pants with a finger pointing up my chest that says "THE MAN" and a finger pointing to my dick that says "THE LEGEND."

"Really Griffin?" I mutter to myself as I pull on the Anaheim t-shirt he left me as well.

Whatever.

They're clothes.

Ella is more important right now.

I throw open the bathroom door and head down his short hallway back to the living room finally feeling refreshed and a little more focused.

"Hey who has my phone?" I ask to the group of guys seated around the room. But the moment they all look my way they burst out laughing.

"Nice pants Blackstone," Bear says with a glint of humor in his eye.

"Nice? Those are fucking amazing!" Ledger laughs, pointing. "I think I need those for myself."

"You could only be so lucky, Dayne," Griffin says to Ledger.

"Besides Blackstone's had a rough twenty-four hours. He deserves to feel good about himself for a little bit."

"Scarlett, what's going on with Ella?" I ask, trying to ignore the snide comments from my teammates about my apparel. "Is she alright? Did she go home? Is that where she is now? Please tell me she didn't take her stuff and leave."

Scarlett shakes her head. "I'm sorry, August. I don't have all the answers for you. I only know what I heard last night because I found her sobbing in the physical therapy room."

I plop down on the couch, my hands in my wet hair. "Fuck."

"She was pretty shaken for sure," she says. "Upset about what happened, obviously, but for what it's worth, she heard the medics trying to help this Jeff guy and heard him shouting about suing you and the entire franchise."

Fucking Christ, if that happens, I'm done for.

"But then she confronted him and put him in his place. Gave him hell and then threatened to take him for everything he has over those photos he took and for slandering you over the years. And then she slapped him."

"That's our girl," Ledger says with a smile. "She's bad ass sometimes."

Yeah. She is.

Not that this makes me feel any better about this mess. Ella should never have had to come to my defense. She shouldn't have been made to feel the need to fix things because I shouldn't have let it go as far as it did. I knew better and I reacted with my fists anyway.

I hang my head, holding it in my hands, and sigh not knowing what I'm supposed to say or do now, but Scarlett kneels down in front of me and places a comforting hand on my knee.

"For what it's worth though, August, I heard her say to Furbling that she chooses you. And that even if and when you hate her guts, she'll still choose you. Because she loves you that much."

My chest tightens, my cheeks burn, and I drop my trembling chin to my chest. "I don't fucking deserve her," I say, pressing a palm over my lips to keep from crying.

"You do deserve her, August," Scarlett tells me with a sympathetic smile. "She's your person. She's always been your person and from the sounds of things, no matter what has happened or will happen in the future, she'll always be your person. You just have to talk to her."

"How? What could I possibly say that would fix everything I said to her last night. I called her a whore, Scarlett," I say, shaking my head. "I said so many fucking terrible things to her. There's no way she should forgive me for that."

Scarlett shrugs. "Maybe she shouldn't. You're right."

I raise my eyes to meet hers because that was not what I expected to hear. "But that's the difference between most women and the one you are in love with. Ella Montgomery is not most women. She loves you with her whole heart and I have a feeling a simple sincere apology would be an excellent start."

"Do you really think that?"

She nods. "Yeah. I do. I really have no doubt that she'll forgive you, August. So maybe an apology followed by something that would make her happy. A nice gesture. Anything. Is there something that comes to mind?"

I have no idea why the universe chooses this moment to toss a thought inside my head but a memory of a conversation we had before she ever moved here comes to mind. I nod to Scarlett and sit up a little more hopefully.

"Actually, yeah."

I spring up from the couch. "I need my keys. Who has my keys."

Harrison leans back over Griffin's kitchen counter and grabs my keys, tossing them to me.

"Thanks. Do you have my phone too?"

"Yep. Right here," he says, pulling it from his jeans pocket.

"Thanks. I've got to go. I'll touch base later."

"Wait!" Griffin calls. "Where the hell are you going?"

I pull his apartment door open and turn back. "I have something I need to do. Scarlett, thank you. And thank you guys. I'll figure out my shit, I promise. But Ella comes first."

Bear gives me a smile—a genuine smile—and gestures with his chin. "Get out of here. And keep us posted."

I'm walking out the door when I hear Ledger shout, "Might want to change your clothes!"

"No time!" I call back with a smile on my face. I break out into a run until I reach the elevator. I'm hyper aware that I could simply walk to my building right next door and maybe find Ella, but I have to make a stop somewhere first so I make a beeline for the parking garage.

Driving down the streets of Anaheim, my phone rings and I press a button on my steering wheel to answer it.

"Blackstone."

"August Blackstone, what the ever-loving fuck did you do to my best friend?"

My brows furrow for a moment and then I see the name on the screen. "Paige?"

"Yeah, it's Paige. Listen, I just got off facetime with Ella and she's a hot mess. Do you know what she's doing right now?"

"Is she home?"

"That depends, asshat! Does she even have a home?"

"What?" I ask with a scowl. "What's the supposed to mean?"

"You told you her you never wanted to see her again. Do you really think she's going to stay in your apartment when you want nothing to do with her? How could you be so fucking cruel? She's not a fucking whore, you bitch-ass little prick. She's fucking ELLA! Your best friend and—"

"Paige! I know alright? I fucking know! And to answer your question, yes! Yes, Ella has a home. And that place is with me. I'm trying to fix this, alright? I don't blame her one bit for being mad and I wouldn't blame her if she doesn't forgive me but I have to try and I'm trying. I've got one stop to make and then I'm going home to her. I want to work this out. I need her to forgive me so I can fix this."

She scoffs. "She's going to forgive you, dumbass. Even if you don't deserve it. She's going to forgive you because she's Ella and that's what she does. She's freaking female Jesus!"

"I know, Paige. I'm sorry, alright? I was an absolute dick last night. I don't have a good excuse because I knew better."

"You should've been there for her, August! She's all alone out there."

"She's not alone, Paige. I promise. She has me. She'll always have me."

"You better fucking mean that."

"I do. Look, I have something I have to take care of and then I promise I'm going straight home to Ella."

"Okay," she huffs. "The next time I call her she better be smiling."

God I hope she will be.

I pull into the drive of the building and park my car. Keenly aware that I look like hell walking inside in these ridiculous gray pajama pants and a t-shirt, I smile at the woman at the front desk who asks how she can best help me. Her eyes light up and she smiles at me and, "Whoa! You're August Blackstone!"

"I am. So, I'm guessing you're a hockey fan."

"Of course! My boyfriend and I have season tickets." She

homes in on my shiner. "Your eye okay? We saw what happened last night."

"Yeah. I'm good. But that's kind of why I'm here."

"Oooh," she nods her head sympathetically. "Mandated volunteer hours?"

"What? No." I shake my head. "Though I'm sure those are in my future and I'd be more than happy to fulfill those here if you need help, but I'm actually looking for the perfect gift for Lumin...I mean Ella. The girl, our mascot. She's my girlfriend. My absolute best friend and I hurt her last night and I really need to apologize to her and I was hoping you might be able to help me with that.

Her smile helps me breathe a little easier. "I would love to! Let's go have a look."

CHAPTER TWENTY-EIGHT

ELLA

"Studio two-bedroom. Fitness center, pool, washer dryer. Thirty-five hundred." I cringe. "That's a little rich for my blood." Scrolling through a few rental properties in the Anaheim area has been eye opening. I have no idea how much August pays for this place but it has to be upwards of ten to twelve thousand per month given where we are and the amenities included. By all means this isn't what I wanted to be doing today but I have yet to hear from August and something in my gut is telling me if he hasn't been in touch yet, there probably isn't much hope that he'll come around.

This entire day so far has been spent cuddled in my bed covered in fluffy blankets. I've only left my room to go to the kitchen for a drink and a snack and then it's right back to bed. I've taken two naps in between calls with Paige. After chatting with her, I decided maybe I do need to at least look around for a new place to live. So here I am scrolling through my iPad and noting any rentals that seem clean, inexpensive, and are in a safe part of town.

"One bedroom townhouse...no, that's not a great area."

Scroll on.

"Three beds, three baths with a balcony. Ugh, not for sixty-eight hundred a month. Do I even make sixty-eight hundred per month?"

Scroll on.

"One bedroom, two floors with pool and balcony for two thousand." I cock my head reading all the rental details and then click the option to save the listing as a favorite. "Maybe? I don't know."

Scroll on.

"One bedroom with walk-in closets..."

I hear the front door open and wonder if it could actually be August.

Do I say hello?

Do I just walk out there?

Should I stay here in my room?

What if it's August and he doesn't want to see me?

Do I want to see him though?

Am I ready for him to be home?

What will he say to me?

Will he be mad that I'm still here?

Will he be expecting me not to be here?

Does he expect me to move out as soon as today?

Maybe not bothering him is best.

He did say he didn't want to look at me ever again

I go back to scrolling through rentals, reminding myself that I do have a few possibilities saved so that if August yells at me to move out I can at least tell him I'm looking. I click on the next listing for a studio apartment with an open floor plan as there's movement outside my bedroom door.

My heart races and my mouth goes dry as the doorknob turns and the door opens just a bit. Nobody speaks and I can't take it anymore so I nervously say, "Hello?"

August doesn't push the door open, nor does he walk

through the doorway. But what does come through makes me gasp, smile, and want to jump from my bed. First it's a little green ball with a bell inside that rings as the ball rolls across my floor. That ball is quickly followed by an eagerly playful orange and white kitten who pounces on the ball projecting it farther across the floor.

"Oh, my God! Look at you!" I squeal quietly to the tiny kitten who runs after the ball with reckless abandon. I climb slowly from the bed, watching its every move even though my heart is pounding, so I don't scare the poor thing. Then I crouch down and pick up my new four-legged furry friend, snuggling him in my arms and petting his tiny little body.

"Aren't you the cutest little thing I've ever seen? And just where did you come from?" I ask, knowing this little thing isn't going to answer me back.

My door opens a little more though, and August stands there on the other side with a few cat toys and a small blanket in his hand.

"Hey," he says.

"Hey."

He swallows hard and then adds, "I'm uh...I'm really bad at apologies so I thought maybe this little guy could help me. They were just giving them away at the humane society."

"Giving them away, huh?"

August bobs his head. "Well, turns out when you make a sizeable donation and promise to volunteer in the near future, they're willing to help you find what you're looking for."

"Mmm." Nuzzling the new fuzzy kitten between my chin and my chest, I walk him back to my bed and set him down. He proceeds to jump around my duvet and then nestles in my lap.

"Can I come in?" August asks, still standing in the doorway.

"It's your apartment, Auggieeeest...August." Fuck. I forgot he doesn't want me to call him Auggie anymore.

"It's your apartment too, you know," he says quietly as he steps inside and over to my bed.

Is it?

When I don't answer, his glance falls to my iPad and the listing I have on the screen. "Ella?"

"Yeah."

He hesitates to answer, so I pull my eyes from the kitten long enough to glance his way and when I do, my heart drops and there's an ache in my throat at the sight of him. His eyes are wide, his chin is trembling, and he bites his bottom lip trying to hold back tears but they slip down his cheek anyway.

"Please don't leave me."

For once I don't know what to say.

I want to tell him everything is going to be okay, but I can't even answer that for myself, so I simply hold out my hand to him in hopes he'll accept the small gesture of comfort.

"How can I help you, August?"

He takes my hand and winds our fingers together before sitting on the edge of the bed next to me. "You can help me by saying you won't leave."

"Are you sure you want me to stay? Because last night you—"

"Please don't say it," he begs, grimacing at the thought. "I know what I said. My own fucking voice has been playing on repeat in my head all day and it's the worst hell you could imagine."

"I can definitely imagine," I tell him honestly.

"Ella." He shakes his head but keeps eye contact with me as tears stream down his face. "I'm so sorry. I was a dick. I don't have a valid excuse for my actions or my words, especially my words to you. I feel like I was having some sort of out of body experience and I'm so, so, so, fucking sorry I hurt you."

I break his eye contact momentarily to check on our kitten

friend who made himself comfortable right up against my other pillow and fell fast asleep. Then I squeeze August's hand and say, "I'm sorry too August."

His brows furrow and he shakes his head. "For what? You have nothing to be sorry for."

"Yes I do," I tell him. "You were right. I should have told you. I should have told you about Furbling all those years ago when it happened." I shake my head this time. "I had forgotten all about it until you said something last night, but I need you to know, to really know, that what you think happened, didn't happen."

He nods. "I know. Scarlett and Oliver got to me. I should have listened to you, Ella. I should have believed you."

"Yeah." I nod quietly. "That did sting a little."

"It was all so fucking much, El. The minute I saw that picture of you I wanted to vomit everywhere. I was so angry at him. Angry for you but then he made me second guess everything. It was too much, and I just..."

"Snapped."

He dips his head slightly and he lets out a sigh. "Yeah."

Lowering my head to meet his gaze, I murmur to him, "Well I feel pretty certain Jeff Furbling won't be seen or heard from for quite some time if that makes you feel any better."

"I don't give a shit about any of it," he says to me. "All I care about is you."

My lips part as I suck in a breath, warmth spreading through my body in tiny waves.

"I love you so damn much, Ella. And I don't want to lose you." He lifts our joined hands to his lips and kisses the back of my hand. "Please tell me there's a scenario where we don't end up apart from each other because I don't want to live without you. I need you. All of you. And I want to be the guy who makes you happy."

"What if I'm not enough for you?" My own question brings tears to my eyes and apprehension to my psyche.

"You're all I've ever wanted, Ella. You're all I'll ever want for the rest of my life. I fucked up, I know. I said some hateful things that I can't take back and I know they hurt you and I'm not sure at this point there's anything I can say to erase that hurt except I'm so incredibly and sincerely sorry." More tears trickle from his eyes and it tugs at my heart.

"August..."

"It's Auggie," he tells me. "I've always been Auggie to you."

I reach up to his face with my other hand and palm his cheek, my thumb wiping away a few of his tears. "I love you too, Auggie. I accept your apology...and I love the furry gift. There's nothing we can't get through together. We're a team, okay? You and me."

"You and me." He nods and then pulls me from where I'm sitting on my bed until I'm in his arms, my legs wrapped around his waist and my arms around his neck.

"I love you, Ella."

"I love you too, Auggie."

TWO WEEKS LATER.

It's been two weeks since the night Jeff Furbling showed up at our game and tipped August's world upside down. Since then, he was benched for the last four games, fined several thousands of dollars by the league, and required to do some community service which, as apparently promised, he chose to complete at the Anaheim Humane Society. Consequently, our new kitten friend, who I aptly named Sunflower—Sunny for short because he's a boy—has a new friend. A white kitten with orange ears and a gray tuft on its tail that I let Auggie name Leo. They're quickly becoming best friends and are ornery as ever, but we enjoy every moment having them in our home.

I watch under the brim of my hat as August steps into the room filled with press members following tonight's game. Watching his body move across the floor to his seat does things to my body. My cheeks heat and my chest flutters as his muscles flex in his arms. Phew! We might not make it to the bar tonight without having to spend a few minutes in my dressing room first.

Or his car...

"August, how did you feel about your first game back after your four-game suspension?"

"Uh, I felt good." He nods. "I spent time in the training room and practiced with the team for tonight's game during the last two weeks so hopefully that showed in my performance tonight."

Totally showed, babe. You looked hot out there!

"August," another press member raises his hand. "Can you tell us any more about your past relationship with Jeff Furbling and have you heard from him at all over these past two weeks?"

Fuck off on the Furbling. He's not talking about it.

"No comment," he tells the man before he sits.

That's right, babe. You tell 'em.

I raise my hand while keeping my eyes glued to my notepad so he doesn't know it's me sitting here.

"Yeah. In the blue hat."

I clear my throat before I begin and then say, "Um, Auggie... can I call you Auggie? Seems like a cute name for you, doesn't it?" I raise my head so he can see who I am and then stand from my seat. The other members of the press stare at me with furrowed brows. Clearly they don't recognize me outside my mascot costume.

He smiles back at me. "Uh, yeah sure. I'll allow Auggie." He winks. "But only for you."

"Alright." I beam, pulling off my hat, my long brown hair falling around my shoulders. "I was actually wondering if maybe you might be interested in marrying me."

The crowd chuckles, assuming I'm making some sort of joke. Even August blinks several times and sits back in his chair watching me, a huge smile widening across his face. "I'm sorry, can you repeat that?"

"Of course. Marry me," I say again. "Because I love you and because somehow I was able to sneak into this press conference with all these professionals and nobody pushed me out so this is me, your unmasked team mascot standing in front of all these press members asking you to marry me."

Cocking his head, he narrows his eyes and shakes his head. "Do you know what you're doing Ms. Montgomery?"

I laugh among a now murmuring crowd with microphones pointed at me. "Well, I'm pretty sure I'm just a girl standing in front of a hot hockey player, asking him to marry her. That was the goal anyway. Am I coming across some other way because this feels pretty cut and dry here."

In the back of the room, the rest of the team comes barging in and somehow I know they just got word that I was in here proposing to August and didn't want to miss out.

Auggie sits up straighter in his chair and clears his throat. "I just wanted you to be sure because I don't want you to ask me to marry you if you're not sure this is what you want. What if I told you I don't want you if I can't have you forever?"

"So that includes for better or worse? Richer or poorer? Sickness and health and all that other stuff?"

"All that other stuff and so much more," he answers with a smirk.

"Sold," I tell him. "Let's get hitched."

August shakes his head with a laugh. "I love you Ella Montgomery. I'll marry you any day, anytime, anywhere."

"I love you too, August Blackstone. How does Vegas sound?"

Want more of August and Ella?
Click HERE to join my newsletter
and receive a special epilogue of August and Ella FREE!

Want a sneak peek of the next book in the Anaheim Stars
Series? Read on for an excerpt of What If I Knew You!

WHAT IF I KNEW YOU EXCERPT

BODHI

"Roses are red, pickles are green. I like your legs, and what's in between!"

Ledger Dayne leads the team in a fit of laughter as I step onto the ice for our last preseason practice wearing a pair of light blue pajama pants with bright green pickles of assorted sizes all over them. The gift from Griffin Ollenberg was waiting for me when I walked in this morning along with a note explaining that it's a team tradition to wear goofy pajama pants for our last preseason practice and that since he forgot to tell me earlier, he took the liberty of buying me a pair.

I had a feeling it was all a joke.

Somehow I knew I would be the only one on the ice today with these Godforsaken pickle pants on, but a tiny part of me wondered if Griffin was being honest with me since he seems to wear pants like this a lot around the arena. It's what he's known for, really. He has this fascination with pajama pants that I don't understand but hey...the fans get a kick out of it so more power to him, I guess.

I could've been my regular asshole self about this whole thing.

I could've refused to wear these ridiculous pants.

But I know if I want the respect of my teammates, I have to earn it, so, pickle pants it is.

"Hey, Kid." Harrison gestures with the tip of his chin. "That a pickle in your pocket or are you just happy to see me?"

More laughter from the guys.

Har, har, har.

"Guess I fell for that one, huh?" I chuckle, skating over to the guys who clearly all got here early so they could stand here and wait for me to show up. I survived much of preseason practice without too much stress in the form of hazing from the guys, but definitely was on the receiving end of a few harmless pranks. They turned off the hot water to the showers during my first week and while I was in said cold shower, someone switched out my underwear in my locker for a pair of granny panties. Last week, before one of our practices, I went to grab some stick tape out of my bag only to find it gone. Lo and behold, the only stick tape that just happened to be lying around everywhere was pink sparkly tape with unicorns and rainbows all over it.

Yeah. That was a colorful practice.

I suppose it could be worse.

They could be giving me swirlies in the locker room toilets.

I may not have gotten the warmest reception from the team but they haven't been cold either. What's a little fun among teammates anyway? Stopping in front of the guys I gesture to my new pants with a smirk.

"You guys want to stare at my pickle all day or are we going to get to work?"

August gives my pickles a once over and then meets Griffin's amused glance. With a shrug of his shoulder, he asks, "Depends, Roche. You got a perky pickle worth looking at?"

Griffin twists his mouth and shakes his head trying not to laugh. "Nah. He's young. He's got to pump his pickle first to make it perky."

August laughs. "Dude did you just say this kid pumps his pickle?"

"What?" I scowl. "I'm not a—"

"He's a pickle pumper?" Ledger asks.

"Hell yeah!" Griffin says with a smile. "All the way to Perky Pickle Palace."

"What the hell is Perky Pick—"

"Alright, alright," Coach Hicks rallies with a slight chuckle. "You guys can tickle each other's pickles on someone else's time. We've got plays to run. Let's go."

"Pickle Pumper," August murmurs, shaking his head with quiet laughter before he skates off to the other side of the rink.

Fantastic.

There's no way that won't become a nickname.

Bodhi Roche the Pickle Pumper.

Oh well. That's the least of my worries now. It's time to show off my skills once again to prove to these guys that I'm just as much of a player as they are. I've been busting my ass during our preseason to show these guys what I'm made of and that I can live up to my hot-shot reputation. I can be a monster on the ice, but every time I go for something flashy or try something they're not used to doing, they roll their eyes or give me a tough time about it. They don't seem too interested in Bodhi Roche the superstar hockey player.

Maybe the joke's on them because that's who they hired.

I've spent years refining my strengths and eliminating most of my weaknesses. I'm bringing notoriety to the Anaheim Stars. They're lucky to have me.

When I was in Boston, if we won it was because Bodhi Roche scored or assisted in more goals than anyone else. If we lost it was because Bodhi Roche had a bad night. Why they put so much pressure on me as the new guy when there were older, more experienced players on the team I'll never know. But, when you come onto a team as a college superstar, and the franchise expects a lot from you, you do what you're told. When I started in Boston I was told to skate fast and score goals and that's what I did.

I won.

Because I'm a winner.

These Anaheim guys though, they don't seem to give a shit about that.

They have no interest in my stats as a player.

And none of them seem to give two shits that I'm out here on the ice with them busting my ass to show them what I can do. I'm showing off all my skills during this morning's practice, but it's almost like I'm not even here.

Maybe they're all jealous of my pickle pants.

"Hit the break, Roche! Hit the break!" Coach Hicks shouts as I speed down the ice. "Be the double threat. Give yourself the opens."

"Ugh, I don't need to be a double threat when I can fucking sink the puck right now."

Harrison Meers swings up behind me and caps my shoulder with his gloved hand. "We don't give a damn how fast you can skate, kid."

"Well, you should because I'm faster than a lot of you."

"Fast is nice," Barrett says from the net, irritated. "But it doesn't get the job done when you end up missing the pass or worse, you miss nine out of the ten shots you take."

Fuck.

He's not wrong, I suppose.

I have missed almost every shot I've taken today.
I'm blaming the damn pickle pants.

"We don't need a superstar out here, Bodhi!" Hicks shouts when he sees I'm talking to Harrison and Barrett. "The guys need a reliable teammate. Someone who can shoot when he knows he can and pass when it's best for the team."

And here lies the difference between the Boston Brews and the Anaheim Stars. Boston didn't stress much about being a team. They wanted to breed star players and that's what I was for them. I'm not going to lie, it's a little aggravating that these guys don't seem to appreciate my competence on the ice. I worked my ass off in Boston in hopes that when my contract was up, I could finally find a team that would accept me for who I am and what I can bring to the franchise.

Anaheim was one of my top five dream teams, so when my agent called and told me I received an offer from the Stars, I was stoked. They've had a winning record and haven't traded a player in the past four seasons. That has to mean something in terms of how this team functions on and off the ice and over the past few weeks I've seen it firsthand. These guys aren't just a team.

They're a family.

Walking into a team that is as tightly bonded as these guys are though; that's a hard door to step through. They've been welcoming, yes, but I can tell I'm not really part of their family just yet. I'm like their annoying little brother that they're forced to play with. They've set their bar high and I know it's my job to do all I can to reach it.

"Run it again," Hicks commands.

"Nice job out there, Pickle Pants," Griffin says to me when we enter the locker room after practice.

I toss my glove on the bench in front of me not sure if Ollenberg is being sincere or sarcastic. "Could've fooled me."

Griffin cocks his head pursing his lips. "Aww is someone a little butthurt that he didn't get to be the super star out there?"

"I'm damn good on the ice. You know it and I know it."

He nods, his expression growing more serious. "Yes. It's true. You have stellar form, Kid but here's the difference between us and you," he says, gesturing between me and the rest of the team. "*We* are a team. *We* have always been a team. *We* will always be a team. We run like a well-oiled machine. It's a give and take. There isn't one of us on this team who is better than the other. We all have different strengths and weaknesses and we know how to use them to our advantage in a game setting."

"It's true," Ledger says as he walks by. "This guy is the king of assist. He'll set you up for the killer shot almost every time and we know we can trust him to always be there."

"Right." Griffin nods and gestures to Ledger. "And this guy can skate rings around me. He's fast as fuck so if I can get him a pass he can take the puck down the ice in seconds. Like I said, well-oiled machine. And you can either learn how the machine works and become a part of it, or you're left standing on the outside looking in wondering where the power button is. You've got a lot of talent, Roche. A lot. But if you want to feel like a member of the team, you've got to act like a member of the team. Got it?"

I huff out my frustrations in a tight breath. "Yeah. I got it."

He pats my back and gives me a smile. "Good. Now clean yourself up Pickle Pants, it's time for lunch."

I hop in the shower, mulling over what Griffin and Ledger had to say after practice and remember what my father once said to me after a particularly frustrating high school hockey practice.

"It's not right," I whine grabbing a can of cola from the fridge. "I work my ass off for him but it's like Coach doesn't even know I exist. He knows I can skate better than any one of them. They all know it. They all call me lightning for a reason."

"Speed is nothing if you can't sink a puck, Bodhi."

"But I can sink the puck! If they would just pass it to me, but they never do!"

Dad lays his hands on my shoulder and gives me a patient smile. "Let me give you a piece of advice, son. You are a fantastic athlete. You're strong. You're hardworking. You're smart and you are kind. But perhaps you're not always coachable."

I tip my head. "What is that supposed to mean?"

"As you go forward in all you do, surround yourself with people who will challenge you to be a better version of yourself," he says. "Listen to what others have to say before making rash decisions. And never be afraid to look at yourself in the mirror to try to see what someone else sees. And if they're not seeing what you want them to see, ask yourself why. Perception is reality, son. Even when you don't mean it to be."

"But maybe they're just perceiving me all wrong."

He nods. "That is absolutely true. And that's what I mean when I say perception is reality. If someone perceives you to be a non-team player, then to them, that's what you are. If someone perceives you to not be a kind person, then to them, you are unkind. See what I'm saying?"

I take in his words and repeat them to myself. "Yeah, Dad. I hear you."

"Great things are going to happen for you, son. One day you will be a star."

A star.

I smile to myself and wonder if Dad knew back then that I would one day be an Anaheim Star.

After I'm showered and dressed, I grab my cellphone and tap the screen for any missed messages. My brows furrow at the lone text waiting for me.

> **UNKNOWN**
>
> Hey Dad. I left spaghetti in the fridge for you. Garlic Bread is wrapped in foil. Good Luck tonight.

"Dad?" I chuckle. "Afraid not, asshat. No dad here." Giving my thumbs a quick workout I text back a reply.

> **ME**
>
> Uh, last I checked I'm 24 and very sure I haven't fathered any children just yet. I'm sorry to say you've texted the wrong number.

Shoving my phone into my back pocket, I make my way to the conference room where the team is having lunch before continuing with the rest of the day's game-day routines. When I sit down, my phone buzzes in my pocket so I pull it out to check assuming it's an apology from whoever just mis-texted me.

> **UNKNOWN**
>
> Dangit! Who's going to eat all this spaghetti then?

I huff out a laugh at the witty response appreciating their sense of humor and text them back.

> **ME**
>
> Well that all depends. Are we talking alfredo sauce or marinara?

UNKNOWN

If I had made alfredo, wouldn't I have told my
Dad there was alfredo in the fridge? *wink
emoji*

ME

Touche. I'm sorry I'm kind of busy tonight or I'd
definitely be interested. I love Italian food.
Perhaps some other time. *wink emoji*

UNKNOWN

Perhaps...

Staring at the reply, I can't help but smile and shake my
head. After a rough practice it's nice to be reminded there's life
outside of hockey.

"What are you grinning about over there?" August asks.
He's seated next to Ella Blackstone, his wife and mascot for our
team.

"Oh, nothin' important. Just a random text."

Ella's brows wag. "From a giiiirl?"

"Nah." I shake my head and then shrug. "Well, maybe.
Whoever it was they were texting the wrong number. Called me
Dad and told me there was spaghetti in the fridge."

"Hey, you got a girl to call you daddy." Griffin winks. "Isn't
that one of those kinky things you kids are into these days?"

"Kids?" I scoff amused. "You know I'm not that much
younger than you, right?"

Griffin waves off my comment. "Semantics."

"So, is there someone special in your life, Bodhi?" Ella asks
curiously as she takes a bite of her chicken. "A girlfriend? A
wife?"

August's eyes grow mischievous. "A secret lover?"

Ella elbows him in his side. "Give him a break. Not everything about Bodhi has to be scandalous, you know. He's a
perfectly normal guy."

If she only knew.

When it comes to relationships I'm probably the most scandalous one here, but I don't mean scandalous in an I'm-fucking-a-forbidden-woman kind of way. Just the opposite really.

I'm not fucking at all.

In fact, I've never fucked anyone in my life.

I'm a twenty-four-year-old professional hockey player.

And I'm a virgin.

What If I Knew You releases on January 17, 2025
You can preorder it HERE on Amazon!

OTHER BOOKS BY SUSAN RENEE
ALL BOOKS ARE AVAILABLE IN KINDLE UNLIMITED

The Anaheim Stars Series

What if We Do: Jilted Bride

What if I Told You: Childhood Friends to Lovers

What if I Knew You: Coach's daughter

The Red Tails Hockey Series

Off Your Game Angry Meet Cute

<u>Unfair Game</u> Strangers/Roommates to lovers

<u>Beyond the Game</u> One Night Stand/Surprise Pregnancy

Forbidden Game Teammate/Best Friend's Sister

Saving the Game Fake Relationship

Bonus Game Single Dad/Nanny

The Bardstown Series

(Prequel) I LOVED YOU THEN: Second Chance at love

I LIKE ME BETTER: Enemies to Lovers/workplace

YOU ARE THE REASON: Second Chance

BEAUTIFUL CRAZY: Friends to Lovers

TAKE YOU HOME: Boss's Daughter

The Camel Club Series

Smooch: One Night Stand/Strangers to Lovers

<u>Smooches:</u> Single Mom/Ex's Best Friend

<u>Smooched:</u> Fake Relationship/Surprise Pregnancy

The Schmidt Load Novella Series

You Don't Know Jack Schmidt

Schmidt Happens

My Schmidt Smells Like Roses

The Village series

I'm Fine (The Village Duet #1)

Save Me (The Village Duet #2)

*The Village Duet comes with a content warning.

Please be sure to check out this book's Amazon page before downloading.

Stand Alone Novels

Hole Punched: Strangers to Lovers/Hidden identity

Total Ship Show

(part of Love at Sea multi-author series)

Kamana Wanalaya for the Holidays: She-grinch/Sunshine

No Egrets: Grumpy/Sunshine

(Part of the Tuft Swallow Multi Author Series)

Solving Us

Surprising Us (a Solving Us novella)

KEEP IN TOUCH WITH ME!

Click to join Susan Renee's Newsletter!

Join Susan's Sweet-Tarts Facebook Reader Group!

facebook.com/AuthorSusanRenee

instagram.com/authorsusanrenee

goodreads.com/susanrenee

tiktok.com/@authorsusanrenee

amazon.com/stores/Susan-Renee/author/B0184I0K3Q

bookbub.com/authors/susan-renee

ABOUT THE AUTHOR

International bestselling author, Susan Renee, wants to live in a world where paint doesn't smell, book boyfriends are real, and everything is covered in glitter. An indie romance author, Susan has written about everything from tacos to tow-trucks, loves writing romantic comedies but also enjoys creating an emotional angsty story from time to time. She lives in Ohio with her husband, kids, three dogs and a cat. Susan holds a Bachelor and Masters Degree in Music Education and a self-awarded Doctorate in Sass and Sarcasm. She enjoys laughing at memes, speaking in GIFs and spending an entire day jumping down the TikTok rabbit hole. When she's not writing or playing the role of Mom, her favorite activity is doing the Care Bear stare with her closest friends.

Printed in Dunstable, United Kingdom

68491411R00178